When I got to the lobby, Tim was waiting for me, strangely silent and pale.

"Did the FedEx package come?" I asked, maybe too loudly.

"I'm lookin'," Al, the package man, hissed from behind a wall of little square mail boxes. "Be patient! You professors!"

Oh, God, Tim looked terrible.

"Look, Jess, I already stashed the book . . ." he whispered, gasping for breath, as he turned to me, his polo shirt drenched in sweat.

"*Jess, tour is . . .!*" His last words. The next second he was sliding down against the package room door. His body slumped on the floor.

"Help him, somebody help him!" Al screamed. How could this be happening? Tim wasn't breathing. As much as I pounded on his chest, there was no movement. Nothing. I held on to my head to steady my trembling as I gave him mouth-to-mouth resuscitation. Still nothing.

Al got Dave, the doorman, to call an ambulance, which, to its credit, arrived in five minutes. As Tim's glazed eyes seemed to stare up at me, I averted mine from his. While the EMS lady performed her CPR, I had to look away from his motionless body. No use. They took him away in their ambulance.

"A suspenseful who-done-it and also a probing exploration of New York City's literary lions, social activists, and provocative artists."
—Sereana Nanda, Co-author with Joan Gregg of *The Gift of the Bride: A Tale of Anthropology, Matrimony, and Murder.*

"A riveting tale with intriguing historical overtones and a colorful array of characters who grab you at every turn."
—E.C. Streeter, Author, *Solving the Solar Enigma*

"After reading this fast- paced and engaging mystery, you've not only learned "who dunnit" but also a treasure trove of fact and lore about the real-life giants of history who have left their imprint on Bleecker Street for today."
—Allan Yashin, Author of *Protected*

"I finally got to meet my neighbors. I've been living in this neighborhood for over twenty years, but I never realized how interesting and colorful it really was until I read Shadows on Bleecker Street and got the proper tour."
—Cousin Bruce Morrow, Sirius X-M Satellite

SHADOWS ON BLEECKER STREET
A Mystery Novel

BY MILTON POLSKY
& WARREN WYSS

Puck Press

ISBN 978-1-932287-76-9

Book design and layout by Paul Sugarman

10 9 8 7 6 5 4 3 2 1

Library of Congress Cataloging-in-Publication Data
Library of Congress Control Number: 2012922869

Puck Press
42 Walter Street
Bloomfield, NY 07003
www.shakespeareinc.com
973-980-2208

For our wonderful ladies who support us in life and literature:
Alice, April, Jenny, Maddy, Olivia, and Roberta.

Acknowledgments

From conception to publication during a seven-year journey, many friends and colleagues helped us along the way. Our thanks, foremost, to Howard Berland for contributing to the depictions of the iconic characters in the novel; scenes with those characters first appeared in "The Spirit of Bleecker Street," a musical Howard wrote with Milton, published by Players Press, Studio City, California, © 1998. Thank you, William-Alan Landes, for permission to use this material.

We are grateful to Maria de Los Angeles for the beautiful illustrations, and Bill Greenfield for the inviting map of the tour's historical events and for his engaging cover art. In the early stages of writing, the astute advice of Randy Levine, Mitch Falk, Middy Streeter, Allen Appel, Jim Story, and Andie Wax was appreciated. Thanks to the African-American Registry for use of the "Jazz is my Religion," by Ted Joans. For their generosity of time and insight, we are indebted to Warren's sister, April Goode; his brother, Wallace Wyss, and niece, Alyce Langley; and to Roberta, Milton's wife, not only for all their editorial acumen but encouragement from start to finish. Our heartfelt thanks to Puck Press and Publisher Paul Sugarman, best expressed in his beloved Bard's words: "Things won are done; joy's soul lies in the doing."

The past is really almost as much a work
of the imagination as the future is.—Iris Murdoch

Up and down, up and down . . .
—A Midsummer Night's Dream

July 1 - 2014

Dear Silvianna,

For a fellow
UFT member —

All the Best

Enjoy!

Nell

TIM'S MAP • BLEECKER ST. BLUES TOUR

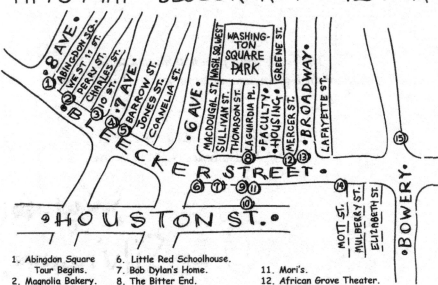

1. Abingdon Square
   Tour Begins.
2. Magnolia Bakery.
3. Old Antique Row.
4. Tom Paine's House.
5. Charlie Parker/
   Cafe Boheme.

6. Little Red Schoolhouse.
7. Bob Dylan's Home.
8. The Bitter End.
9. Lenny Bruce/
   Cafe au Go Go/
   Hot Dog Place.
10. Picasso Statue "Sylvette."

11. Mori's.
12. African Grove Theater.
13. Walt Whitman &
    Charlie Pfaff's.
14. Margaret Sanger.
15. C.B.G.B.'s.

PART ONE

Publish or Perish

Chapter One

Thursday morning

"In memory everything seems to happen in music." Tim loved that Tennessee Williams quote. I'll never get it out of my mind because that's how my story begins—with a song. A sweet memory, all too soon overshadowed by tragic loss.

Even though I was late again for class, I felt assured Tim had everything in control when I heard his voice coming through strong.

Oh Canaan, sweet Canaan
I thought I heard 'em say
There were lions in the way
And I don't expect to stay
Much longer here— Shun the danger,
Run to freedom!

I made my way over to the lectern and stood next to Tim, who was getting ready to move into his role. Lean and handsome, his caramel-colored face was darkened now in the room's diminished light, but you could see his eyes ablaze with passion. I faced Tim and flicked my hand for him to continue. He leaped off the small raised stage, and, as he crouched near the front row of seats, I started my narration. "Who are these lions? What were these dangers?"

We were a team, good enough, I will say immodestly, to hold the attention of these savvy students enrolled in our "Seeds of Slavery, Fruits of Freedom" course. When Tim and I taught the class together at the Greene Street Graduate Center, students not only got interested, they got involved.

I had encouraged Tim to call his own shots for our last class of the school year. But why he chose Frederick Douglass as the topic puzzled me, since we covered him fairly well two weeks back.

"Jeff," Tim said softly, "where were you? Raben's 'trolling the halls!"

"Take it easy, I'm here now."

"Okay, good, good, 'cause our man's ready to fly!"

Tim played a young, twenty-year-old Frederick Douglass escaping from Maryland to New York City, back in 1838, probably hiding somewhere in a safe house for fugitives in lower Manhattan.

Darting over to the corner, Tim, as Douglass, rubbed his hands like he was huddled over a fire, warming up his mind with a new thought. Students heard his velvety baritone voice all the way to the back of the classroom, crying out the words that Douglass recalled when he was still a slave on the eastern shore of Maryland, yearning from the deepest place in his soul to be something that the students took for granted:

Free ... when I was a boy, and those slave bosses weren't breathing down on me, I used to sneak off, and watch all those ships sailin' out from the harbor ... I was praying, O Lord, if I could just sail away—or maybe—fly! With the wings of a dove—and be free!

In character, Tim asked some students to join him around the mimed fire. He whispered to them how he had enough of the whippings, the humiliation, being treated like a thing. "I'm gonna fake them papers, disguise m'self as a free black sailor—and find my way to freedom."

Renee, one of our more eager students, said, "Gotta be careful, Fred, they be lions in the way! They'll be after ya, to bring you back to your master."

"*So-called* master, you mean. I'm leavin' now ... Gotta!" Tim-as-Fred said.

Another student joined in. "How you gonna do it, Fred, bein' your master's property? No diff'rent from the trees in the woods here."

"His property? Hell, then I'll steal *m'self* away."

That got a big laugh.

"Don't do it, Fred! They shoot you in the foot if they catch you."

"Let 'em! I'll drag m'self to freedom somehow," Tim said.

The students wrapped themselves around every word. Quickly, I stepped in to remind them that they were Underground Railroad agents now, helping young Fred Bailey—his slave name—find freedom here in New York.

As Fred, Tim bobbed and wove, crouching some more, looking for places to hide among the students, who were now standing up like buildings, casting bouncing shadows on the side wall. No safe place to hide! Slave catchers, rifles in hand, were prowling around the city—yes, like lions after their prey—searching for runaways to turn into cash by returning them to their so-called masters.

Some students made the sound of the chilly wind, while others intoned the inner voices of Fred.

Hide . . . run . . . wait . . . watch out . . . hide . . . run . . . wait . . . hide!

The class continued on for two hours. With these sharp grad students so engaged, we covered a good portion of Douglass's life, not only as the country's foremost abolitionist, but also as author, newspaper editor, orator, and public servant. I got a good laugh when short, burly me played thin, tall Abe Lincoln being chastised by Douglass, who considered the freed four-million slaves as "stepchildren" of Lincoln.

At one point I projected a transparency of the younger Douglass onto the screen wall. His features were strong—a dignified firm chin, penetrating eyes, and crown of thick matted hair. Tim spoke his words, " 'Those who profess to favor freedom, yet deprecate agitation . . . want the ocean without the awful roar of its many waters . . . ' "

Tim added his own words. "As a human being, an African-American, and foremost a teacher, I can only hope to accomplish one-tenth of what Douglass achieved." He wrapped up with a zippy pep talk on what students could do for their community.

Then he asked me to say a few more words. I did. Two. "Agitate, agitate!" Douglass' words.

That ended the class on a real high. Applause, hugs, a few toasts of the wine students had brought in, return of term papers, and the class and year were over.

I was standing near Tim when Renee handed him a plastic cup of wine. She tried to smile, but only managed to say, "I'm sorry," then she turned quickly and left the room. All too emotional for her, I guessed.

"What was that all about with Renee Alvarez just now?" I asked him quietly.

"Oh, she's angry at me 'cause I failed her for plagiarising her term paper. The school was gonna kick her out, y'know. She didn't give me time to tell her I planned to ask Max to give her a chance to make up for it. Do something special on the Bleecker Street tour I lead—and write it up."

The applause in the classroom was just dying down when Max Raben, the college's elderly Social History department chair, passed by the open door. By his side clung Doree, the young department secretary, toting his books as he traversed the hallway in search of any poor instructor with "unstimulating" classes.

"Superb job, Tim," he said, entering the classroom. "I happened to pass by and heard a bit of your class. Fine! You really get your students into it! In a few minutes, come up to my office for a short while. We have something to celebrate!"

Here I was off to the side, waiting for, maybe, just one word of acknowledgment for devising the course and shepherding Tim through it. But, no, all Max said to me was, "See you next week, Jeff." He was referring to our conference regarding my long-overdue tenure book that I *still* hadn't produced.

All I had now were the good wishes of these students bidding me a great summer, a long line of them.

Well, I was going to miss them, especially the cute gal with an iPod stuck in her ear, who told me the course was "totally awesome." I had helped her out with some counseling when she was depressed about keeping up with school work and her part-time job. I told her to thank Mr. Hartknoll for giving the class its dynamic energy. She hugged Tim and daintily shook my hand good-bye, chirping, "Enjoy your summer, both of you!"

"See, they love you, Jeff," Tim said. "The school does too. We need you!"

"Isn't up to me, Tim, whether I stay or not. Depends on whether I can write a book this summer for my tenure."

"Don't worry, partner. Max knows how important you are here."

I had to laugh at Tim's noble efforts to make me feel better. But he was blowing hot air. For years I was struggling to come up with just one workable idea for a book that I'd write for tenure. I repeated the boring mantra that Max so often buzzed into my ear: "Publish or perish! Without that book, you're gone!"

"Ah, you can do it," Tim pronounced, as he jabbed me playfully on the arm. "Listen up, Jeff. I have some fantastic news for you—that just may make this problem go away—fade away entirely!"

"Fantastic news? Don't kid me, Tim. We know that you're going to be promoted."

"No, it's not that!" He picked up his briefcase, his eyes brightening. "Let's go someplace, uh, where we can have some privacy."

In a few minutes we reached my office down the hall. Tim motioned for me to sit in my old beat-up swivel chair.

"Jeff, wait here for fifteen minutes or so, will you? I have to go up to Raben's office."

"Yeah, well . . . we all know what it's about, Tim. Good luck!"

As he grabbed his briefcase and headed for the door, Tim flashed a warm smile. "Thanks. You know what? I have a feeling both our lives are gonna change today—big time!" I could only wonder where this high was taking him—and what was in his briefcase.

Chapter Two

Twenty minutes later

Tim had once joked that the faculty offices here at Greene Cent resembled the sweatshops this SoHo building once housed, but instead of sewing machines, computers were the instruments of labor. I would have laughed, except my grandfather might've been one of those very immigrants bent over his sewing machine for fifteen grueling hours a day. More of a reminder were those old loudspeakers on the walls for bosses to keep their workers on unrelenting task.

Tim returned from Max's office with his face all aglow. He made sure the door was closed shut as he entered my cramped office.

"Sorry, I'm late," he said, delicately laying his briefcase on my desk. "I got tangled up with some business...and all that. On the way down I ran into someone I knew from the tour, and celebrated briefly with him—just for a minute."

Noticing his wobble, I said, "Man, you've had a lot today with all that wine you gulped down. You souse it up with Max, too?"

"With him? No, we toasted my appointment with his famous non-fat milkshakes."

"Congrats, Tim, or should I say, *Professor* Hartknoll!" I whooped, giving his back a couple of hearty pats.

"Jeff, my ace friend and colleague. Your tenure will come soon, believe me. I just called my family about the good news and they'll be meeting me later at the apartment, takin' me out to a grand Village lunch. You're welcome to join us."

Tim got a bottle of water from my little fridge and took a swig. He was still out of breath as he reached into his briefcase and held up an old tin box, about the size of a shoe box. It was faintly grayish with a few scratches on it.

"*This*, my friend, is gonna change our lives forever!"

"Really? So what is it? One-shop, nonstop porno?"

"Whoa, partner," he said. "*Change* our lives, not *derange* 'em."

"Slow down then, Tim. Take some more water." I hadn't ever seen him like this before, so heavy in overdrive. He wiped some droplets from his mouth and moved his chair closer to mine.

"Last week, I was leading my walking tour about authors in Greenwich Village—y'know, my part-time gig—and this tall, sweaty construction worker, maybe in his thirties—Antonio—never gave me his last name—suddenly comes up to me and shows me this box here, right? Said he saw me a couple times on the tour I lead on Bleecker."

"Wanted to unload a bomb, or something?" I couldn't resist it. He punched my shoulder.

"Shut up, will you? So this Antonio says he found it when he was bulldozing the basement wall of an old building somewhere in the Village. Could hardly get his English out, okay, but I got what he was tryin' to tell me."

"What did this dude look like?"

"Sorta tall, thin, beardless, probably Latino. He has this jagged scar on his right cheek, just below his eye."

I fingered my shaggy beard, then motioned for him to go on.

"I did a double-take because he was wearing an *I Love New York* T-shirt and baseball cap. Just like you do, Jeff."

"Lots of people do. So?"

Tim smiled. "I think I told him my friend Jeff wears one too, but it always has lots of spots on it."

I agreed with him on that one. I was not one acclaimed for any neatness, compared to Tim's perpetual preppy look.

He paused, then ever so carefully opened the box, like what one of those super-slick TV CSI forensic lab investigators does.

A small black book. It looked old. Smelled musty. Inside, on the first page, there was an illustration of a woman in some sort of negligee, with wispy Breck-girl curls, standing like a semi-nude fairy next to a pond or lake. The title and author were clear, set in the old-fash-ioned lettering of those times: *Lady of the Lake* by Sir Walter Scott.

From his briefcase Tim pulled out a pair of those CSI thin latex gloves, slipping them on like an old pro working the evidence.

"What the fuck—what are you *doin'*, Timothy Hartknoll? Whoa there, slow down. We just did our show for the class!"

"Keep your eyes on the prize, Dr. G. Don't move. Don't—"

I read the inscription on the second page. Boom! It knocked my eyes out.

"C'mon, c'mon, slowpoke, read it. Out loud, Jeff."

"With this book I have a new name and a new life and hope for ever-lasting freedom."

I almost pissed in my pants. It was signed *Frederick Douglass*, with that bold, even-handed writing of his that was so recognizable. In script, under the signature, was scrawled *New Bedford, Mass., 1838*. I wanted to hold the page, run my fingers over the heavy plain paper. It looked so simple, and yet so amazingly profound—if it was real-whatever that overused maligned word meant today. Tim flipped gen-tly through the pages. Clean, no stains or tears I could see.

I nudged him to hold the book under our so-called energy-saving florescent lights, in order to check for watermarks. Walking over to the window for better light, Tim coaxed me to follow.

"That's the thing. A paleographer checked all of that out, too, of course. Here, take a look for yourself."

"Paleographer? Handwriting expert? This some kind of a joke, you brainy numbskull? A going-away present for me, maybe?" I joined him at the window, and sure enough, the watermarks, so clear in the sunlight, were there.

"You're not goin' anywhere, Jeff. This book will get your tenure for sure!"

"Ha-Ha, if it does, my friend, excuse me for not laughing." I was too stunned.

Tim started dancing around like a pro football player who just scored a touchdown.

What was this crazy ball of energy—Timothy Hartknoll—up to? It was too much for me to swallow in one sitting. I got up and walked over to him, resting my hand on his shoulder. "Yo, this can't be for real, my friend."

"So Antonio shows me the book, and right away wants to sell it to me. Once I laid my own eyes on it, I knew I had to have it. The greedy bastard had me, Jeff, hitting me for every last cent he thought he could squeeze outta me."

"Well? How much?"

"To begin with, half a thou—"

"Five hundred bucks for what could be a hoax? Are you out of your effing crazy skull, Tim? What was the total he asked for?"

"Well, he said $2,000. Then there are the additional expenses. Like paying for the book's authentication . . ."

"Wait a minute," I almost shouted. "Aren't you going a bit too fast on this deal?"

"Don't give me that, Mr. Cautious! We're talkin' a first—FIRST—1810 edition. You dig what *that* means? Signed by Frederick Douglass himself! Could go down for a hundred thousand or more!"

"If it's worth that much, why didn't he keep it for himself, this Antonio creep? And how do you know this guy's not a sleazy con artist?"

"Not to worry, Jeff. I told him I'm a professor here. That's why he's letting me deal this."

"Alright, maybe he's okay, maybe he's an illegal immigrant, maybe he's this or that. I don't know. You don't know. Jeesuz, maybe you're latching on to some kind of nasty lawsuit or something. Did you check all that stuff out?"

"Hold on, I'm comin' to that. Listen, Jeff, the way I see it, it's a win-win all the way. Old is good! Awesome! We can get credit for the discovery, or get some money and put it to good use. Maybe some-thin' for your own book."

Tim held up his prize again. "Douglass could've bought any num-ber of these books back then. But this one we got is signed. By *him!* *Frederick Douglass!* Incredible. God!"

"Bullshit! How do you know?"

"Are you ready for this? I had the same doubts, Jeff. Of course, I wasn't going to fork over one dime to this Antonio cat until I had some idea that the book was authentic. He wasn't gonna trust me with the book either—until I kicked in a down payment."

"So it looks like you had a stalemate—"

"Not so fast, bro. Together, we took the book to a dynamite bookstore in town, the Odyssey, y'know, the one that also appraises rare books. They said enough to convince me ninety percent that both the book and signature look authentic But to be sure, they'd have to send it to the RaraVista lab in Princeton for tests. For a cou-ple days. Two independent professors there would work on it along with a highly respected conservator. You know, carbon checks on the paper, ink tests, signature analysis—the whole megillah—yeah, the whole thing. They'd even run the paper through the latest fiber-optics tests."

"Let me get this right. This guy Antonio—a total stranger—agreed to all this?"

"Yeah. I told him that I'd pay for the lab work. It would be best for all our interests to get the book properly checked out—authenti-cated—the right way. So they did all these optic tests, with UV lights, everything. Two seven-hour days of lab tests, from stitching to even glue checks, for chrissakes!

"Well, did you get any results?"

Tim stopped and released one heck of a loud burst of laughter. "Yes, yes, it was confirmed to be authentic—the book, the inscription, and the signature! All real! And in great shape. Can you believe it? The book didn't go through any stress all those years."

"None at all? How come?"

"Well, you see, the paper's not parchment, so it's not fragile—and this metal container was like an airtight sealer of sorts."

I nodded for him to go on, expecting a catch somewhere.

"Believe me, it's amazing. Just one tiny smear, can hardly see it. Spectrometry came up with no structural damage; the red Moroccan leather binder, tight. Amazing! Antonio and I went back to the Odyssey bookstore three days later to retrieve the book. All we have to do now is wait for their certification papers."

"We? Whoa—! Don't you mean you and Antonio?"

"Of course not, partner! You and me! I made sure to pay off Antonio $500, so he'd release the book to me. That's the down-payment he asked for. He was getting pretty damn anxious to have that bread, threatening me to close down the deal if I didn't give it to him immediately."

"$500 out of two-thousand?"

"Yes, yes, Jeff. Here's the thing. I didn't want to lose the deal, man, so we went to the ATM machine, and I gave him the down-payment right then and there."

"Okay, okay, just hold on a second. How do *I* come in all this?"

"Well, y'know, man, I'm dead broke—dropped my last red cent on that down-payment. So I thought if you want to be my partner, help out, you know . . . Shady Lady could be our passport to—"

"Shady Lady—? Isn't that a brothel in Nevada?"

"No, fusspot! *The Lady of the Lake*, Jeff. Our code name! Once I get that certification, I got to pay RaraVista and Antonio the rest of the bread I owe him . . . by next week."

There it was, the pitch I was suspecting all the time—and the hook! It made sense to me now, his choosing Douglass for our last class, to warm me up for this.

"So that's why you waited 'til now to tell me—partner! You need my *money*, not me."

The pisser thought he had me. Well, not quite.

"Tim, give me some time to think this over okay? Lots of other problems with this deal we gotta discuss. For one thing, it still bothers me a lot, gettin' mixed up with anything . . . *dishonest.*"

Saying it that way was as discreet as I could put it, but I just wasn't sure of all the legal bullshit.

"What do you mean '*dishonest*'? Antonio found the book and is selling it to us—fair and square, without a doubt!"

"Oh, yeah? How do we know he just didn't cop it from some place?"

"We don't. But his story *seems* legit."

Tim's naive enthusiasm wasn't enough, at least for me. "Face it, Tim. Even if it was dug up like this Antonio said, that doesn't mean it *belongs* to him—or to us—for that matter."

"Jeff, c'mon, you've never heard the expression, 'Possession is nine-tenths of the law'?"

"Now you come on, you hard-on! Ever hear 'Let sleeping dogs lie!'? Even *pedigree* ones?"

"Don't go on provokin' piss, Jeff! Whoever originally owned the book has long been dead and gone!"

Tim got up and paced around my office. "See, the world has completely forgotten about this lost treasure buried in the crumbling walls of some old obscure basement. Man, it might have been stuck there for another hundred years if not for an immigrant construction worker bumping into it by accident. You see, it's finder's keepers. All the way." Tim's eyes were blazing now, as I held on to keep my cool.

"No, I disagree, Tim. The deal may be legal, but not exactly ethical. Here's my take on it. We've got to pass it on to the Douglass Foundation, or maybe the National Archives. That's my deal. Take it or leave it. Period."

"Of course, of course, Jeff. Or maybe to Greene Cent Grad Center. But remember, we're in a time bind now. Just a couple of days to fork over the rest of the money to Antonio before he . . . . He said he'd catch up with me somewhere on my Village tour to arrange a time when and where we can finalize the deal."

"Wait a minute, Tim, just a minute here! We can't do it until we get the certification papers, right?!"

"Within the week. Not a problem."

"I know, I know. The Princeton people said they'd deliver them by FedEx. I'm checkin' my mailbox every day now."

This was heavy stuff. My tenure was already slipping away, and this deal could muddy up the waters real good. But, on the other hand, maybe it all could be on the up and up, even helping me with my tenure. And, if Tim was right—everyone could benefit.

I guess to clinch it, I reached down to the last drawer of my desk and pulled out a bundle of tattered papers—all a grand part of my many aborted attempts to write a book for tenure.

He sat down and put his hand gently on my shoulder again. "Well, don't worry now, 'cause this book will help you get a really dynamite topic."

He meant well, of course, but it didn't help. My anger was rising against the whole messy college system—all these old fat so-called professors, half asleep in their cozy life time, getting raises for fifty years, sucking up the treasury, maybe writing one learned little article, and never lifting a pen after that. It didn't matter if they couldn't teach a damn because they'd already published, usually something with abundant proofs of the obvious. But Max still pushed his staff to do *fundable* research.

"Alright!" I put my head down on my desk, exhausted. Six years, coming to an end if I didn't do *something*.

Tim put the papers back into my desk. "Stay cool, Jeff."

"Dammit, Tim, stop tellin' me not to be worried about it. I *should* be worried! *You* are one lucky son of a bitch. First, this precious book falls into your clutching hands and then you get this great job offer! What about me? At my age, with my years of experience, I should get priority. Instead they choose you—a newcomer to the staff—'cause you're young and—"

I caught myself from finishing. Stupid venting. So dumb of me to say that. I could tell Tim was hurt and angered.

"What made you bring *that* up?" he said under his breath. "I guess the Civil War isn't over yet. Lincoln may have freed the slaves, but he didn't free black people with shit like that spewing outta your mouth."

"I'm sorry, forgive me. It's just that, well, nowadays, that does give you an advantage. I don't mean you personally, I mean, hell, I don't know what I mean. I'm really sorry, Tim. C'mon, you know me."

"Great advantage," he scowled, his lips curled down. "Anyway, they pay me less than you just because I'm newer."

He was right. Dammit, he was always right. Why couldn't I keep my big fat mouth shut?

"Let's forget it—the whole damn thing!" he burst out.

But why the hell was *he* pissed? He had a job. I was the one who would be out of one if my meeting with Max went sour. I was a realist—yeah, an ex-idealist with a separated wife and a thirteen-year-old to support. My job was like the air I breathed. Tim was right. I needed this teaching job to stay alive. I didn't need him to tell me how to do it, but there he was, in my face again.

"Come on, Jeff. Don't let this chance get away from you. Douglass didn't. He took risks. He made a new beginning."

"You drunk or somethin'? Comparing me to him?"

"I just meant . . . you can begin again."

"Were you listening, Tim? Don't tell *me* what to do!"

"You cut all this crap out then, old man!" Turning sharply away from me, he leaned his back hard against a bookshelf, and with his arms flailing around, knocked down one of the iron busts of Shakespeare bookends, which landed square on my toe. It hurt like holy hell.

Doree, our ever-efficient department secretary, heard my scream, and knocked loud on my door. Thank God, she was always there, just when I needed her. Quickly, but carefully, Tim placed the book back into the tin box, then into his briefcase.

"Hold on, Doree! Be right there!" he shouted, scrambling to pick up the books scattered on the floor before letting her in.

Promptly sizing up the problem, Doree rushed to my rescue. She sat me in a chair in the corner, then gently removed my shoes and socks. My whole left foot started to turn red and swell up, but, thank goodness, it wasn't bleeding and it looked like the bone never pierced the skin. She rinsed my foot in warm water, and fitted me with a sandal she found in my cluttered office closet.

My foot hurt like a red-hot iron, and when I got up, I could just about hobble. A ridiculous sight, to say the least.

"Close the door!" I yelled. I don't want anyone to see this!" Doree complied, but then started acting like a saintly Mother Superior.

"Professor Gardner, how did this happen to you?"

"Just celebrating a bit too much, Doree. You know, Mr. Hartknoll's promotion . . . "

"This looks serious. Let's get it taken care of."

"Never mind," I murmured. "I can handle it myself."

"No way, sir! I'm taking you to the infirmary."

Imagining the grand sight we would make, I hastily said, "That's alright, Doree. I'll, uh, toe the line. Thanks. You can go now."

She looked puzzled. "That's not what you tell your students, Dr. Gardner. You always say safety before studies—health before homework, abstinence before—"

Nice try, Doree, but I didn't feel like laughing. "Thank you, really, but I'm okay. Seriously."

I took in her frown. No choice there. I had to go with it.

"Come on, sir, let's get you to the school infirmary." She had the drive and the girth to hoist me up, all two hundred pounds of her. As

I struggled to stand up, I made a stab at a little humor. "Lovely to look at, delightful to know . . ." I sang out blithely.

Sensing my embarrassment, Tim said, "I'll take him, Doree. You can go back to your stuff."

Doree gave us a disgruntled look and started to leave. "Make sure you go to the infirmary—now!" she said, storming out.

I cursed myself for being such a hot-headed slob. All this pain served me right, And, of course, Tim was giving me warm, fatherly encouragement, even though he was half my age.

"You win. I'll go," I said, with a begrudging smile.

""It's gonna be good, Jess," he slurred. "But you havta get a hol' of yourself, Jess. Really. Less go."

What the hell was wrong with *him* now? He was speaking too damn slowly, and his mumbling was really bothering me, but I had to make light of it.

"Look who's talkin'," I mock-scolded. "You can't even hold your fancy wine, Tim.

Hey, look at me! I'm an old pro at it. Plus, I've a lovely repertory of other bad habits."

"What d'ya 'spect, Jess? I've been celebratin' all mornin' now!"

"You need to go home and get some shut-eye. But first, when you get home, hide your book good."

"Ha! I was thinkin' somewhere along the tour I lead—"

"No, you tickle-brain son-of-a-gun, *at home!* "

"Like in my bedroom?"

I nodded okay to that. His new-found romance. So close to him.

The doctor at the infirmary in the adjoining building took care of my toe, wrapping two digitals together like twins. I was good to go.

Chapter Three

2:30 p.m.

We inched along to the Bleecker Street Apartments in the Village, where we had faculty apartments. Tim seemed so mellow now, more so than I had ever seen him all morning, but he still clutched his briefcase as if his life depended on it.

"Y'know, we're gonna make so much ridiculous moola from selling Shady Lady—a humongous barrowful. You know what I plan t'do with my share—?"

"Your share? I thought we agreed that the book would go to a nonprofit outfit."

"Like I said, I still want to help those homeless kids I tutor. High school dropouts, but good kids. What about you, Jess? How ya gonna spend your share?"

I just kept on walking. Tim was so gung-ho about his cause, but it was much too early for me to share his euphoria.

"Don't know yet. Let's cross that one later."

I tried to keep up with him. Framed against the sturdy cast-iron Soho buildings we passed, one after another, I noticed him tipping from side to side a little. Some pedestrians gave us quick, smirky looks over their shoulders.

"Fussy fools," Tim said, referring to the thick crowds thronging the entrance of an electronics store that we passed by. "Wastin' their money on the latest cellphones and iPods! Throwin' away all that money on conspic . . ." I thought he was trying to say "conspicuous consumption," but the words came out mangled.

Another thing. He seemed to have trouble trying to stand up straight, as if he needed help. Of course his pride wouldn't permit it. When I put my hand on his shoulder and offered to carry his briefcase, he backed off like he felt an electric shock.

19

"Can I help you, buddy? You've had way too much to drink."

"You should talk, *Jess*, in your condition! Ha! I'm okay. Thing is, I gotta go ahead, man, to check the mailbox for those cert-, certification papers for Shady Lady."

I had to laugh. With all that wine in him, I didn't blame him for going ahead. In my new great shape it would take me forever to hobble to our building. Why slow Front Man up more?

Twenty minutes later I got to the Bleecker Street Apartments. Some of the Greene Street Cent office staff, like Doree, had apartments there too. The building looked like a big tacky checkered box, but had the prize-winning Sasaki Garden with breathing space and stone chess tables. Down the block was the NYU Recreation Sports Center. As NYU alumni, Tim and I used to swat a few tennis balls there.

When I got to the lobby, Tim was waiting for me, strangely silent and pale.

"Did the FedEx package come?" I asked, maybe too loudly.

"I'm lookin'," Al, the package man, hissed from behind a wall of little square mail boxes. "Be patient! You professors!"

Oh, God, Tim looked terrible.

"Look, Jess, I already stashed the book . . ." he whispered, gasping for breath, as he turned to me, his polo shirt drenched in sweat.

"*Jess, tour is* . . . !" His last words. The next second he was sliding down against the package room door. His body slumped on the floor.

"Help him, somebody help him!" Al screamed. How could this be happening? Tim wasn't breathing. As much as I pounded on his chest, there was no movement. Nothing. I held on to my head to steady my trembling as I gave him mouth-to-mouth resuscitation. Still nothing.

Al got Dave, the doorman, to call an ambulance, which, to its credit, arrived in five minutes. As Tim's glazed eyes seemed to stare up at me, I averted mine from his. While the EMS lady performed her CPR, I had to look away from his motionless body. No use. They took him away in their ambulance.

I wanted to go with him, but they insisted that was not the procedure. Only members of his family would be allowed to accompany him. They were due any time soon—expecting to take Tim out to celebrate—and now . . .

Amidst all the confusion, Doree walked into the lobby and quickly put her comforting arms around me. As consoling as she and the other tenants were, I felt hopelessly alone, torn by my shattered thoughts.

Hold on—Shady Lady! Tim said he hid it. I had to go right up there and find it before the police sealed the room against anyone entering.

Breaking away from Doree's grasp, I excused myself, telling her I felt sick and had to go to my apartment and lie down. I asked her to look out for Tim's family's soon-expected arrival—and break the news to them. I was no good at that sort of thing, but she was always in control. She would do it.

I limped to the elevator, fetched an extra set of Tim's keys from my place, and headed for his apartment on the floor below.

The minute I entered, I froze up. Everything was turned upside down. *Ransacked* was too tame a word for the mad disarray. Papers strewn everywhere, table and chairs turned over, pictures and some of Tim's precious African artifacts scattered on the parquet floor. My heart was jumping and my foot killing me as I got into his bedroom to check the place where he had told me he would stash the book— in the middle drawer of his dresser. Nothing there but a pile of old socks. Just as I feared, Shady Lady was gone.

No sight, either, of his briefcase. Facing me on top of his dresser was the funny cap he wore on the tour he led. Compulsively, I grabbed it, stuffing it into my pocket. God, I was losing control. I pulled out my pill container and forced down a tranquilizer. There went his fortune and my great academic boost. To hell with all that materialistic crap, what about my friend?

There was no time to think about it now. I had to get out of there before someone caught me.

I took the flight of stairs up like a numb zombie, the nervous pain in my head burning worse than the spasms caused by my injured toe. Once in my apartment, I fell onto the couch, unable to rest my thoughts about Tim, who, only an hour ago, had been so full of dreams, at the cusp of a glorious future—and about his family who had made the long drive from Long Island to celebrate with him. They were probably in the lobby now, steeling themselves to make the painful ride to the hospital.

The phone rang. It was a cop, asking me to meet him and his partner tomorrow morning, to find out what I knew. His *partner*? I slouched back into my pillow. I hated that word.

But it was Tim's last two words, *tour is,* which kept me up most of the night.

Chapter Four

Friday morning

In spite of yesterday's nightmare, I somehow managed to get some sleep. Eventually I was aroused by the clatter of pans coming from the kitchen and the scent of hot coffee and eggs cooking. Sweet Sasha, of course, making a lovely breakfast. Too bad I wasn't hungry.

"What time is it?" I called out groggily from my bedroom.

"Almost ten, honey. C'mon, get some breakfast. I made your favorite—egg whites, onions, and kippers."

Ten? I remembered yesterday's phone call from the police—not much time before they'd get here. I quickly showered and put on an old pair of jeans before joining my girlfriend in what passed for a breakfast nook.

"That poor man," was all that Sasha could muster, as I greeted her with a kiss. "I found out what happened to Tim when I came over last night. So sad. Some students were placing flowers on the sidewalk . . . and your doorman told me . . . " She paused for just a second, pouring me a cup of coffee. "When I dropped in, you were sleeping so soundly, I didn't have the heart to wake you up."

"Yeah, I still can't believe it." We wrapped our arms around each other. I slid mine around her slender waist and held my breath.

"Was he sick? I mean . . ."

"I don't know . . . I just don't know. It happened so fast, I—"

"You saw him die?"

"Sash, please, I—"

"You don't have to talk now, Jeff," she said, as I limped to the counter. "Eat something, and—good God—what happened to your foot?"

"Oh, that? Nothing. Clumsy accident, that's all."

"How?"

"It's nothing."

"I need to take a look at it."

She headed to my bedroom. That was my Irish-Latina beauty, always on call. Sasha and I were an item for three months now, since Nan and I separated. I met her when my dad came up from Florida to be treated by a retina specialist for his macular degeneration condition at the NYC Eye Center, where Sasha is the receptionist. Quite an eyeful herself, I reminded myself, as she placed the footstool in front of me.

"Make sure you lift your leg up for circulation, honey."

Resting my foot on the stool, she checked out my toe. Satisfied, she encouraged me to eat, while waiting, I suppose, for me to tell her how it happened.

A long silence. We just played with the food.

"Listen, Sash, the police are comin' over soon."

"Cops? Why? What's really going on, Jeff?"

"Nothing to be alarmed about. They just want to ask a few questions, that's all."

"Questions? Is there something wrong?"

"I'll know, sooner or later, Sash. I guess they need me."

Why were they coming? Some foul play concerning Tim's death? Do they know about Shady Lady? Was I in trouble? I was getting nervous all over again.

"Well, then," she said, "I'll clean up. And I better go off to work. I called earlier and told them I'd be a little late."

"Thanks. Oh, don't worry about the dishes. That warm dish water should help calm my nerves."

"Good. Why don't you do some of those deep-breathing exercises I coached you on? They might help you." She was into every conceivable kind of alternative health remedy concocted by man or earth goddess.

"Thanks, Sash. I will."

"You know, you should keep off your foot today, give it a chance to rest. Why don't you go back to bed?"

"Jeezus, Sasha, I told you—the cops are comin'!"

"Just take care of yourself!—I'll order a take-out lunch for you from Silver Spurs."

"Okay, honey. I appreciate your concern—now go to work!"

"Don't forget to call me as soon as you can," she whispered, throwing me a worried one thumb up as she left.

I finished soaking my hands in the soothing dish water, when the buzzer sounded. My heart racing, I hoped I was up for it. I buzzed the doorman to let the cops come up.

Chapter Five

Five minutes later

I let in the two police detectives—a man and a woman—who apologized for bothering me at this hour, but their schedules were tight for the coming week and they needed to ask me some questions.

The detective in charge was a tall black woman, maybe in her early thirties, almost as pudgy as me, sporting a page-boy haircut, blue blazer, and gray slacks, and prominently on her face, a pair of fashionable silver-rimmed glasses. She introduced herself as Detective Jameson, and her partner, Detective Gerard.

"Thanks for meeting with us, Dr. Gardner," Jameson said. Her eyes veering to my foot, she asked if I was alright.

"I'm okay with this," I said, looking down at the tightly bandaged big toe sticking out of the sandal on my left foot.

"This won't take long—just preliminary," said Jameson.

"I know how overwhelming all this is for you. Thanks for letting us talk with you now," Gerard added.

I put him at forty, around my age, short and muscular. Nice angular features, big smile, upbeat. Neat crewcut. His partner evidently didn't believe in smiling at all. I straightened myself up, determined to make this interview as friendly as possible. "Can I offer you anything? Just put up a pot of fresh coffee, a super new Brazilian roast."

"No thanks," Jameson said. "We won't take too much of your time, Professor."

I motioned for them to sit, while I pulled up a chair and adjusted my footstool, facing them on the sofa. On the wall behind them was a painting that Rachel, Tim's sister, had given me. I gazed up at it, "Beach Party"—a full-figured brown-skinned woman in an orange swimsuit, standing in the sand, while a pale yellow sun mimics her smile.

While my eyes lingered on the painting, Jameson took out her pad and pen.

"You can call me Jeff."

"Well, then, Jeffrey . . ."

"Jeff would be more to my taste."

"Alright, then, Jeff," Gerard continued, as Jameson prepared to write down all my precious words.

"You okay, Jeff? I know you and Mr. Hartknoll were colleagues. So it has to be quite a loss," Jameson said.

"Thanks for your sympathy. It was an enormous shock."

"Just a few questions."

"Go right ahead, I'm perfectly calm," I fibbed. "Whatever you'd like to know."

They got right into it. Jameson first. "Where were you yesterday morning?"

"I was co-teaching my last class of the term with Tim. That was about 10 a.m. After the class, we celebrated a bit. You know, had a little wine, chatted with the students, then we split. Tim had to go up to our department chairman for a few minutes, and I went to my office."

"Did you see him again before you left for home?" she said. "Was he depressed or angry about anything?"

"No, just the opposite. He returned about twenty minutes later with, uh, some very good news."

"Oh?"

"He had just been promoted to professor, with a full-time job. We cut loose, dancing 'round the room, then I stupidly bumped into my book shelf, and that Shakespeare bust landed on my toe."

"I see," Gerard said, looking down at my open sandal. "Happened to me once. I was fishing off a dock in Red Hook, and got all excited when I began to feel a big one on my line. I was jumpin' around so much with joy that I knocked over a heavy tackle box onto my foot. Boy, did that knock the sense into me. Lucky for the fish . . . it wiggled away." His valiant attempts at humor were not lost on me.

"So, what happened then, Dr. Gardner, after Shakespeare hit you on your toe?"

"Well, luckily the boss's secretary, Doris Utrick, heard my scream and came to my grateful rescue with a handy First Aid kit. Wrapped up my toe good in a bandage."

"Umm. Doris Utrick. I noted her name among the witnesses in the lobby yesterday," Jameson responded, searching her notebook for further information.

I tried to be nice. "Doree can be very helpful to you. Do you need her number? She also lives in this building. A lot of Greene Cent faculty and staff do. I can call her if you want."

Jameson motioned for me not to bother. "We already had a talk with her. We also contacted some of the students in your class from a roster she had provided. Of course, everybody was shocked to hear the news."

"The students we reached looked like a very decent lot, Jeff. How do you like teaching at Greene Cent? The students call it that, right?" Gerard chuckled. "It should be Green Dollars, maybe?"

"Yes, *after* they graduate," I answered. The rest of the joke, which I spared them, was that most of them would end up in the red after paying off all their tuition loans. It was still a ton or two cheaper than NYU or Columbia, I mentioned.

Gerard laughed out loud, going into a spiel about one of his nieces, majoring in tax law, who had gone to Baruch, also a City University school. She was now a lawyer in the city. As he rambled on, I still didn't know what to make of this guy.

I interjected, "Greene Cent is a poor man's—I should say poor person's—New York University. Very good for a public college graduate school—an experimental division of the City University system, its focus on information technology and media studies. We only have three buildings, but a pack of good instructors, I might immodestly add. And we're close to a lot of cultural institutions in Soho, like museums, the Angelica Film Center and—"

"I'm sure it's a fine school," Jameson snapped, cutting my commercial short. Her turn again. "How well did Mr. Hartknoll get along with his students?"

"Fine. I saw nothing." I stopped cold. Walking on the bad foot was continuing to take its toll, and my toe was throbbing full blast now beneath the snugly wrapped buddy-tape. My footstool wasn't helping any.

"You said you saw nothing—?" she continued, not missing a beat.

"Nothing," I repeated, hitting the first syllable hard.

"What d'you mean, Jeff?" Gerard asked. "You saw nothing? Take your time."

"Look, Tim got along wonderfully with all his students, as far I observed. And that goes for the staff too, including Doree and our chair, Dr. Max Raben. Everyone respected him. Nothing untoward about him. *Nothing.* You should know that since you already spoke to his students. He was one of our most popular young instructors. A tough grader, but everyone loved him. An exemplary life, always for the underdog and—"

Jameson, who made a big deal about my interruptions, rudely burst right in. "Someone said he had trouble with a student. A young lady in that class you co-taught with, Mr. Hartknoll. A Renee Alvarez. Do you know if there was, uh, anything between them?"

"What are you insinuating?"

"Just what I asked. Some difficulty with her maybe?"

I mentioned the small imbroglio after our last class when Renee left in tears. God, did I get her into trouble just now? Who were they going to unearth next?

"Before yesterday, when did you see Mr. Hartknoll last?" Jameson asked.

"I think at a department meeting about a week ago. Then there was the end-of-term party for the Greene Cent staff in Central Park later, on Wednesday."

"I see," Gerard said.

What did he see? Had I said anything important just now? Was I saying too much? All these questions. Was I some kind of *suspect?*

Jameson reached into her sling bag. What the hell for—an electronic tracking device for my ankle to keep my toe company? The way she delicately palmed her hand, it could be a GPS homing device to plant on me later. Sasha should be here. Or maybe I *should* get a lawyer. Hiram, Nan's brother? No, no way! My friend, Steve, who lived down the hall? No, he practiced corporate law. Gerard's niece? No, she's a tax lawyer ...

The detective was, oh, so delicately popping another dreary Chiclet into her mouth with the grace of a fussy wine taster. "And you weren't with him any other time?"

"Officers, I do have some things to attend to. Can we wind up this interview?"

"Just a few more questions, Dr. Gardner," Jameson said, peering at her little notebook like a fortune teller. "Is there anything more we should know? About his relationships that you may find disturbing? Involving friends? Colleagues? Relatives? Other students? Anything any of 'em say that strikes you as important?"

"No, I told you Tim was an exemplary man. In his teaching and life he fought against injustice, but still, no enemies for all that." Why were they making such a big deal about this?

Jameson nodded for me to continue.

"He prided himself on bringing different people—blacks and whites—together. That's why he loved examining the period leading to the Civil War, when African-Americans and whites worked together to combat the white terrorists who brutally oppressed their slaves—and former slaves. That's what his proposed thesis 'We Shall Not Be Moved—Black and White Together' is all about."

"Some students said he had quite a temper," Jameson cut in, a little softer.

"No, not really. Tim was even-keeled. Above all, for academic freedom, free speech. You know, very Voltairean."

"Voltairean?" Gerard asked. "Some kind of electrical current?" Big smile.

" 'I despise your view, but will defend to the death your right to express it.' That kind of thing. Hated extremes from left or right."

Jameson eyeballed me good, her voice measured, intent. "Are you aware that Mr. Hartknoll's apartment was violently trashed?"

How could I forget it, ransacked that horrible way? I put my head down for a second, and took some deep breaths. They paused for me to come up for more air.

"Did you go up to Mr. Hartknoll's apartment after the ambulance left?" she asked.

"Well, I had to get to my own apartment. I was upset." I pulled out my trancs and gulped two on the spot. Gerard looked at me quizzically. "Sorry, my toe's acting up again," I blurted. Damn, why weren't the pills working? I was sweating like Quasimodo at the stocks.

"May we see that?" Gerard asked softly.

My pillbox? Were they crazy? I managed a nice frosty smile. "If you need a pill, be my guests. Help yourselves."

They nodded comfortably to each other, comparing the pills with something in Jameson's hand I couldn't see.

Then dear, nice guy Gerard murmured so smugly, "Yes, they match—same brand, same tranquilizer. Thorazine."

Turning to me, holding up a tiny pill inside a small vial, Jameson announced, "We found this in his bedroom. On the floor."

Damn, was I *that* stupid, to have dropped one there?

"Maybe it was Tim's?" I wasn't normally such a devious dissembler. At least such a fumbling one.

"No, it wasn't, Jeff," Gerard said. "We've looked in your friend's medicine chest. There's no evidence that he took tranquilizers."

Jameson stopped chewing. Thank God. Her face was a glacier now. "Mr. Gardner, will you please answer my question? Why don't you admit you were in his apartment yesterday?"

"Well, okay, I was. Why are you bugging me this way? Why all these incessant questions?"

"Because we're trying to find out what really happened."

My cellphone rang. "Hi, Popster! It's Nellie." I'd better calm down for her.

"Sorry, I can't talk now, sweets."

"You okay, Popster? Mom told me what happened yesterday to your friend, Tim."

"Thanks for calling, but not now. Later, darling. Want to see you soon . . . tonight. Promise." I hung up the phone, breathing heavily.

"That was your daughter, right? Detective Jameson, here, has an adorable five-year-old daughter. You know what her favorite story is? *Pinocchio!*"

Very funny. Gerard put his hand on my shoulder, halfway between a gentle pat and a nagging tug. "C'mon, like your daughter said, Tim was your friend, wasn't he? Don't you want to help? What're you hiding?" he asked, in a tone halfway between pleading and commanding. "C'mon, don't pull a Pinocchio on us!"

I wasn't going to drag down Tim. Now or ever. So, I let go, like an avalanche. Told them *everything* about the book—Tim's encounter with Antonio, their drive to authenticate it, my promise to go in with the deal, all up to its theft in Tim's apartment. Everything.

"Thank you, Jeff," Gerard said, "we appreciate your coming clean—and telling us what really happened. But why didn't you from the get-go?"

"Frankly, I was embarrassed, Detective Gerard. I didn't want you to think I was more concerned about the book than . . . staying in the lobby and consoling Tim's relatives. I just wasn't thinking.

"Okay, okay," Jameson said, flipping a page in her notebook. "Now, go into some more about what you encountered in Mr. Hartknoll's apartment."

"Well, you gotta understand how important this book was to Tim. The last thing I said to him as we were walking home was to find a good hiding place for it. In his bedroom! So, once I realized that Tim was . . . gone, I suddenly panicked and went up there looking for it."

"You had a key to his apartment?"

"Yeah. We exchanged keys, in case of any emergencies. When I got there, and saw how it was trashed, it hit me that the book was missing. I just had to sit down and take a tranc to calm myself. When I noticed his tour cap on his dresser, I impulsively grabbed it and stuffed it into my pocket, then got the hell out."

I jerked out of my chair and hobbled to the front closet. A minute later I returned, clutching Tim's tour cap. "This is all I have left of Tim," I confided, lifting it up into the air like evidence at a trial.

"Quite a story, Jeff. Yes, sad . . . " Jameson paused for a second or two and whispered something to Gerard.

"Hold onto the cap, Jeff. It's okay. Keep it. And you might as well know, it'll soon be in the news. Do you have any idea what caused Mr. Hartknoll's death?"

"No, only—I mean, when I last saw him—he looked terrible."

Mr. Hartknoll ingested too many sleeping pills," Gerard said matter-of-factly. "Strange, there was no evidence of sleeping pills in his apartment." He went on and on, but I couldn't take it, didn't want to even listen. My head was in a nether-zone, making me hear words through a vertigo-like dizziness, but they weren't attached to anything I could take in. Did he say sleeping pills? Was it accidental? Suicide? Murder?

My cellphone spared me for the moment. It was Rachel, holding back her grief, asking me if I was coming tomorrow, giving me directions to the church. "Yes . . . of course, Rachel." I let her go on talking as I looked at her "Beach Party" painting again. I sensed the detectives' impatience with me, but I had to take my time writing down her directions.

While I was still writing, Jameson put away her pad and pen and Gerard started to get up. "Yes . . . I'll be there, Rachel. Speak? Say some words at the service? I don't know . . . I'll see you then . . . Take care of yourself."

I put away my cell and waited. What the hell was next? Would I be escorted to police headquarters for further questions? Did they suspect me of poisoning Tim? Was this the real reason for their visit today?

"Thanks for your time, Jeff." The good cop again. "You've been very helpful. If we need you for further questions, we'll contact you."

Of course, Jameson had to add her own cookie-cutter remarks. "Oh, Dr. Gardner, I wouldn't travel too far, if I were you. In case we need you."

Good luck to the cops. I prayed with all my mixed-up agnostic heart that they would come through quick.

Five minutes later, a knock on my door. Why? The cops coming back to dog me some more? So soon? No, thank God, it was Doree.

"Are you okay, Dr. Gardner? Poor Mr. Hartknoll. I had no idea what a sick man he was. Maybe he should also have been checked out in the infirmary, along with you!"

Did she notice the police leaving my apartment? I didn't feel like going into what the cops related. She was getting all emotional again.

"Oh, Dr. Gardner. Some painkiller pills for you. I went to the drugstore . . . "

As she handed them to me, we tightly hugged each other in shared sorrow.

"Thanks, Doree. I'll see you tomorrow at the funeral. Take care."

Chapter Six

Saturday morning

Under other circumstances, I would've been glad to get away from the city for a beautiful Saturday in the sun, lured to the southern Long Island community of Copiague with promises of relaxation and sports. But there was no sun in store for me on this trip.

I decided to take the train. I didn't want a lift from anyone else from Greene Cent who had a car. It would be easy for them to remind me about my tenure review meeting coming up next week, and I was in no mood to think about *that* now. I needed to be alone to collect my thoughts and grieve in my own way.

At least the slow thirty-five mile train journey gave me some time to think. Yes, about those cops, but more about Tim.

I still couldn't get it out of my head. Why did I encourage him to even proceed with Shady Lady? When I agreed to help him pay for it, didn't I do just that? Sure, I should have known better.

My mind drifted to Tim's family in Copiague—a stepfather, a mother, and an eighteen-year-old sister, Rachel. "My lifeline," he used to say, referring to the tight bond he and his sister had developed over the years He never said much about his parents, except that they were hard-working and serious—and expected much from their children.

His real dad died five years ago, just about the time I met Tim. Mine, like the father in *The Glass Menagerie,* was a "distant" dad, so we had that much in common. Except Tim loved his, while I barely tolerated mine. Pa was a brewery worker in Milwaukee, who wanted me to make something of myself—meaning make lots of money. We had a falling out in '88, my first year of college, when I supported Jesse Jackson running for president. One hot summer night, we were watching the Democratic Convention on TV, and I cheered wildly when Jesse spoke of keeping hope alive. "He's for the little guy, Pa," I said.

"Yeah, little—like me? Bull! You're sticking up for the guys who are taking our jobs away! That nigger Commie bastard!" my dad yelled at me. Dumb move, but I cheered some more, and Pa reached for an empty beer bottle like he was going to hit me with it. I froze. He stood there, shaking, drops of sweat all over his face.

"And another thing! Don't ever call me *little* again, you Commie bastard!" he shouted, taking another threatening step toward me. I fled the house, my mom screaming for me to come back.

After he retired a couple years later, I headed for New York and never made much money, choosing instead, after a brief stint as an actor, to become a high school teacher in the South Bronx, getting my Ed.D. on the side, and finally joining the faculty of Greene Cent Graduate School, getting promoted by *teaching,* not sucking up, I'm proud to say.

Tim's mother had remarried after his father died. His stepfather was an ex-Marine, who, according to Tim, sometimes acted like a drill sergeant to his children. Still, even he would have been proud of Tim, with his academic career, his dedication to civil rights, his uprightness as a human being—a perfect son! Except for Tim's *problem,* as he put it.

Bethel African Methodist Church claimed to be the oldest black house of worship on Long Island. I arrived late to a crowd that had overflowed the red-roofed, shiny white-shingled church. I managed to find a little space in one of the back pews just as a hymn was finishing. Looking around, I spotted a few people I knew—Max Raben, some of Tim's Greene Cent colleagues, Doree, and of course, a score of students who must have been Tim's. The majority of mourners looked like relatives, friends, and neighbors in this small, tight-knit black community. My three gals—Sasha, Nellie, and Nan, my almost ex—had claimed their own excuses for not coming.

I was in time for the testimonials, informal platitudes of praise to Tim. Relatives, friends, students, and Raben, of course, went up to the dais and spoke of their treasured ties to Tim, little stories that brought him briefly back to life, such as his volunteer work with homeless kids. Laughter intermingled with the tears. I should've gone up myself to speak, but I had a lousy excuse—my dumb toe.

I looked up to see family members join the minister in the pulpit. Tim's frail mother was too distraught to join them.

A budding portrait artist, Rachel herself was a picture of graceful simplicity, with a dancer's classic figure and the face of Nefertiti—soulful brown eyes, full red lips, and finely-sculpted cheeks. She wore a tiny bird pendant pinned on her black cashmere sweater. When she got up in the pew to remove her suit jacket and take out some tissues from her purse, I noticed she was wearing white gloves, adding to her subdued elegance.

Rachel held her mom close as the gospel choir sang their hearts out with a favorite hymn, "Lift Ev'ry Voice and Sing," which Tim himself used to belt out in the choir. Next was a soulful Sam Cooke song, "A Change Is Gonna Come," that Tim used to sing as a kid. A surprising choice, I thought, considering Cooke had died from a gunshot wound back in 1964, at the young age of 33. The circumstances of his death were cloudy, some saying it was an accident, others claiming it was an attempt to silence him for being one of the first entertainers—black or white— to refuse to sing for segregated audiences.

The end of the service was very spiritual and uplifting. The pastor talked about Tim seeking out God to do His bidding by caring for others. When he intoned the words, "Surely goodness shall follow me all the days of my life and I shall dwell in the House of the Lord forever," everybody was in tears, me included. He spoke passionately of love, justice, and mercy, all qualities which Tim had in abundance. A few more words by one of Tim's favorite uncles and the service was over.

As the mourners slowly left the church, I managed to briefly greet those I knew and offer my condolences to both parents, who were unmercifully shaken with grief. But it was Rachel I wanted to spend some time with. Hugging her, I looked into her sleep-deprived eyes and mumbled, "I'm sorry." What else could I say?

She was pleased to see me. We moved over to a corner, where Rachel asked if I had some time before the reception. "There's something important I want to talk with you about," she put it simply.

I told her that I had to get back to the city, so I couldn't stay, and asked for her forgiveness." There is nothing to forgive. I'll drive you to the station after the burial and maybe we can stop for a few minutes along the way."

I nodded that it was okay.

The burial service was eloquently brief and simple. Rachel said good-bye to some of her friends and family, and then returned to me.

"I have to tell my parents." I looked over to a cluster of mourners as Rachel approached her mom and stepdad, Donny MacNeil. He didn't look too happy about her leaving now, but she promised she wouldn't be long, and would meet up with them later. His disapproving eyes followed us like a cold beam as Rachel and I made our way to the church parking area.

Chapter Seven

Ten minutes later

We were sitting in Rachel's compact Chevy, silently making our way to Amity Harbor. "Let's sit on a bench over there, overlooking the ocean," she said. "I come here whenever I want to sit and think. Or do some painting."

The waves gently rolled in, soaking up the sand. The noonday sun was teased by a wisp of a cloud in an otherwise clear blue sky. In spite of the inviting beach scene, there was nobody there, as if nature respected us on this somber morning.

With a warm smile, Rachel's eyes met mine for a second. "Thanks again for coming, Jeff. I know that Tim would've wanted it."

I recalled the few times that I had been with her, when she visited her brother in Greenwich Village. Though there were eight years between them, they were tight. In spite of their age differences, the similarities in their appearance and character were so clear. A natural portrait of grace, simplicity, and tenderness.

"Quite a service, huh, Jeff? Oh, such wonderful words about my brother! A good person, but, of course, not as perfect as his eulogy made of him."

"Who's perfect, anyhow?" Yeah, Rachel, sure as hell not me, I admitted silently to myself.

"Did Tim ever tell you why we moved to Copiague?"

"No."

"Well, it had to do with an incident when he was fourteen. You know, we once lived in a bad neighborhood in Brooklyn. My brother used to run with a pack of boys, always getting into trouble. One day they started to sneak over a turnstile at the subway station like they often did, but this time were caught. A cop blew his whistle. All the boys ran away . . . except Tim. He just had to *prove* himself—show off his manhood, I suppose—by jumping over it. This cop—he must've had something to prove to himself as well—ran after Tim, yellin', 'Nigger, stop!' "

Rachel's eyes began to tear as she continued. It was so painful for her to go on, I wished she would stop altogether.

"The cop must've tripped, falling right at the end of the platform, with his arm dangling over the edge. And there was Tim, five feet away, frozen so bad he wasunable to help. Oh, those honky newspapers had a field day blasting Tim for not rescuing the cop. All he had to do was pull him away from the track! Yeah, right. What in the hell do you expect from a fourteen-year-old! He just couldn't move. It was pure fear! We couldn't live with all those blame games going on, Jeff. So we moved away from Brooklyn the next month and then came here to Copiague."

Tim never said a word about it. I guess it was just something too hard for her to talk about. I extended my arms to her in an awkward attempt to comfort her.

"Well, it looks like your family—and Tim—recovered nicely. Look at what a wonderful person your brother turned out to be."

"Yes, I guess you could say that movin' out here brought some positive changes to Tim."

"How so?"

"His whole personality changed! He was no longer the wild rebel, but the star, the shining bright star. He began to excel in everything— academics, sports, even sang in the church choir. Y'know, the same kind you heard in our church today."

"So after you moved to Copiague, Tim was okay?"

"Basically, yes. Except he had trouble sleeping lately."

"I don't—"

"Well, the police said that, according to the lab report, there was an excess of sleeping pills in Tim's system. He took the pills because of sleeping problems, right? The newspaper reporters have been calling day and night, pestering us. Did you see that terrible story about the professor taking his own life? My Tim! No, he wouldn't—"

"You're right. He couldn't have done that." But how could I be sure?

"To top it off, Jeff, I got a phone call yesterday. From a Detective Lynda Jameson."

"Jameson? Can I ask what she wanted?"

"She told me they were working on the case as . . . a possible . . . homicide. Oh, Jeff . . ."

I held Rachel close to me. Looking out into the unending expanse of the ocean, I said as softly as I could, "He must have loved you very much."

"Tim was so thoughtful. He even told me he was taking on an extra job as a tour guide in the city to help me out when I was in trouble once."

She paused again, a tiny tremble.

For a long minute, I held her in my arms, both of us staring into an empty ocean. A little boy strolled onto the beach with his dog.

"Jeff, who would want to . . . harm Tim?"

"That's what I'd like to know."

Unexpectedly Rachel laughed. Her eyes followed the boy as he tossed a Frisbee into the air for his excited pet to chase.

"I was thinking that my parents will be in for some surprise when those detectives started prying into Tim's life. They won't be able to take it. Things are going to come out to the public."

"Well, I already know that Tim was gay, and frankly quite at ease with it."

"You do? Well, I'm not surprised. Tim was much more open about it in the City, but not at home."

"Yeah, your stepfather, the tough-as-nails ex-Marine wouldn't tolerate it, would he?" Tim wasn't so beloved by every family member after all, from what I knew of Tim's negative feelings about hard-balls Donny.

"They had a big blowup. Led to Tim's final break from the house. But not before my brother helped me. Big time. Left him with quite a debt. Jeff, I thought that Tim had mentioned . . . I recently had an abortion." Her face was flushed. She turned away.

I shook my head. I had no idea. The little boy and his dog ran off when his mother called. A flock of seagulls swooped down, looking for . . . whatever. I waited for a few seconds before I could continue.

"Did your stepfather know about . . . your condition?"

Her face tightened up when she turned to me. "I don't want to get into that."

"Yeah . . . well, it must be hard for you to be still living at home."

"Yes, Jeff, but it was harder for Tim. Not only do we have to act 'perfect' at home, but we always have to watch our backs in the community. Can't have any scandals. It's the 'black' thing. Being a minority in a white town."

"Oh?"

"Yes. Think of it. Only four percent of Copiague's population is black. That means we have to go to white schools, shop in white stores, play with goody white children. We'd better be good, we'd better be smart, we'd better be clean, we'd better be—"

"Better than better—"

"There's only one little niche where we can be ourselves around here—and that's the church! 'A mighty fortress is our God!' But to our pastor, Reverend Johnson, being gay is an abomination against Christ. And his being against gays with AIDS is even worse. His so-called *purity* makes me sick! He's such a terrible hypocrite."

I nodded.

"You see what an ordeal being in the closet here was for Tim—"

"Yes, of course."

"Being forced to lie, live a double life. I detest that too."

The waves were still rolling in gently. She slipped her white gloves on again.

Rachel got up. "Listen, Jeff. I have one more thing to tell you. Tim has a boyfriend in New York. He needs to be found. Someone has to let him know him about Tim."

"Who is he? Maybe I can reach him."

"His name is Derek. I don't know his last name. Tim just met him. I never had the chance—"

"Some tall order, Rachel. How d'you expect *me* to find him? I mean, I can try."

"I only have one clue. Both he and Tim were working for that tour company, City-Wide, or something, the one that deals about the artists and writers in the Village."

"Hmmm. I know where Tim worked. I'll check it out."

A slight smile on Rachel's face. I said, "That's better, Rachel. You just have to know that I'm here for you . . . and Tim."

One more embrace. I didn't know when I would be seeing her again.

"Jeff, it was rough. Tim was going to help me pay off my abortion from something he was going to sell. That's all I can say. He called me last week, all heated up about some old book he found that he was going to unload somewhere."

"Did he tell you anything 'bout it?"

"Well, he did mention that it had something to do with a lady. We laughed about it. He used to call me his 'regular little lady.' Funny, isn't it? I hardly deserve that title . . . but since I'm eight years younger, it still kinda fits. Jeff, my stepfather knows about the book too."

"Yeah? Really?"

"Yes. Tim contacted Donny 'bout a week ago, asking him to witness a transaction between himself and another man."

Her tears were welling up again, ruining her mascara, as if she cared.

"The hell with it, let it run," she joked. "Thanks, Jeff. I gotta go now. My parents will be wondering where I am. I should be with them at the reception. I'll drive you to the railroad station, okay?"

When we got back to her car, Donny was waiting for her, his eyes lacerating into her. He motioned for her to get into her car and said he'd drive me to the station.

"I'll talk to you soon, Jeff," she said faintly, as she squeezed into her seat and drove off.

Ex-Marine Major Donald MacNeil motioned for me to get into his PT Cruiser. Once I was inside, I noticed he was playing on his cassette player a fitting dirge, Mahler's "Ninth," the last before the composer died so young and so sad. MacNeil turned the volume down.

"Jeff, I'm glad you could make it to the funeral."

"Why not? Tim was my friend. It was the least I could do."

"You and me—we got to meet again, real soon."

"Oh?"

"Yes. About the book. You know. I think we very well might be able to set up some kind of deal, mutually beneficial to both of us—"

"May I ask you, sir, what you know about the book?"

"Sure. I've known about it since last Thursday, the day he—"

"Well, thanks Mr. MacNeil. Maybe. But now's not the time for us to talk about it."

"Hold it, Jeff. I just want you to know that Tim got me involved from the moment he asked me to be with him and this guy—Antonio—I think his name was, at an East Village diner at 8:00 a.m."

"Why?"

"The way I understand it, Tim told me he had made some kind of a book deal with Antonio, but the guy didn't seem satisfied, and wanted to speak with my son further about it. Tim was scared that Antonio would cheat him out of their agreement, maybe demand more money, so he asked me to join 'em, for my imposing presence, you could say. Just so things went the right way! And they did, at least then."

I could see that this bully ex-Marine might've scared the shit out of Antonio.

"Oh, Tim mentioned you also."

I flinched. "Why?"

"Well, it turned out that Antonio called the meeting because he wasn't sure Tim had the balance to pay him, based on something Tim said when they were at the ATM."

"What . . . ?"

" 'Don't worry, señor,' he told the immigrant. 'I gotta partner who can help out.' "

Meaning me, of course. Pretty confident of Tim, to deal me in before he even asked!

"The next time I heard 'bout the book was when Tim's mail clerk handed me his mail. Something very amazing—a letter of certification, addressed to Tim—and *you!*"

He drove to the station without a further word. I got out of the car, wondering if he would show me the letter—and try to squeeze me on some deal.

Chapter Eight

A few minutes later

I was surprised to see Doree on the train already. When I greeted her, it was like I had awakened her from a deep sleep.

"I took a cab over. I didn't know you got a ride, Dr. Gardner. Nice car, " she said, with what sounded like a tinge of envy.

She said she was happy that no one in the funeral service had talked about what Tim had done when he was a kid. I was surprised that she even knew about it. But, then again, she did do a lot of extra work for Tim, word-processing his stuff, so he must've shared some of his boyhood misadventures with her.

"It was such a beautiful service, Dr. Gardner."

"Yes, it certainly was, Doree. Let me ask you something. Do y'know his friend Derek, by any chance?"

"Yes. He and Mr. Hartknoll worked on some things together. I helped 'em."

"Oh? At Derek's place?"

"No, in Mr. Hartknoll's apartment, Dr. Gardner. In fact, he's sitting behind us, right now."

As I looked back, a skinny, young black man put down his Backstage newspaper. I pegged him to be in his mid-twenties, but he could have been younger.

"Hi, I'm Derek."

I didn't remember seeing him at the church service.

"So glad to finally meet up with you, Dr. Gardner. Tim said a lot of good things 'bout you."

I shook his hand. He held onto mine for a moment, firm and strong. He was wearing a plain grey cotton suit. His tie was hanging loose, and there was a spot on his white silk shirt—from tears or sweat? He looked uncomfortable in his suit, like it was choking off his blood vessels. His nice smile seemed genuine.

"I see you weren't planning to go to the reception either."

"Me? I'm an outsider. Like no one even knew I was in the church, stuck there in the back pew. Tim's stepdad wouldn't dig it if he knew I was involved with him. The tough ex-Leatherneck doesn't approve of his son being 'that way.' And that goes for the uptight Reverend Johnson dude too."

Derek removed his black, square Poindexter glasses and polished them like his life depended on it. "People see what they want to. Can I call you Jeff?"

"Of course." I wanted to move next to him, but Doree, snuggling close, rested her neat curly head on my shoulder and fell soundly asleep. Noticing a Long Island newspaper wedged in between the seats, I wondered if it carried any more news about Tim. But I was too wiped out myself to look now.

"There was so much Tim and I were gonna do together with music," Derek began, with a little laugh. "You know, I thought we'd hook up on an AIDS relief project for Africa. But Tim convinced me to keep the focus on the devastation, y'know, of AIDS on black people right here in *this* country, like helpin' the kids hangin' around my block at night. Brave soul, Tim was, workin' with them tough screwed-up kids. That was his number one project."

Derek's voice trailed off as he slumped down into his seat. All I heard now was the rhythmic sound of wheels slowing down.

When we got off, Doree asked me if I wanted to share a cab back to our building.

I had other plans, I told her politely.

"You sure I can't help?" she dutifully asked anyway.

"No thanks, that's alright, Doree. I'll be okay."

She said good-bye to both of us. As Derek and I rode up the escalator to the street level, I asked him if he knew anything about a rare book that Tim had discovered.

"Hmm, the only book I know about is the binder of personal notes he keeps 'bout the Bleecker Blues tour he leads. Y'know, I'd only been on the job a couple weeks when Tim shared it with me."

"Do you know, uh, where I can see it?"

"Maybe in the CWC, Ink office. Could be. Why?"

"To know more about him." What I thought was, maybe I'll find some clues about who did that to Tim . . . or where I could find Antonio—maybe.

"Okay, man. Hey, did you ever take the tour Tim led?"

"No."

"You might want to check it out, man. See that great material he put together. The tour'll be startin' up on Monday. Though it won't ever be the same without him."

"Thanks for checking on Tim's personal Bleecker Blues binder, Derek. I—"

"Hey, don't mention it, brother. Not a problem. I'll hold onto it for you, if I find it."

If the cops hadn't got it already, I thought. I waved good-bye to Tim's lover. Or his— I quickly chastened myself for even suspecting him, but at this point, there was no reason not to.

I told the cab driver to hold on a bit as I waited for Derek to go into his apartment building off Christopher Street in the West Village.

* * *

When I got back to my apartment, a ton of e-mails sat waiting for me: one from Doree, thanking me for keeping her company on the train, another from Rachel, just thanking me. My phone messages were clogged up too.

The eighth or ninth was one I had to play over and over. It started with "Dr. Gardner," so at first I thought it was from one of my students. But it went on: "Dr. Gardner, this is Reverend James Johnson from the Bethel African Episcopal Church, where Timothy Hartknoll's beautiful funeral service took place this morning. I didn't want to disturb you then, but this is a matter of great concern. Timothy's father mentioned today something about a rare book that Timothy owned—a book that would benefit the African-American community. We would like to talk with you about this, at your convenience, of course, as soon as you're able. There's also a Derek Molson, Tim's friend, who might be part of this team too. If you would kindly help us with that . . ."

I had to play his phone message back five times, it was so hard to believe. Contact Derek Molson? How the hell did *Derek* get in the act? On the train, he had denied knowing anything about the book. It was Tim and I who got the book deal together and as far as I was concerned we *alone* were going to put it on the market—or maybe even donate it to a worthwhile nonprofit organization. Tim never even mentioned Derek.

So he might be mixed up in this whole thing! Okay, that got me thinking that I needed someone on my side. Someone I could trust, share my doubts and questions. Sasha. Sure. For her, sharing with people she cared about was real, not the so-called phony kind of sharing a lot of people did on their Facebook connections.

I decided to call her on my cellphone, leaving my other phone free to record any messages. I got into bed, propping up my leg like she told me. She listened patiently as I went over everything as cooly and matter-of-factly as I could, a very condensed story of what happened between Tim and me the past few days—right up to the funeral today. I played down the cops' visit, since it seemed now that I was, thank goodness, in the clear with them. I also left out Antonio's plan to meet Tim in the Village—to take care of "unfinished business." There'd be too many questions about this, and I didn't want to needlessly worry her.

"Wow. Heavy, Jeff. I gotta take this all in," was Sasha's first response. A pause, then, "Anything else you need to share? Feelings about . . . anything? I'm here for you. If you'd like, I can come over . . ."

"Not now, Sash, there'll be loads of time later." I was relieved she was eager to help out, but still wondered how deeply her involvement could ever really be.

"I understand, honey . . . take your time."

"Thank you, Sash—I'll work it out."

"If you want to make it work, don't work *on* it, Jeff. Let it loose, let it come to you. Try concentrating on relaxing, dear, okay? Do what makes you feel comfortable. You know, the best way to relax is to focus on positive things . . . for instance, people . . . people you like . . . you love . . . "

"I know . . . I know. Thank you."

"Brunch tomorrow?"

"Yeah, great idea, Sash. The Open Bagel?"

"All the way here to the East Village ? What about your toe? I can come over there."

She wanted to be "close," she said. Yes, meaning going all the way, something I had unfortunately been avoiding, in order to honor the no-sex clause in my separation contract with Nan.

"Don't worry. I'll hop on the crosstown Eighth Street bus."

"Usual time?"

"Yes. Take it easy, Jeff. Love you."

That's all I needed to hear for now.

Chapter Nine

Sunday morning

I tried to put the funeral behind me, but Rachel's words kept coming back, "Who would want to hurt Tim?" I spent the morning reading the papers and noshing with Sasha at The Open Bagel in the East Village. But I was not quite through with ventilating my feelings to her about yesterday's events. I confessed how choked up I got at the funeral, but said pitifully little about meeting with Rachel afterwards. Too disturbing. Sasha was content to cut me the space and we let it go at that.

As sometimes happens in this nabe, a Greene Cent student passed by our table, thanking me for his grade. A warm shake of hands, and he was off to another trendy East Village spot. Sasha was happy that I was so appreciated. But this brief encounter only brought back the Greene Street blues.

We settled down on the topics of the day featured in the Sunday Times. *Surge. Pull out the troops. The pain of Hurricane Katrina.* Too much for me, too many contradictions of hope and despondency to deal with now. Easier, in a way, to go back in history to consider something at hand, more real, if the book could be found. Poking my fork in scrambled egg whites, I had a sudden vision, that if the story of the book and Douglass were available to readers across the country, it could renew a dialogue about the pain of slavery and the pride of fighting for freedom in so many forms, here and around the world.

Sasha snapped me back to Earth. "You okay, honey?" When she was assured I was, we got back to chatting about her job and what was new in the macular degeneration field. (A lot of new studies promised some breakthroughs. Too late for my dad, though, who had an advanced case of it.) We finished our brunch on a high note of starting the crossword puzzle.

After she reminded me of our plans to attend a rock concert in Tompkins Square Park that evening, I gave her a peck, assuring her that I would be there in ample time.

As she started back to her apartment, I caught a cab over to Nan's place to pick up Nellie for our once-a-week visit.

Nan and I had our usual curt exchange.

"How was the funeral, Jeff?"

"Beautiful."

"Sorry I missed it."

After a brief pause, we awkwardly embraced, just as my teeny-bopper Nellie bounded in with her usual high energy. She seemed delighted in catching us in this pose.

"Hi, Popster. Where we goin' today?"

"We have a couple of choices. I'll let you call it."

Nan shooed us out the door. "Have a good time, you two. And, Jeff, don't forget our group counseling session on Saturday."

"Yeah, I won't. Remember, I'm meeting Max Raben the next day about my tenure. That oughta make you happy!"

Nan smiled. "Good luck with it, Jeff."

I know why she was wishing me this. One of the reasons why we broke up was my neglect in getting on with the damn thing.

Nellie and I couldn't make up our minds whether to see a new circus movie uptown or a live street theatre performance in Washington Square Park down the block.

Since it was a nice warm, breezy day, I opted for the latter so we could schmooze and catch up. Trying to explain, with my limited knowledge, Einstein's Special Theory of Relativity for Nel's science class had stiff competition with her gawking dreamily at the lanky young white-faced clown juggling oranges at the edge of the park's fountain. Looking at boys now was a big part of her rather crowded social life. At school she still liked the geeky thirteen-year old Aerosmith knockoff with the smelly bandanna wrapped around his head. I owed her a talk about that, but now I kept things light.

"What's the big deal about Einstein anyway, Nel? All he did was juggle the three letters—E, C, and M—together, and add the number two, squared. C'mon, any kindergarten kid could do that, right?"

She giggled and hugged me. One of the clown's oranges slipped from his hand and rolled a bit over the fountain floor.

"Embarrassing . . . but the dude doesn't seem to care, Dad."

"Of course not. What goes up, comes down, that's all. And starts all over. Life goes on. Like your graduation comin' up in a couple weeks."

Nellie laughed at that too, but what I meant as a joke flashed on me how Rachel's life was thrown so suddenly into a windfall of despair.

She must've sensed something was up with me when we started baking cookies in my apartment. I told her how much I looked forward to our weekly ritual of guilty pleasures. My daughter was plump like me, although you could tell from any number of photos on my fridge door she was far cuter, with her dangling brown curls, bright eyes, and dimpled cheeks. Heaven forbid if Nan found out about our weekly criminal cookie caper!

"Roger that, dude!" she said, handing back the box I had put out on the kitchen counter. "But, Dad, unless we want those cookies to be as hard as rocks, we better use baking powder instead of baking soda. Just a suggestion."

I don't know what touched it off, the word *just* or *gest* in suggestion, but what came through to me was *Jess*. Nel had no idea, of course, why I suddenly spooked and ambled over to the couch to lie down. How could I shake off Tim's last words, *"Jess, tour is . . ."*

"Hey, Dad, I was only kidding about the baking soda. You're an okay baker, the best!" she said, plopping down next to me.

"I'm tired, that's all."

"Then mind if I hit you with a couple of knock-knocks. Ready? Knock, knock!"

"I give up, who's dere?"

"Esther."

"Esther who?"

"Esther . . . a doctor in the house? And I don't mean you, Dr. Gardner!" she roared, mussing up my already tussled hair.

That got me up and we finished the baking, while attempting to sing, in harmony yet, some songs from *Hello Dolly*, which Little Red Schoolhouse, her intermediate school, had recently produced. Later, snuggling together on the couch while munching on the calorie-loaded cookies and watching America's Top Whatever, she ventured, "Anything wrong, Dad?" so innocently that my heart went into melt-down. I put on a smile, promptly changed the subject.

How's school, Nel? Not much left of the school year, huh?'

"It's okay, Dad. They're showin' some great movies for us graduating eighth graders during lunch period. *Citizen Kane* was on last week. Did you know Orson Welles was only twenty-five when he made it? Did you see it?

"More than once, honey."

"Remember Kane's dying word, 'Rosebud'? What does it mean?"

"Sorry. That's for the reporters in the story to figure out. And you."

I put on another smile and continued making silly wisecracks about the television show. During an ad about adopting dogs lost in Katrina, I resolved to get Nellie one for her upcoming graduation. After returning Nellie to Nan's apartment, I called Sasha, who reminded me again of our concert tonight at Tompkins Square Park. I told her that I'd meet her there, but first I had to get some solid shut-eye for a couple of hours. So I shut off all my phones and crawled into bed. Trouble is, I slept 'til morning—too hung over with some troubling dreams about keeping my commitments. Later it bothered me that I couldn't remember any of them.

Chapter Ten

Monday, 9 a.m.

The next morning, I was set to cab it up to CWC, Ink, a short hop to Times Square. On the way out, I was pleasantly surprised to see Doree placing some more flowers on the little memorial that was concocted for Tim in front of our building. After exchanging some somber greetings, I told her I was heading uptown in a cab.

"Oh, do you mind if I hook a ride with you, Dr. Gardner?" she asked. "Won't take a minute to get my things. It's important. This won't take you outta your way." In three minutes she was back again, toting a hefty Greene Cent gym bag.

We went out to fetch a cab. On the sidewalk in front of the building, there were more flower bouquets, candles, and messages written in different colored chalk: *When will we learn to love?—You will always be in our hearts, Professor Hartknoll—Rest in Peace—Beautiful Tim, we will love you forever.*

A newspaper intern who had been there from day one stopped us. "Pardon me, sir. I'm Joe Chiang from the Daily News. You knew Professor Hartknoll, didn't you? If I can ask you—"

"I've already given my statements. Sorry, uh, nothing to add."

"One minute! Just—" Joe started—and finished—as a cab thankfully rolled by.

Doree was at no loss of words as she rattled on about her mission this morning. "I didn't get any sleep last night, thinking about Mr. Hartknoll and all. My mom was up too, fretting about me. She spilled some tea on the floor and had a bad fall. It's all my fault. I'm going out to buy her a back brace near Grand Central. That's what this bag is for."

I got off at CWC, Ink on West 45th Street and wished Doree well, as the cab turned east. Sweeping by was one of City Wide Culture, Ink's red, white, and blue double-decker buses, with its logo in big bold letters, the W spanning the two C's like the wings of an eagle. Americana culture vultures flying high, I mused.

I craned my neck to see if anyone was following me, though it seemed ridiculous to me that the detectives would be on my tail. They were hopefully off my back now, giving me some room to see what I could uncover.

The building, right off Broadway, was sandwiched in between an Indian restaurant and a musical instruments shop. I took one more backward glance before entering, to make sure I hadn't been trailed. My heart was pounding like one of the drums in the shop's window.

I still wasn't sure this was a good move, but CWC, Ink was the only place I could reasonably check out now. Tim's apartment was sealed off as a crime scene, as was the package room area, where Al had tried to bring his body back to life. Most of the Greene Cent students and staff were already gone for the summer. It would be hard to reach those not enrolled in summer school as they scattered to apartment sublet cubbyholes all over the city or to resort jobs across the country.

With clues so scarce, I had nothing to lose checking out this place. I would talk to a few people, maybe take a tour. The security guard, an old black guy with a bent back and a sand-papery, whiskered face, took me up the creaky elevator to the seventh floor. I was buzzed in right away.

A youngish-looking, gum-chewing (no, not another Jameson!) receptionist, with peroxided hair, thrust a clipboard at me and said curtly, "You here for the job? Word gets around fast when we have an opening."

I didn't suspect that Tim's position was up for grabs. I had just come there to take a tour, that was all. But now, how could I pass up this big break falling right into my lap?

"I'll take your résumé now," the receptionist said mechanically.

My mind went into overdrive—gotta fix up my old résumé from my acting days. "I'm having it typed fresh. Can I bring it in tomorrow?"

"Sure. Fill in the application. Like, don't leave any blanks." She motioned me to sit in one of the three straw-covered moldering chairs inside, which shamelessly passed for a reception room.

Addressing my toe sticking out from its sandaled foot, she finally said it. "You know this position is for a *walking* tour? Like, you have to walk a lot. And you have to know a lot about music. History of it and stuff."

Of course, I knew. "This fabulous tour—great!" Tim proudly said to me more than once. I also knew that he had practically designed the Bleecker Street tour all by himself.

I looked around the reception room. Big headlines blared from all the walls, "LET YOUR IMAGINATION DO THE WALK-ING—FUN AND INFORMATIVE—INTERACTIVE AND EN-TERTAINING!" with jazzy graphics highlighting the glossy copy, proclaiming how the tours really get into the guts and souls of the artists and activists in New York history. The tour would take you up-front to the places "where they lived and worked and wrote and painted—and where some even died fighting for their belief in free expression." I surmised how perfect a guide Tim must've been for this tour adventure.

There was a poster entitled "Join the Ghosts of Gramercy Park," which featured writers such as O. Henry and Washington Irving— and tie-ins with Pete's Tavern, where short-story writer O. Henry once dined and knocked out stories. Another poster, "The Best of Brooklyn by Bus," highlighted resident writers such as Thomas Wolfe, Harriet Beecher Stowe, Carson McCullers, Arthur Miller, and Norman Mailer—and also proffered enticing breakfasts or lunches.

Tucked in the corner of the beige wall was Tim's itinerary, "Bleecker Blues: A Stroll Down Freedom Street." There were blown-up illustrations of Charlie Parker, Tom Paine, Lenny Bruce, Margaret Sanger, Frederick Douglass, and Walt Whitman. My heroes! I had lived on Bleecker Street in Greenwich Village now for close to twenty years. Hey, I could lead this same tour blind and backwards! But in my heart I knew why I was applying for this gig. And if I had to fib a little—what the hell! In this case, the ends would justify the means, so I gave myself an easy pass.

"It's like an inventory worksheet," the receptionist said, prodding me on. "Later you'll be taking a test. Here's the form. Like I said before, don't leave any blanks."

I focused my head on not leaving any, but also making sure I didn't include anything about Greene Cent.

I took a chance and used my real name. Vanity of vanities! But, whoa, red light! Address could be a problem. I filled in Sasha's, in the East Village, reminding myself to tell her later. Occupation. I put down unemployed actor. It was sort of true. At this moment, having just finished for the term, I was technically unemployed. And like lots of people who eventually went into teaching, I had done some acting when I first came to the Big Apple. I remembered Tim saying the tour owner liked actors because they were gabby and outgoing.

References might be an issue. I put down Bob Laprone, a boyhood friend from Milwaukee, as someone I knew when I attended New York University, where he taught now. Bob owed me for covering his classes when he got back late from an out-of-town conference tryst with a woman not his spouse. I would be sure to ask him later to say that I was a great teacher and lapped up history like a thirsty camel at a watering hole. The other reference I put down was my spinster aunt in Paterson, New Jersey, whom I hadn't seen in years.

Another woman, about sixty or so, wearing an oversized CWC, Ink T-shirt, introduced herself as Mrs. Jones and ushered me into her office, which was one of six or seven cubicles laid out in a row, all tendered by young employees busily taking reservations for tours. She went over my inventory worksheet and asked me why I thought I was suitable for the job. Time to do some more acting now. Oozing sincerity, I told her I loved people, which was half-true anyway. It depended on what people, and in which of my manic-depressive moods I was in, down and out, or giddy to go.

But I *loved* history. That was true. A double pump dunk! I was the only history major at Washington High School in Milwaukee, and my dad protested when I told him I planned to be a history teacher. "Be a lawyer, make some money!" he used to nag. Of course I didn't tell Mrs. Jones, and could tell no one else there—if I got the job—that I was an Associate Professor at Greene Street Grad Center of City University.

Mrs. Jones seemed pleasant enough, but had bad breath, and could have been a YouTube moment by the way the skin from her shoulder rolled back and forth when she pointed her nifty CWC, Ink monogrammed pen at me. I answered her questions briskly. She told me that there was an opening on the *Bleecker Street Line* (her words) and while the company cleared my references and fingerprints, I would be part of a *test run* (her words) tomorrow, to see how it worked out. The *trials* (her word) would take three days.

With the finesse of a sumo wrestler, she thrust a plain black binder in my hand and motioned for me to take out the papers. "Bleecker Blues—A Stroll Down Freedom Street. Conceived by Timothy Hartknoll." I glanced through it, but, no, this wasn't Tim's personal binder, the one that I was looking for—his notes written in the margins. Just a copy for office use. Damn!

Mrs. Jones buzzed back the receptionist and asked her to get me some other information from a file. Then she adjusted the surveillance camera in the corner and strode over to me. Looking up at the camera, for a split second, I wondered if she had been recruited by the detectives to keep an eye on me. Yeah, silly me.

"Be careful of what you say on the tour," she said in a guarded tone. "Stick to the facts on those info sheets when you lead, okay?"

I nodded, smiling compliantly. And then I mused, what if Shady Lady was really some place around *here*? I looked over to the almost barren bookcase lining one of these cracked walls. It could be anywhere. I would have to snoop around . . . somehow.

"Pay attention," Mrs. Jones said. "I'm tryin' to explain."

And then she was talking about this young man who everyone "absolutely adored," as she put it. "One of our tour directors on the Bleecker Line—Tim Hartknoll—was so wonderful. We all loved him. You must have read something about him in the newspapers. He died . . . poisoned, it was believed." She reached for a tissue.

Should I have told her that I knew him, that I was his colleague, that we shared a secret? Or that I felt guilty that something he got from someone on the tour might have led to his death?

"Did he mention the name of a book by Sir Walter Scott?" I asked.

"I don't know what you're talkin' about," Mrs. Jones said. "We have no Walter or Scott working here. C'mon, we gotta tend to business. Let me introduce you to some of our staff."

Chapter Eleven

Right after

Mrs. Jones led me into another small paint-cracked room, where some other applicants at a long table were taking a test. The four fans scattered around the room were supposed to cool us. Not much.

The test consisted of general questions about the Big Apple and on some specific areas, like Greenwich Village, Soho, and Tribeca. Scanning the sheets, I knew that it would be a breeze, but I didn't want to come on like a Jeopardy whiz in front of Ms. J. Recalling the advice of a long-ago acting teacher, "Whatever you do, make it *seem* real," I chewed on my pencil, bit my lip, and scratched my head. "Bogus. Overacting! Not normal," my teacher would've scolded. In due time, I handed my completed test to Mrs. Jones, whose eyes brightened as she got to the third page. She must've known the multiple-choice answers by heart.

"Good, you passed the written test, one-hundred percent," she said. "Now we'll see about the practical test. One of our staff—it might be Mr. Jankowitz himself—will meet you at the Bleecker Street Playground tomorrow morning. Here's a map of the area. Learn it inside out. You'll get your Tour Director Kit—including cap and T-shirt—*if* you pass the trials. At that time, you can also learn how the mike works." Surveying my damaged toe, she added, "You sure you can get around . . . with that?"

I didn't have time to tell her anything. Three young tour guides, all wearing CWC, Ink T- shirts, burst in from the other room. Hey, one of them was Derek, who shot me a side-glance wink. Mrs. Jones introduced them as the actors who did scenes along the tour route. Derek motioned me to the bathroom, where I joined him directly.

"Jeff! What's up?"

"Derek, listen, this is serious and I have to know. Now! Remember, on the train back from the funeral, I asked if you knew anything about a rare book that Tim had?"

"Sure. And I said that I knew nothin' about it. Only book we worked on together was his personal binder for the tours!"

"Yes, as I recall. But then yesterday, I got a telephone message from Reverend James Johnson."

"You mean that dude that covered Tim's funeral?"

"Exactly. The message said he wanted to get in touch with you about the book Tim found. Will you please explain that? Now don't jerk me around!"

He wiped his glasses hard. "I just told you, I don't know nothin' about that book! Word! And further more, Jeff, I had no conversation with no reverend. Never even met him. I swear on my momma! Look, I'll show you somethin'."

He put his Poindextors back on and pulled out a stuffed three-ring blue binder from his sling bag.

"Look what Tim left in my apartment. Take a gander, Jeff. Tim's personal—"

"Binder," I said sheepishly, feeling foolish that just a minute before I was hard on Derek's case. "Thanks," I added, leafing through it. Many of Tim's hand-written notes were in there. "This is something, Derek! This will really keep me stickin' to the tour!"

"That's okay, man," Derek said, pulling the book from my hands. "But I'd like to hold on to this for a bit, if you don't mind."

"Wait. I need to look through it, Derek. When can I—? "

"No time now. Later! How 'bout my pad? I need to talk to you more . . ."

"What you two doin' in there so long for?!" Mrs. Jones thundered, as she knocked on the men's room door. "Come out! Mr. Jankowitz wants to meet you, Jeff. He's waiting!"

"Come out, come out, wherever you are," Derek merrily trilled, as we bounced out the door. After the perturbed efficiency-expert

Mrs. Jones headed for her office, Derek kissed Tim's personal binder and put it gingerly back into his CWC, Ink sling bag.

"See you soon," he chirped again "Hope you bag the gig." He quickly joined the other actors in another room to go over their tour scripts.

Tim filled me in earlier about the owner of CWC, Ink, Hank Jankowitz. His background was, to say the least, idiosyncratic. A man from the Deep South who is born Henry Smith, changes his name to Jankowitz, drops out of college, becomes a one-person encyclopedia, wins a small fortune on the quiz show *Jeopardy*, and starts City-Wide Culture, Ink in four different cities, including his native Atlanta, Georgia.

"Come in, come in," he fairly shouted, "and leave the door open. I'm expecting some other hopefuls later."

I was surprised to see how handsome and well-preserved the man appeared at seventy or so, until I noticed a motorized polished chrome wheelchair in the corner of the room. I liked this guy the minute I saw him. Everything about him was a mismatch, from his shiny bald head to his faded smudgy penny-loafers. A pair of soft, paisley suspenders barely held up his big-buckled cargo shorts, leaving just enough room for him to tuck in his spotty CWC, Ink T-shirt. Jankowitz motioned for me to take a seat. He ran his massive head down my personal data sheet, without once looking up at me.

"Hmmm," he said hoarsely, "history major . . . actor . . . what else?"
"What?"

He leaned forward from his antique oak desk that was littered with all kinds of maps and guidebooks. There were some family pictures on his desk as well. The pale, rose-colored walls were covered by manning boards, schedules, and photos of the multifaceted tour routes that made up the widely strewn empire of CWC, Ink.

"What else you got goin' for you? What's the story on that toe? 'Crown to toe, dire cruelty.' *Macbeth*, right? Ha! Tell me, when's the buddy-tape coming off? Soon I hope. There's a lot of walking. Walkin' and talkin', talkin' and walkin'—as Fats Domino might have sung it. Get it? They're walking tours of New York history, like the great ones Joyce Gold conducts, only we act them out."

He didn't give me a chance to answer, but went on and on how he grew up in poverty and supported a dysfunctional family and started his business single-handedly. His unstoppable oratory reminded me of how I had once applied for a job in Arizona and the chairman of the history department went on and on about it for an hour-and-a-half without asking me one solitary question.

Finally, Hank admitted he had a "good feeling" about me, that I even had the guts to apply for a walking tour with a "stubbed toe"— his words—and then he paused.

"I should talk. I'm reduced to using that wild speed wagon over there," referring to his wheelchair. "But, in my case," he said, "I just get around *faster,* a whole six miles an hour. So, I don't expect your little problem," pointing to my toe, "should be any real problem." I felt my toe shriveling into my shoe.

Hank chortled, changing the subject. His face lit up, exposing cherry dimples and a network of furrowed creases. "Well, Mrs. Jones told me you got a 100 on our test. Mmm, the *only* one I know ever to do so. That's good because, if you're hired, you'll be replacing an excellent man on that tour—one of the best. But, sadly, he passed on. I just wanted to tell you that, before I give you a live demo and a couple of trials. I mean, the cops and a reporter were here yesterday, asking me about him. It's okay, but I just thought you should know, in case you spot the police around. His name is Tim Hartknoll. Black guy. Really smart."

He held up what looked like a paperweight of the world and fiddled with it, his nervous energy getting to me.

"Tim's special tour was Bleecker Street, the gleaming jewel in our entire tour package. It wasn't always the case. When I handed Tim that tour to redesign, I initially resisted his kooky ideas. But it turned out he was right after all. God bless him. Whoever I hire to replace him has to make sure that this tour remains the jewel it is. He's got to be an exceptional tour guide, *vehrsteh?*, *comprende?* Got it, Sunshine?"

Hooray! He finally put the paperweight back on the desk.

"I'll lead the tour—Tim's tour—tomorrow. Dig, I'll model it, and you'll observe, like the rest of the applicants. Are you free the next three days? *Three Days of the Condor*. You ever see that spy-movie with Robert Redford? This'll be three days of *candor*. Just the facts, ma'am, thank you. By that time, we should have a pretty good idea what kind of mighty good guide you can be."

I felt committed, though I wasn't sure if my foot could take it. I said okay. *Okay*. The most over-used word in the English language.

"You're not the only one applying, you know. If you don't pass everything, you'll still be on your way. But the *other* way. Dig?"

I dug. Okay.

Jankowitz pulled a brochure from a pile of them on his desk and pushed it toward me. "This is a brief description of the tour you'll be following. Look it over carefully. Hilda Smithers, my assistant, will give you the particulars about your role on the tour as we go along. Bring a notebook and some index cards. You know, when I started in this game, our company never used notes. But now with Googling and all that overkill, we got to keep up. Googlin'—never use it myself. Computer phobia!"

Thank goodness for that—he won't be Googling my name!

"Oh, and your own clothes—neat, not like mine! Dinner'll be on us." That, I was glad to hear.

"There'll be four job applicants in total coming on board this week. You and another guy. Also, two gals. Nice." Pointing out the designated tour in the brochure, he added, "Note where and when the tour starts out. Be a half-hour early! See you tomorrow. Good luck!" We shook hands on that.

Oops! My cell rang. Nellie, I thought, keeping track of me. Not a good time. No, It was Max Raben, and he wanted to see me, *pronto*.

Had to be important, otherwise Doree would've called me. As I put away the cell, I offered a lame "excuse me" to him.

He shot me a withering look. "*This* time okay. But no cellphones on the tour when you are trying out—only me and Hilda. *¿Capiche?* No distractions!"

No computer, *no* cellphone. *Sí,* one *poco loco.*

He jabbed his forefinger to the door, and I was out of there.

I managed to get down the rubber-matted stairs. The security guard flipped off his well-worn Yankee cap and waved it at me. I guess his good feeling bolstered the snap decision I made upstairs. Didn't Yogi Berra once advise, "When you come to a fork in the road, take it"? I didn't know exactly where I was going with this, but at least it was a start, a stab at doing something.

As I crossed over the curb and walked into the heavy traffic looking for a cab to take me down to SoHo, I suddenly felt a hard push against my back that sent me crashing against a car stopping for a red light, inflicting a sharp cutting pain across my forehead when it bumped into the fender. No time to think about who did it. Reeling against the side of the car, I managed to spot a guy in a raincoat running across the street—the bastard who pushed me! I tried to get a good look at him, but he'd already disappeared.

My eyes were closing down, my head spinning as my feet found the curb again. I managed to plotz down to the pavement in a swirl of black dots, barely conscious of where I had been, where I was going.

I felt a gentle touch of my shoulder and looked up hazily. A stranger, a teen-aged girl, looked down at me and spoke. "Wow, I saw that, mister. You nearly got killed! Can I help you?"

"If you could, just let me rest a few minutes . . . and call a cab, okay?" I managed to find a bill in my wallet to offer her.

"No thanks, Mister. I'll just stay with you until you're, uh, ready to move. It looks like you only have a bruise on the head. Are you lucky!"

Within a few minutes, my Good Samaritan had hailed a cab. I got in—dizzily—and rested my head in my lap. It was too damn sore to touch, but there was no blood—yet. "Crown to toe," I crooned to my dazed self, "what a day this has been!" And I managed to mutter the words "Greene Street, in SoHo downtown, Sunshine . . ." to the driver, before slumping back into the seat.

Chapter Twelve

Twenty minutes later

The cab driver, a spunky refugee from an eastern European country, knew where SoHo was, but was unaware that Greene Street was split in the middle, broken up by some buildings running east and west, including where I live on Bleecker Street.

"Here ve are," he bellowed. "Greene and Eighth Street!"

I must've been out hard, letting him get away with taking me to the northern end of Greene. The wrong end.

"I am zo zorry, mist-ur," he kept on repeating.

"No problem, really," I tried to assure him. He probably thought I was drunk. The bump on my head reminded me I was very much sober. Enough to make me wonder if whoever pushed me was trying to kill me! And . . . why? Of course, tin brain, the book! Obvious, someone didn't want me to get Shady.

I told the cabbie to continue right along on to Broadway and then head south to Broome and a few blocks over to Greene. All the way there, 1010 News announced the latest bombing or natural disaster somewhere in the world, but my thoughts were closer to home, worrying about why Raben was ordering me to see him right away. My tenure could very well be on the chopping block.

I decided to keep my cap on, lest there be any questions about the new prize on my head. I didn't want to be blamed for that too.

Teetering around the garden, I approached the alabaster statue of Nathaniel Greene, after whom the school was named. He was Washington's favorite and most trusted officer during the Revolutionary War. The Greene Cent powers-that-be who erected the statue modeled it on the figure at the Washington Square Arch. Like the Washington statue, Greene had a burnished sword in one hand, and a big book in the other. The engraving on the statue cried out in bold letters, "Use Technology—Trust Men for Creativity!"

Back in the nineteen seventies, this naturally pissed off some of the women graduate students so much that they molded a humongous plastic penis, and in the dead of a winter's night, attached it on old Nat's groin with a sign, "TRUSTING MEN LIKE THIS AIN'T EASY!" With my head swirling full speed around from the bump, the sword looked to bleary-eyed me like a limp penis. I raised my imaginary glass of brew to dashing Nate.

I entered Greene Cent by way of the side entrance to avoid bumping into students. A couple of construction workers were putting up a wall that would eventually be part of a new student cafeteria, for which I could assume some credit. It was tough for students and faculty to find a low-priced decent meal in the midst of all the SoHo posh boutiques, wine bars, and art galleries. I was kind of proud to have served on a school building committee that would give the students a break.

I was greeted by Jackson O'Rourke, the pot-bellied, pure-bred Irish security guard who had been at Greene Cent from day one. His standing joke was that this cast-iron building once housed a huge six-story factory devoted to making textiles, and now the whole scene in SoHo was *sex* styles. "Sex this, sex that, Jeffie, m'boy," he said in his native brogue, "and I wish I was gettin' me some."

This time Jackson said nothing, just patted me on the shoulder, his way of acknowledging the loss of Tim. As I made my way to the elevator I noticed him scratching his graying head. Was he thinking about my infirmed toe? Or maybe he thought I was off the wagon. For any—or all—of those reasons, I reminded myself to act particularly sober in front of Max.

Highlighted on the main lobby bulletin was an announcement about Tim. Some candles on the floor were still burning, and scattered all around were flowers and notes taking the place of the usual announcements of the summer events. Under the "Jobs and Sobs" section, there were a few notices of dwindling employment opportunities. A foot-long plaque above the entrance stated the mission of Greene Cent was to unite technology and humanity through creativity "in the spirit and service of society." Easy slogan to say, harder to pull off, right?

Just as I reached the elevator, two reporters rushed toward me. I waved them off as best I could as I stepped into the elevator.

I got off on the third floor, checked my letterbox, and stopped off at my office to retrieve my Yankee cap, lest the great Max, or even Doree, whoop up a fuss about my latest embarrassment. Doree loved the cap. She played softball herself and was a whiz-bang pitcher at our faculty picnics. Then I headed for Raben's outer office, trying to steady myself with the heel-and-ball of my foot.

Doree seemed to have recovered from the rigors of attending the funeral. On the old-fashioned wooden squawk box, laced with over-done angelic swirls, she announced me in with that professionally-practiced purr of hers, "Dr. Gardner is here to see you, sir." But switching to a more personal tone, she warned, "He's miffed about something. Careful." Then she added, "Your foot okay?"

That was Doree, to the letter, always thinking about others. Tim had adored her. Max, always. She even kept a supply of heart medicine for Raben's elderly wife—when she made a rare visit to the school.

"You know, Dr. Gardner, my mom wanted to come to the funeral, but she was in no condition." Her mother was in a sorry state, so Doree had to keep a watchful eye on her. No one ever saw her anymore since she stayed hunkered down in bed most of the time.

"My mom would've loved the flowers. I take after her in our love of plants."

"Yes," is all I could say, recalling Tim's white satin-lined coffin suffused with all kinds of lovely flora, mainly dahlias and white roses.

I turned in my grades and hastened into Max's office. He was ensconced in his favorite overstuffed grey leather chair backed by his favorite brocaded handsewn pillow, tapping his fingers, his gruff voice ready to greet me. How, I could only guess.

Chapter Thirteen

Immediately after

"Hello, Jeff," he said testily, turning full face toward me. "Good to see you." Maybe.

His back was turned away from me. I figured he was playing chess with himself, which he managed to do every available moment he wasn't teaching, advising, writing, or "grabbing for grants," which he hated. He was an old folksy Socialist, who believed the struggle for high ideals set standards for others to live up to, even if they were impractical to carry out. His real interest now wasn't politics, but a good replacement—chess, "the people's game," he called it. Max's faculty was quite used to waiting for him to complete a move—or a thought.

I hoped he'd get to the point quickly. His cramped office, overrun with folders and books of every description (half of which he had authored), wasn't air-conditioned.

"I asked you to come in for a reason, Jeff."

I recognized Bach's Suite in G major floating from a tiny radio on his desk and nodded my approval.

"He wrote it between making twenty-two kids, at least," Max quipped.

The chessboard was empty. Only a lonely rook stood off to the side of the board on his shiny teak desk, cluttered with papers and more books. Contributing to the sense of ordered chaos were prints on the walls of Victorian scenes, decrying, like Dickens himself did, both the squalor and pretentiousness of London life. Balancing these severe images were some serene modern Japanese prints—bucolic and refreshing to my tired eyes.

Max was a truly charismatic presence, with a full mane of white hair, a neatly trimmed goatee to match, and a cratered, weathered face that was ruggedly handsome. He looked a lot like Papa Hemingway, who was supposed to have said that he loved sleep because his life had a tendency to fall apart when he was awake. Max, at seventy-five, had energy to burn and worked around the clock. He was rumored to be afraid of no one, except perhaps his own shadow when he went off the deep end after tipping one scotch too many. Sure, we had that in common, but more telling was the way he stuck up for me all these years, like a father protecting me. Unlike the one who kicked me out of the house while I was in college, Max was always there for me.

Slurping one of his famous frosted—supposedly diet—milkshakes, he snapped off the radio and bellowed in his deep, fear-inducing voice, "I got a favor to ask you, Jeff. But first have a shake. Non-fat, you know."

I laughed. "Come on, Max. Plenty of sugar in that artful concoction."

He didn't want to argue the point, as he'd done so many times when Nan and I visited his Riverdale home for dinner. Vania, his Italian-born wife, older than he, made the best Chicken a la Capricciosa in the world, with tons of oily carbohydrates. "It didn't hurt my kids," he boasted. They were all doctors and lawyers, his grandchildren, too—except for the druggie grandson Max helped push into a rehab center for substance abusers.

I nodded to one of the realistic Victorian prints on the wall behind his desk. "What kind of favor, Max? You want me to deliver your Charles Dickens Humanities Lecture in London next week?" I ventured, hoping for a good-mood riposte.

He waved a curt "no thank you, " pointing to a new silk scroll on the wall.

"I'm into Japanese art these days, Jeff."

"Or write the whole lecture for you, Max?" I went on amiably.

He nodded a mock energetic okay to that, and got down to business.

"What I need for you to do," he said, putting down his shake, "is to mind your own *fucking* business when it comes to the Timothy Hartknoll investigation that's swirling 'round here."

How much did Max know about my snooping around? Obviously enough.

"Listen, John Harkins, the History Chair at NYU, just called me. Twenty minutes ago."

Damn it all! The all-too-efficient Mrs. Jones must've called my references right away.

"Harkins said you wanted a fake reference from one of his professors . . . a Bob Something or other for a part-time job at CWC, Ink—where Tim worked part-time."

"Bob's an old friend of mine from Milwaukee." So much, I thought, for trusting buddies from my dear old hometown.

"I don't care if he's from the Lost City of Timbuktu! John Harkins is an old friend of *mine* and extremely influential. He was right there, in his NYU office, for chrissakes, when you called Bob Whoever, who turned pale pink, and told Harkins what you were asking for. God help you! Are you off your freakin' rocker? Well?"

"It's for Tim. I'm doing it for Tim."

"You have to be kidding," he smiled wanly, shaking his head. "You're up for another tenure review this Friday and you're foolin' around with stuff like this? In our academic community we're tighter than that iron fire escape out there. Mixing things not your business into your academic life is one way to get a good swift kick outta here! So, what *are* you doin' anyway? Talk!"

"I'm trying to find out if anything happened to Tim out of the ordinary last week, but keeping it all hush-hush for now. I didn't want anyone at CWC, Ink to know I knew Tim."

"Oh? Playing gumshoe, are you? Great! Well, lay off, Jeff! The cops and reporters interviewed practically everyone here at Greene Cent—including an hysterical student whom Tim had had a tiff with over a supposedly plagiarized term paper, the matter never fully resolved. They even hauled away Tim's computer hard drive and discs. I'm hoping the police won't be coming here anymore. Let 'em do their efficient job somewhere else!"

Damn it! I had wanted to check all that computer stuff out myself. I should've come here first, instead of going to CWC, Ink this morning.

"Jeff, you know—well, maybe you don't see—these little lies all add up. Faking references is no laughing matter." He paused to swallow the rest of his milkshake.

"I didn't ask Bob to lie, just focus on my work at NYU . . . and not mention anything about my job here at Greene Cent."

Max exploded. "How could he write a letter of recommendation for you and not mention *that*? Deny that he really knows you work here? It's a lie! Alright, a sin of omission! You, of all people, as an historian, should know that what you leave out is sometimes as important as what you put in. History has more holes than Swiss cheese, but that doesn't make it right to fudge it, does it?"

"Funny, Max, don't you say in your seminars that little lies grease the wheels of history?"

"Not in this case, Jeff! Listen, you know what chutzpah is? A cop sees a young guy lying on the grass and says, 'Can't you see the sign, "Keep Off the Grass"?' The guy, still lyin' on the grass, says, 'Yes, I saw the sign, but it didn't say *positively*.' Well, I'm giving you my *positively* sternest admonition to cut this shit out! God, what do I need to do to make you see what I mean! Maybe I have to call Nan to get on your case."

"People take chances, Max. History's not for sissies. You gotta believe that, too." Feeling the throbbing from the bump on my head, I was speaking from hard experience.

"Here's something you may *not* know. Jeff. As a colleague and a friend, let me duly inform you now. You've seen the press, the nice obits that have appeared lauding Tim's contributions, like me and him and his grad students working with high school kids?"

I nodded I had.

"Well, you won't see much, if anything now, about his poisoning—until it's clear exactly what happened that day."

"I won't?"

"No, You won't, and that's because both NYU, where Tim went to grad school, and City University don't need—and don't want—that kind of publicity that has our staff meddling into police matters. We're in the education business together and that kind of monkey business hurts us when parents see what they perceive as negative news about nosy personnel being splashed all around."

"Parents? We cater to *grad* students, Max. Meddling parents are out of the scene."

"Don't kid yourself. Parents are never really out of it when things get down and dirty, even if they say so. So we don't need you to unnecessarily stir up the pot. I mean it. Period. So end of comment, end of commentary!"

Gotcha! I was up for tenure. So, right, end of comment, end of commentary for me. I was psyched, period. No messing up now. I wanted to get up and get the hell outta there, but Max wasn't through with me.

"Hold on a sec, Jeff. Got to get something from Doris. Be right back."

What's this? More third degree, another p or p harangue?

He got up without his cane and returned in a minute, a very long one for me, with a bulging manila folder in hand.

"There were some beautiful words spoken at his funeral, Jeff. We're all in an incredible funk about what happened to Tim. He was a wonderful person, a rising scholar, a true humanitarian. You'll help us, of course, prepare the memorial we're planning in the fall, when the faculty is back won't you?"

Was he giving me a subtle tip-off that I might *actually* be on the road to tenure—or at least getting another extension? Max had tremendous pull on the school divisional tenure review committee. This venerable body of pseudo scholars that he coordinated included a bizarre bunch of weirdos: an old-timer who'd be lucky to remember the day of the week; another fossil, whose last book was published thirty years ago; and two humorless spring chickens who didn't know their beaks from their itchy ambitious claws.

"Hello! Are you still with me, Jeff?" Raben must've noticed my mind drifting.

"Of course I am, Max. Got a question. When the cops were here, did they say anything about a book Tim found . . . that was worth a lot? Did he mention . . . any special kind of book to you, Max?"

"Not to my knowledge . . . no." He paused, picked up the rook, and turned it over. "Jeff, didn't I just tell you to get off this already?"

"I know, I know, but—"

"But *nothing!* We all have to get on with our lives. Period. Get back to *your* book, Jeff. When you gonna get it done, for God's sake? I can't hold off the divisional tenure committee year after year. Sorry, but this is the part of my job I hate. I have to have something to give the committee, don't I?"

He paused, turning the rook over again, and flipped on the radio, turning up the volume. Just what my bruised head needed, something or other blasting out. Seeing me wince, he turned down the volume.

"Hate to be in such a treble-some mood for you, Jeff." He turned the radio off. Sorry."

For what? The bad pun, or the lecture that was coming up? Anyway, I was prepared to listen carefully to whatever blast was coming.

"Yes, write a book! At least some decent chapters that show you can do it. For the 'Big T,' remember? So I can at least inform them that you're actively working on it instead of farting around like you tend to do. What's your hang-up? Why can't you do it, get it out?"

"I have trouble reading my own writing."

"Be serious," he said, with a not-so-endearing chuckle.

"I am. Trouble is, Max, I write so much, I get tired of reading my own stuff when none of it adds up."

"Adds up? Why does it have to add up, for chrissakes? You know what we tell our Ph.D. students about their dissertations? And faculty grant writers? Just get it down. 'Get black on white,' as de Maupassant said. And I say it too!"

He held up the chessboard and waved it past my face. "Have a look. What do you see? Sixty-four spaces here—for all those moves, possibilities, positions, options." He paused, pouring another drink for himself.

I waited. I needed to see his point.

"Some great moves in there . . . *Wunderbar*." Another pause. He seemed to be in a far-off place, all alone, with whatever memories were in that chess box.

"Where was I? Oh, yeah. Fine. You don't have to be consumed with the game like the warrior Napoleon or Duchamp, the artist, to find *something*. Isaiah Berlin, with whom, as y'know, I studied at Oxford, said it all started with *one* move, but then you gotta keep on moving! Sure, he beat a *patzer*, an amateur like me, but he taught me something else—to get moving, to make some spontaneous moves like the Romantic-style players used to do. Man, that got me interested in the whole Romantic literary movement. Moving, movement, it's all there. But you can't wait for the muse to tickle your *tuchus*! You gotta roll up your sleeves and work at it! See my storage room over there? I had to wade through a ton of books there just to find my lead paragraph for my upcoming speech in London." He paused for another sip.

The only word I caught from his gentle tirade was *Romantic*. Max was no international grand master in chess, but he was one of the leading international Romantic and Victorian scholars. He could piss Coleridge, Dickens, and Wordsworth inside out. Waiting for him to slow down, I decided to go for it.

"Max, I've come across some new information about Frederick Douglass that could become the basis for me to explore and write about."

"Hmm, Interesting, Jeff," he said measuredly, gently squeezing the lonely rook. He kept fingering it, and then, ever so tenderly caressed the chess box.

"Interesting." His lips tensed up a bit, enough for me to see he was uncomfortable. Nudging me so much to work on my own stuff. That's why I went on cautiously.

"I'm just in the early, exploratory stages . . . the opening gambits, you might say."

"Yes, Tim told me he was honing in on something about Frederick Douglass, too. Were you two working on something *together*? I caught a bit of the class you, uh, did with him. Oh, yes, he was talented." Max put the rook down gently on the last word.

Where was he going with this? Chess was not my game, and he was the expert.

"What did Tim tell you, Max? Do you mind sharing? "

"Most interesting. You know how Frederick Douglass was harshly abused as a slave—starved, whipped, denied every basic right? Even as a so-called 'free man,' he was still mightily discriminated against. On the ship over to visit England in 1845, he suffered tremendous prejudice from the American passengers. Humiliating. But when he got to the UK, he fell in love with the English people because they didn't reveal any disfavor against blacks. Sure, Douglass recognized that the British workers labored under horrendous conditions themselves, but they saw him as a *man,* not a thing to be sold or bartered."

"Is that what Tim told you? That's pretty common knowledge, Max."

"That's true, but there's something else. The British people loved Douglass as much as he loved them. As a matter of fact, did you know they raised the 700 pounds to pay off his so-called master in Baltimore? So Douglass had sailed to England a slave in actuality, but returned to this country free from the fear that he could be recaptured and returned to Maryland as a slave. You know what Tim told me Douglass said?"

"You tell me, Max."

"Douglass fiercely loved the Poets Corner at Westminster and other monuments of British freedom."

I stifled laughing out loud. The irony, "British freedom." Tim and I had uncovered the book written by a *Scottish* author that had given the fugitive slave his new name of freedom—Douglass. I knew I was pushing it, but I had to ask him again—*forte*, but not in his face.

"Max, are you sure Tim didn't give you a book to look over, *Lady of the*—"

"Stop it! Timothy Hartknoll gave me nothing!" Max slapped his full palm down, and stood up, all in one motion. "And you're going to have nothing if you don't focus on *your* writing!"

Max sat down, extra slowly. He ran his fingers through his wavy white mane and then shook his finger at me.

"Grow up, already, you booze-head! You're the best damn teacher here, but you're at a fuckin' standstill without the tenure book you're supposed to produce! Taking the treadmill nowhere fast!"

Yeah! On that cannon burst, I felt like running over to the bar on the corner and downing a few quick ones 'til my insides were soaked with blessed balm.

"I know how you feel about Tim. We *all* miss him, sorely. You know, we gave him a full-time job for next year." Max rubbed the rook again, just for a second or two.

"I know."

"Jeff, keep focused on your own career. Remember, you have a little girl. I would have been her godfather if your brother-in-law hadn't beaten me to the punch. Think of her."

Whisking the palms of his hands up and down like a frenzied conductor, he motioned me to raise my slumped shoulders. As I straightened up, he repeated in a hoary whisper, "Get up, get up, and do something—finish it!"

Mockingly, I lisped, "Thanks, Max, for keeping your integrity alive."

"I'll see you on Friday for the tenure review meeting, Jeff."

"I'll be there—on time."

"Shave . . . wear a tie, and, for godsakes, don't be so damn sassy. Hear?"

"Yes, Max, I'll be a good boy."

"I got a lot to do still," Max said, imbibing the last shlurp of his shake. "My wife's coming along to England. I just hope it's cooler there. Doris will help take care of her."

I said good-bye and hobbled to the door.

On the way out of the department reception foyer, I noticed Doree was holding a framed picture of her dad, a cop, who had died when she was about thirteen, the same age as Nellie was now. "My dad, in the line of fire," Doree said. She never went into it, but traditionally around July 4, she always placed a sweet family photo on her desk. Wrapped in her father's arms, she held some little American flags.

I tiptoed around her, but, noticing me, she looked up with soulful regret. Kissing her on the cheek seemed to brighten her up a bit. On the way out, I wondered how much she'd heard of Max and me sparring. Her little tan squawk box, after all, was connected to his office. But I thought I had seen him turn off the outlet when he turned down his radio. Departmental paranoia was getting the better of me. So calm down, Jeff, chill.

On the way to my office, I ran into a student Tim and I had taught. Tim had helped him come out, to recognize and be proud of his homosexuality. I think he had toasted Tim with wine last Thursday. A lot of students had.

"Jeff!"

It was Max again. In the hall. What the hell did he want now?

"I need to ask a favor of you."

"Yes?" I asked, pausing at the door to my office.

"Can you teach Tim's summer class, Brit Social Lit? He was planning to go into depth on *Julius Caesar*. Ordered the Brando version for an Angelica Film Center screening and—"

"Can I let you know Friday?"

"You can let me know in *ten* minutes! Doris will bring you his syllabus. "

Chapter Fourteen

Minutes later

I rummaged through my shelves for books on Shakespeare, joined in my task by the bust of the Bard, once more sternly gazing down at me.

Julius Caesar, Max had mentioned. I was going through ideas already on how to teach the play—a revisionist interpretation of how our knowledge of conspiracies today might reflect those going on in the play. It would be Globalization Theory, seeing the world of the Roman Empire from today's perspective. I could go into how the two empires—then and now—stacked up against each other with a little American Exceptionalism theory, whatever that is, factored in. Is America really different in its shock-and-awe brand of imperialism? I would definitely use active learning, with lots of role playing. Tim would've liked that.

Two of the photos on the wall behind my desk reflected benchmark teaching experiences we had together: one of him and me waving our hands from the steps of Washington Irving's nephew's house on Irving Place; the other showing us hanging out with our students sitting on the stoop of Louis Armstrong's home in Elmhurst, Queens, where we'd co-taught the Living History Through Music course.

I thought back on some of those projects, all involving active learning, with students playing out historical and contemporary events, like having live press conferences with characters from different periods. A favorite was Walter Cronkite's "You Are There"-type reenactments of key historical moments and turning points. Tim and I could've had a lot of fun with *Julius Caesar*, acting out plots in low-voiced *sub rosa* meetings in dark, twisting alleys—all taking place in the classroom or maybe in nearby Little Italy, for a pseudo-realistic noir effect.

Max moseyed in and immediately spotted the books on the table. "Ah, I see you may be interested in teaching that summer course. Marvelous! Just a suggestion, if you do, Jeff. Take it easy on reading too much of today's history into the past. You know what Wilentz says, 'That's good propaganda, but lousy history.' Remember the logical reality and the evidence of the times you're studying."

"*Julius Caesar's* a play, Max. A play has its own rules of logic and probability. It's a drama of feelings, not a factual document of how things might have actually occurred. We're talking about probability, not actuality."

"But, still, drawing implications about real events of today."

"C'mon, Max, present-day events are always reconfigured by the events of the past, whether real or perceived, just as history is written and rewritten in each generation to fit its own mindset. In *Julius Caesar*, Shakespeare was reflecting concerns with Elizabethan England. Today's audiences see parallels with their own politics."

"Right you are, Jeff. He was a man of his times—and ahead of it too. Just keep the students on their toes with questions; for example, 'Is assassination ever justified?' "

Pointing dramatically to his Shakespeare bust on the top shelf, he added, "Just don't reduce the Bard's elegiac poetry to mundane politics."

"Oh, you know I would never do that."

"I know, I know, Jeff. You don't pontificate, you don't go into politics for its own sake or to influence others, like those Neo-Cons accuse us of doing. I like your open-minded inquiry . . . always have. Fine. If only you could put your thoughts down on paper and *publish*, for God's—and our—sake."

He headed for his desk. "Now, how about looking at that syllabus for your class? I'll buzz Doris." There it was—his charming, cheery side.

I nodded a casual okay, but inside I felt a tinge of excitement. Who knows, there could be some clues in Tim's syllabus and notes about Shady Lady that might help me in my own writing.

The truth is, I knew myself to be a better teacher than writer, at least of academic books. I thought about my depository of stacks of false starts to academic tomes in my bottom desk drawer, trials and errors leading nowhere except to countless bouts of booze. Yes, maybe Tim was right. With Shady Lady as my talisman I could finally find the antidote for that persistent writing block dogging me.

I remember Nan, just like Max, constantly goading me with "C'mon, Jeff, give yourself permission to write a crappy first draft." Trouble is, *all* my drafts turned out that way—crappy. No angels of clarity were to be released from the dense uncertain sculptures I was trying to carve.

I sat down and began to think about writing something worthwhile. It would have to do with how a young man, running away from his life as a slave, took a name from a character in a poetic novel by Sir Walter Scott and found new hope in challenging an American empire built on the miseries of others. I could get into the idealists and realists of the time in the expanding saga of a country marred by terrorist slavery, its imperial ties with England, and a unique voyage to England that changed the man's life and the life of America.

I would repay a painful debt to Tim with this book. Strange, I really felt him now. The way he used to cheer me on, the memory of that, buzzed in my brain. "Go for it, or forgo it, Jeff, you ol' fart!"

As I remembered it, *Julius Caesar* dealt with a similar theme, a rebellion supposedly based on idealism—"freedom from, freedom to"—but enacted by all sorts of people with both base and noble motives at work. This too I could easily fit into my tenure book.

A knock on my door. I got up to let Doree in. She was holding a large ring of keys. Max excused himself, reminding me to meet him in eight minutes now.

"The syllabus should be in Mr. Hartknoll's cubicle. I have the keys," she said.

Of course. The whole cubicle wing had been turned into a crime scene, everything locked up tight.

"You know, no one is supposed to go in there without Professor Raben's expressed permission," Doree acknowledged. "The police are really clear about that. Professor Raben has to approve everyone nowadays, what with those newspaper reporters still snooping around."

When she opened the door to the wing, I felt like an Egyptian tomb raider. One light in the back cast an eerie glow over the whole office, which consisted of compact little cubicles. Tim once jokingly remarked that the part-timers' cubicles were constructed to hold only one person, to cut out any fooling around.

Tim's cube, at the end, was virtually bare—nothing on the shelves, nothing in the drawers, nothing. What was I expecting? In the back of my mind I had a vague suspicion that Tim could have taken his own life. In that case, a note, a letter might pop up any place. That usually happened. But now—I took another breath—nothing. My mind snapped back to what I was really looking for—anything at all leading to finding the book.

"I helped Mr. Hartknoll with his *Julius Caesar* syllabus," Doree said. "I wonder where it could be?" She suggested that we go to her office to look for any notes that Tim had passed on to her, to help prepare the syllabus.

"Great, here it is!" Doree fished out a folder from the bottom drawer of her desk and handed it to me. "I put all his articles and notes in this handy folder."

I'd read most of them before. Wonderful articles. Especially the ones on how Toni Morrison wrote so many splendid novels about the African-American dilemma throughout American history—two steps backward for every proud step forward.

Doree paused several times as she skimmed through Tim's work.

"I especially like this quote on that sheet," she declared, handing me one of the notes. "I read it again after Mr. Hartknoll died." She knocked me out as she recited by heart, " 'Since Cassius first did whet me against Caesar, I have not slept. / Between the acting of a dreadful thing / And the first motion, all the interim is / Like a phantasma or a hideous dream.' "

Starting to get too emotional, I felt I had to get out of Tim's cube. But first, one more try. "Did you ever help Tim with his notes for the Bleecker Blues tour he led?"

"A little bit. The notes he wrote with his friend Derek. I still have some stuff in myapartment."

"Yeah, I see. Do you mind if I look at 'em sometime, Doree?"

"Call me tomorrow, sir," she replied, ever on-spot. "I'll bring them to you."

Max, waiting outside the door. lifted his cane towards me, like Moses raising his rod, waiting for my momentous reply.

"Well, it's past ten minutes, Jeff. Did you decide? "

"Yes, I'll do it, I'll teach the course. Thank you."

He smiled. "Fine. It'll take your mind off things."

What things? That he knew more than he was telling me? Like what else he and Tim talked about besides his promotion last Thursday? What else did he know and what was he hiding, and why was I acting like such a damn paranoid fool?

My cellphone rang. It was Derek, with some good news.

"Fifteen minutes. In my lobby? Catch you soon."

Good old Max wished me well. "Let me know if you need a toga."

"*Pax*, Max. I'll call you if I do, sir," I told him, along with the best stiff-armed Roman salute I could muster.

Chapter Fifteen

Late afternoon

It was after 4 p.m., the toughest time to get a cab, so fortunately for my toe, only a short walk to where I lived, on Bleecker and Mercer.

Dave let me know that some visitors stopped by.

"Sasha?"

"No, she's upstairs, Dr. Gardner. It was another woman and two men."

"Thanks, Dave." Couldn't be Jameson and Gerard, who worked as a pair.

Two men? Who could that be? I had little time to think about it as Derek appeared in the lobby, his face all lit up. On the way up to my apartment, he sprang the good news. He overheard Hank Jankowitz tell Hilda that he liked me and wanted me aboard as a tour guide. Jankowitz told her to have me report in the morning to the Bleecker Street Playground in the West Village for the start of the model tour, which the applicants would eventually have to lead themselves.

"Wait 'til you catch me in the lead-off scene," Derek said. "A scream. You'll fall down. I wreck the place!"

"Does Jankowitz have any idea I knew Tim?"

"C'mon, man, I told you, mum's my word on all that. You still don't trust me, huh?"

I shrugged because I honestly didn't know at this point.

"I'm for you. And Tim," Derek said, wiping his specs.

I nodded. "Yeah. For Tim."

In the apartment, I introduced Derek to Sasha, who looked like she was about to absolutely explode. Yeah, I remembered she was counting on time with me alone. Derek made a strategic retreat to the kitchen while I tried to ramp down Sasha's hot temper.

"What is it with you! You stood me up last night. Remember, we were supposed to go to the concert in Tompkins Square Park! To top it off, I haven't heard from you all day! What's goin' on?" She continued in my face until she noticed the red radish-like bump on my head when I took my cap off.

"Omigod! how did you get this?"

"It's alright."

"Wait a minute." She headed for my bathroom and zipped back to me.

"Naturally, the medicine cabinet's empty. I'm going to the drugstore and get some ointment for that bruise. How'd you get it, Jeff?"

When I told her I ran into a car, she threw up her hands and called me a "careless ass," swearing that the "car should've hit me harder." She was way too good for me.

My cellphone rang. Doree, reminding me there was going to be a preliminary meeting on Tim's memorial program. She had also volunteered again to help me with my summer school course. Okay, I'd call her tonight at home. It made me feel a little better that I was being consulted about the memorial for Tim.

Even my toe was feeling a little better, the swelling going down considerably. With more confidence, I walked to my bedroom to check my crazy wall-chart with the five M's to see if I was in the red zone:

Moving around—yeah, constantly—fidgeting big time now. Well, at least the cab companies were getting rich on me— status: Excellent.

Mouthing off—pretty good, had managed to piss off, with my big mouth, the cops—Jankowitz and Raben—some were silent screams, though—status: Good.

Manners down—still impulsive and rude interruptive behavior—status: Super sucks!!

Mindset—sure, not paying attention, distracted easily from my task, not finishing tasks—status: Paranoia, revving up for full blast!

Murder Suspects— Antonio Whatever—Hank Jankowitz, and Max Raben just added—status: Dangerous!

Without knocking, Sasha (to put it delicately) stormed into my room and stared at the wall. "What are you doin' with that? Get off it already!"

"It was your idea—to be self-reflective, get things down to look at 'em—to steady and improve myself."

"On paper, Jeff! Not on the wall! And those charts—silly categories like that. Especially the last one, murder suspects—*estúpido!*"

"Okay, okay—"

"I'm going to the drugstore. Try being just … *still.*"

I sat sprawled out on my bed. Maybe she was right, maybe Raben was right, me trying to play Sam Spade. But I couldn't help thinking that Max, a pretty slick dude, was offering that Shakespeare seminar to keep a close eye on me. Well, I would turn the tables and keep close tabs on him. Wait a minute—recalling Tim's last words, "Tour is," I thought about it some more. What did Max have to do with the tour? Maybe it was Jankowitz who did Tim in. I'd be better off at CWC, Ink., keeping tabs on *him*. So where to spend my time—at Greene Cent or on the tour? One or the other? Or maybe both?

I pulled off the wall chart and folded it neatly into my dresser drawer. After Sasha left the apartment, I trotted back to the kitchen and made sandwiches with what was left in the fridge. Derek, still there, apologized for "causing trouble" between my lady and me. I told him to forget it and enjoy his snack.

Time to check my calls. Hilda called to give me the good news about the tour. Nellie reminded me she was heading straight home after school to Nan's place, further up on Mercer Street. Nan was on my case again to cough up the remainder of our daughter's camp fee—due last week—and also the balance for Nellie's graduation party next week. Two Greene Cent grad students left me heated voice mails, probably complaining about grades, always the ones who turned in their papers late. Hard to believe, some of those students evidently hadn't heard about Tim yet—or were giving me some respectful space.

My cellphone again. A bad connection. It sounded like Rachel.

"Hi, Jeff. Rachel. I'm in the neighborhood. We were there earlier, hoping you'd be in. Can we come up?"

"Who's with you?"

"My stepdad and Reverend Johnson."

As I repeated the names, Derek's "what-the-hell!" look spoke volumes to me.

"Sure, Rachel. Come on up. I'll be expecting you." I got up.

"Time I was splittin'."

"No, do me a favor. Go into my bedroom and listen to what goes down, okay? This would be very helpful. Very helpful, indeed."

Derek scooped up the rest of his sandwich, bounded for my bedroom and slammed the door shut. Time to see what kind of real partner he could be. Or me, to him.

Chapter Sixteen

Right after

As much as it was great seeing Rachel again, I felt uneasy about the other two visitors barging in here. Rachel's stepfather I had already unhappily encountered after Tim's funeral, but now he seemed over-friendly as he shook my hand warmly. The second man I recognized as the minister who officiated at Tim's funeral—Reverend Johnson. Medium-size build, maybe in his early thirties, eloquently garbed in black, with starched white collar befitting his station, a radiant smile across his face. What were they up to? Whose side was Rachel on? I stood on my guard.

The reverend held tightly onto a large-sized manila envelope. What the hell was it? The certification letter that MacNeil mentioned to me on the day of the funeral? Tim's father must have sensed I was interested because he drilled his eyes into mine for a long second, backing away when Rachel raised her hand slightly.

She took a small wrapped package from her purse and handed it to me, whispering, "A little painting I did a while back. I always meant to give it to you, Jeff. A miniature water color. Don't open it 'til later . . . ." I thanked her, placing it on my dining room table.

Moving into my living room, I offered them drinks, but no takers. MacNeil asked the reverend for the envelope. I noticed a large silver ring conspicuous on his pinkie as he gave it to him. Then MacNeil signaled his stepdaughter to lead off. She paused, looking nervously, I thought, at her stepdad, and cleared her throat a bit.

"Jeff, my father got all of Tim's mail from the package man the day Tim died. An envelope delivered to him that day contained Certification of Authenticity papers. That means the book that Tim found is an authentic first edition, and, more important, the signature and inscription inside are authentic, too."

"I know Tim would be pleased."

"You know then," the reverend said, pointing to the envelope MacNeil clutched, "that the signature is of a great black abolitionist and humanitarian."

Was the good reverend trying to trap me into admitting I had the book in my possession? "Yes, sir," I said, cooly as I could.

"Don't be so coy, Gardner! Let's cut straight to the point without your bull. The book is not yours to keep!" MacNeil thundered.

"Yes, I agree. "It's Tim's . . . or was . . . or should be." I glanced over at Rachel, still undecided on whose side she was on.

"Now that book belongs to African-Americans, Dr. Gardner," the reverend said in a soft, even voice. "It belongs in a cherished place where our people can visit with pride and respect."

"It belongs to *us!* " MacNeil roared, a vein popping out of his neck.

Rachel winced at his outburst. The reverend got MacNeil to calm down. I noticed that she hadn't looked at Johnson once since they entered my apartment.

The reverend stepped in front of MacNeil, gently holding Rachel's jittery handsand spoke quietly.

"Dr. Gardner, I'm sure you understand the significance of this potential discovery: the signature of America's leading black abolitionist. Our beloved hero, born into slavery, enduring every kind of abuse and indignity as a young man, running away when he was twenty to New York. Self-taught, he became one of the best-known orators in the United States, starting the antislavery newspaper 'North Star,' a leading advocate and activist of the Underground Railroad. His voice thundered for freedom. Few antislavery militants, black or white, did so much as he did to advance the cause of liberty to the people of this country and Europe after the Civil War. He was a lion roaring for freedom. Certainly you understand."

This was all too familiar to me. Rachel politely reminded MacNeil that I was an historian and had worked with Tim.

"Then you *know* how important it is for our people to have the original published book from which he took the name Douglass," MacNeil calmly said.

Sure, he made the same good points I myself had considered. But his well-intentioned swagger-stick sanctimony was frankly getting to me.

"His slave name was Frederick Bailey. Do you know he took the name Douglass after running away from New York and then went right on to New Bedford, Massachusetts? He says in his autobiography he got his new name from the character of Douglass in *Lady of the Lake* . . ."

"Yes, *I know all that.* It's common knowledge, revealed in his own brilliant slave narrative . . ."

"Okay, okay, Jeff. Good," Johnson said. "We just wanted you to understand our passion on this. But there's something you have to explain to me. Major MacNeil told me the story of how Antonio found the book and gave it to Tim. My question is how did it end up, way back then, in some basement hiding place?"

"It could've been that Douglass had *Lady of the Lake* with him at a speaking engagement somewhere around here, where he autographed the book . . . to raise money for a good cause, perhaps. But I don't know who buried it in the basement, or why. It's all a mystery to me. I wish I could help you on this—"

"Then, let's just say that the book is a gift from God," Johnson was quick to reply. "And God works in mysterious ways!"

MacNeil got up from his seat and faced me squarely, with his deep burrowing voice. "Let me put it this way. You don't really know what Frederick Douglass means to our people. When I served in the Marines, I had a picture of him tacked onto my wall—and when I faced discrimination at times, and I did, I remembered his righteous words, 'If there is no struggle, there is no progress . . . . Power concedes nothing without a demand.' "

"Dad, please . . . " Rachel said, trying to calm him. MacNeil sat down slowly, taking turns facing me and Rachel. He handed the reverend the envelope, treating it as if it were the Holy Grail.

"No, it's true," her stepfather went on. "Well, take the Fourth, coming up in a couple of weeks. A time of celebration for all, right? Not for Frederick Douglass. Not for him. You know what he said back then? 'The Fourth of July is yours, not mine. You must rejoice. I must mourn. It is inhuman mockery to drag a man into slavery and then call on him to join in joyous celebration . . . The man struck is the man to cry out!' He spoke out against injustice, time and time again, and now, *I'm* speaking out. We want what is ours! *Now!* Do you read me, Gardner?!"

I read him, alright. This hard-ass ex-Marine was scaring the piss out of me, as he did back at Tim's funeral. Rachel held up her hands firmly for MacNeil to cool it. Good for her!

Still I had to give him some respect for the way he pissed passion in buckets. He believed in what he wanted. But Scotty, our neighbor's terrier, was a passionate believer, too, when he trapped a rat in the laundry room last week.

The reverend reached into the envelope and retrieved a letter. "Do you know what Douglass wrote in that book? "

I shook my head. But of course I did.

He went on in a softer voice. "It's all on the certification summary sheet: 'With this book I have a new name and a new life and hope for everlasting freedom.' What a wonderful statement!"

"May I look at that certification letter?" I asked.

"Yes, but first let's see if we're in on this together," MacNeil said. "Why don't you just get the book, so we can all have a look at it? I suppose it's somewhere here, in your apartment, right?" MacNeil asked, looking around the room.

"No it's not here."

"No? Then where is it? We don't have all day!" Reverend Johnson losing his cool?

"It was . . . stolen."

"What? Oh, come now—!"

"The day Tim died. Tim had it. His place was ransacked."

"Well, I know who stole it. *You!*" MacNeil said, rising from the sofa.

"I've been looking for it myself. I wish you would respect me for that."

"Well, you'd better damn well find it!" he shouted.

Rachel calmed MacNeil down again. The reverend put his bony hand on his shoulder, his voice firm and steady. "Major MacNeil, you told me Tim had a partner who was in on this. Could it have been Derek Molson, his boyfriend? Maybe *he* has the book. Do you know where we can find him?"

This was too much for Derek, who emerged from my bedroom, making a beeline to the reverend.

"That's a downright damn lie," Derek said. "I didn't know nothin' about that book. Nothing! I don't know where you got that information. Tim never mentioned it to me! Never!"

Everything stopped. MacNeil looked like he was going to throw a grenade at Derek.

"Uh, Rachel, this is Derek Molson, Tim's friend."

She seemed too scared to say anything.

"What the hell is that fag doing here?" MacNeil asked. I hadn't heard that word used since *Midnight Cowboy*. The reverend, looking at him, mumbled, "But isn't he also on the deal?" MacNeil responded with a puzzled frown.

Rachel finally looked up, still shaking, as I opened the door. "Jeff, I'm so sorry about this whole unpleasant business."

"It's okay. It'll all work out in the end . . . somehow," I said. They left.

Derek came over to me. "I heard it all. Damn, what liars! Saying that I was in on it 'bout the book!"

Now I got it. "Derek, could it be that Johnson misunderstood MacNeil's report on what Tim said at that Lower East Side cafe? He mentioned that he had 'a partner' who'd help him pay for the book."

"Oh," Derek smiled, "I see. MacNeil thought he meant *me*—"

"When he really meant *me*. Jeffrey Bonehead Gardner."

"Those creeps!"

"Yeah, Derek, but not Rachel. She's alright."

"Those cats rant and rail—and call it justice—when it's just plain envy!"

"You heard 'em, blabbing on and on how they want the book for their people—don't believe it! They want it for themselves! Grade A greed!"

"Don't feel bad. He never told me either."

"I think they'll do anything to get it, Derek."

"Hey, we're gonna kick ass together. Don't be so down, Jeff. Things will look brighter in the morning—you got that tour gig—remember?"

"Brighter? Yeah, for the shadow of the man I am—I should've been . . . more forceful with those guys."

"Keep goin', man. We'll get 'em! 'Put some color in your cheeks.' Now, that's a Shakespeare quote I like. I put my arm around his shoulder. "Come on, sidekick, we got more some sandwiches waiting for us. I'll ask Sash to join us when she gets back."

Later I would remember to add two more names to my list. And not forget I was on theirs.

PART TWO

Bleecker Blues

Chapter Seventeen

Tuesday morning

Hank Jankowitz, in his sleek motorized wheelchair, met me at the Bleecker Street playground, in the West Village, the starting point of the tour. It was only 10 a.m., but the sun was already blazing. Even this early there were signs of life—A few frisbee-tossing stoners, a couple of bongo drummers, some young moms, of course, and older nannies, eyes glued on the tots.

I felt energetic enough, despite the shaky dream I had last night of Orson Welles' massive head taunting me with Kane's last dying word—except it wasn't "Rosebud" he was saying. It was "tour is . . ." over and over, until I woke up in a sweat. If someone was telling me to watch out, I better do . . . what?

This morning, the group consisted of ten business people from Japan, all wearing walking shorts and T-shirts and clutching cameras and camcorders, two women carrying dainty parasols. Soon we joined the other prospective tour job applicants, all young: Francesca, Mindy, and Arthur. Francesca was tall and willowy; Mindy, short and feisty. Arthur could've been Woody Allen's kid brother. After Jankowitz introduced us to the tourists, he paused to let one of the Japanese businessmen translate. That was supposed to make us feel good. Mindy called out, "Maybe you can show us Tokyo someday!" Off to a campy good start. Yes.

Hilda, Hank's administrative assistant, was on hand to take the tickets from the tourists. Eyeing me, she gave a little nudge about submitting my résumé. I told her my computer was down, so I couldn't print it out. "Better than the proverbial dog story," she quipped. "But I hope *he* buys it," pointing to His Eminence, Sir Hank Jankowitz.

My cellphone rang. Doree again. Before I could answer her, temperamental Hilda reminded me again to put it away—Jankowitz didn't permit applicants to have them on the trial-run tours. "Didn't he warn you? Too distracting for beginners," she scowled.

She was right. I didn't want to start off with a bad impression, so I hastily turned my cell off and stuffed it in my pocket. My mind went into overdrive. I had to find a sharp way to endear myself so I could nail down this job. I figured since he came up with that Shakespeare quote so easily yesterday, I myself would lay on the Bard at the opportune time.

Jankowitz gathered the group around his wheelchair and began, his talk oozing out smooth as misu soup. No need for any amplification with a headphone. His stentorian voice, alone, would carry the day. He rattled off that before there was a street, there were forests here, and the earliest inhabitants of the land were native Algonquin people. He sure knew his stuff, but considering how much of his talk was connected with Tim's itinerary, it looked pretty tame so far— basic history.

My head drifted over to Francesca, blonde and sinewy, who, I admit, did distract me. Anyway, Hilda spotted my wandering eye and motioned me to pay better attention to Hank. Ah, another demerit.

Jankowitz signaled everyone to get ready to head down Bleecker Street for the time of their lives. Seizing the moment for my Shakespeare ploy, I piped up, " 'Up and down, up and down!' " That got Hank's attention. "From *A Midsummer Night's Dream*," I added proudly.

Locking his eyes into mine, he shot back, sharp as an Algonquin arrow, " 'If you *will* . . . laugh yourself into *stitches*'—*Twelfth Night*." He laughed a bit too, as he glanced down at my bandaged foot.

We strolled across the street. Pointing to his right, Jankowitz remarked that the east-west paths were known as peaceful thoroughfares for native tribes. One such path became Bleecker Street. Doffing his fancy CWC, Ink tour guide hat, Jankowitz invoked everyone to breathe in the pure cosmic Spirit of the Sapokanican, and in one smooth breath say, "Peace." Corny, but it seemed to work, sending a message that this tour would not be an ordinary one. I was game to see what Tim had prepared, alone, or with his partner Derek, nowhere in sight now.

As we crossed the street, Jankowitz said the primitive paths would later become the rest of Bleecker Street, where you might hear at least eight different languages—just like in the Village today—including the diverse dialects of the Munsee Indians and regional speech of newly-arrived Africans. He pointed out that some of these Africans that privateers brought to New Amsterdam as slaves earned their freedom by working the land and building the early wooden houses. Pausing for a gulp of air, Jankowitz said, "Others got jobs as freedmen right from the start of their new lives here. And I mean right *here*—where you are now standing, folks."

Hank said we would be visiting the ten blocks on Bleecker that were the crucible of social change in America. We would also stop off for a typical Bleecker Street nosh, where we would see the gardens that were enjoyed by a very famous singer who in the mid-1960s lived on Bleecker and MacDougal Streets. This will be a surprise."

"Who?" one of the tourists called out. Someone who, uh, sang at the Village Gate? That's on Bleecker Street, right?"

"Well," Hank snapped back. "I did know the Gate's fabled impresario, Art D'Lugoff. Matter of fact, I sold encyclopedias with him a long while back. Special guy. The sign on the Gate's last show is still up. We'll pass by it later and chat. But sorry, that's not the surprise, folks."

"Well, then, who is it?" another tourist asked.

"Hang in, it's just down the road," Hank replied. "You'll see in a while."

Suddenly, he started to whistle a bit from "Blowin' in the Wind," and, turning to the applicants, asked if anyone knew the song. Skinny, bespectacled Arnold sang out, "The answer, my friends, is blowin' in the wind, the answer is blowin' in the wind." Some of the tourists joined him energetically, off-key, with a rousing "browin' in the wind."

Coming toward us now, I spotted a squat, well-built and deeply tanned mustached guy in walking shorts and tank top who was looking the scene over—or was he just looking at me? Without any warning, he brushed within a hair's breath of me and distinctly whispered into my ear, "You Jeff? You knew Tim?" I nodded, but before I could continue, he slipped a small envelope into my hands. Then he was gone, leaving me, frozen, to ponder what this meant. Antonio? No, couldn't be, didn't fit Tim's description of him—a tall man with a scar. And, damn, how did he know me?

"Jeff! C'mon, let's go!" A voice from the distant present. I pushed the envelope into my pocket, planning to get to it at my first free moment. It was Hank, who else, tapping me, like little pellets, on my shoulder. "You okay? Get your motor goin' !"

Some of the tourists were dying to see the Magnolia Bakery Shop, of "Sex and the City" TV fame. I was not so anxious, since a lot of teenagers—my daughter Nellie included—were emulating all those TV stars smoking on the show. In any case, Jankowitz, to keep things moving, one-upped the tourists. He already had Magnolia's red-velvet cupcakes in a bag, which he distributed as he whistled the familiar opening tune from the TV hit—mixed in with the Sapokanican chant he had made up.

The freedom part of the tour revved up again, with me, of course, trailing just a little behind. Since my toe was almost healed, I didn't think it was very sporting for Jankowitz in his speedy chariot to shout, "Hey, Shleppalong Shakespeare, come on! Get the lead outta your shoes!"

Easily keeping apace with the group, he jiggled his sky-blue joystick like a pinball whiz, tilting his super chair in a go-position. " 'People, get ready!' " he sang out, from the Simon and Garfunkel oldie. The tourists kept on walking, but more slowly, randomly peering at the showy store windows. I adjusted my toe to fit more snugly into the sandal's cloth-band. I felt good.

We headed for Old Antique Row and the hot-shot shops, from whose stacked shelves the tourists could cram their pockets and purses with small souvenirs of New York and "Freedom Street." They seemed to be more intent on gawking at the Lulu Guinness $400 gold suede shoes, the pink metallic slippers, and $800 handbags at Ralph Lauren. I smiled to myself. No trinkets like these for Sasha or Nellie. No, not with the possibility of losing my teaching job. Dang it, I should be home preparing my tenure materials. But no, here I was, passing blithely by the hallmarks of conspicuous consumption that once housed cozy delis and boisterous laundromats for the locals, peopled by aspiring artists of all types, armed with spiral notebooks or sketch-pads.

Thank God, a breath of fresh air. Jankowitz rolled into a bona fide antique store—something real—on the corner of Charles Street, the kind I remembered flourishing ten years ago, in the last millennium. Here was another one of Hank's "surprises," Warren's "Big One," which turned out to be the silver telescope of Peter Warren, a British pirate turned New York Colony governor, whose mansion in the Village was the gem of the 1740s. The tourists had fun looking through the scope at each other, mugging their faces and taking pictures nonstop before Hank encouraged them to amble around the store a little. "This stuff is very old," he jokingly barked. "Even older than most of you, so enjoy!"

While the tourists carefully examined the delicate pictures, maps, lit-up globes, and statuettes, I glanced around the store, trying to discern if there was anything in there that might've interested Tim, clues to where Shady Lady could be now (especially old artifacts, old books, old whatever). Details, details!

Here's where I got a chance to look inside the envelope Mustache Man handed me. All the note said, in a scratchy handwriting, was, "meat you were the wind is blowin' on Bleecker. Food place. Tonite, 8." Weird how we were just singing that song on the tour. Did he mean the Pizza Box on Bleecker and Sullivan?"

I was mulling all this over, my image reflected in a Louis XVI bronze-gilded mirror. Funny how I looked—with my T-shirt and pants and neatly trimmed hair that my cleaned-up cap thankfully covered—so far from that that conspicuously royal age. Fortunately, the ridiculous oversized sandals that clung to my feet were not in view. Of course! My "I Love New York" T-shirt and Yankee baseball cap! That's how Tim had *described* me to the construction worker. And that's how this mysterious mustached dude knew me now.

My mirrored image smiled back wanly: "Jeff, who the hell do you think you are, so darn neat? That's not the real you, looking like one of these tourists sashaying down to this pseudo-hip micro-neighborhood of high fashion and big bucks." What it all had to with freedom was hard to fathom. I couldn't imagine why Tim included this stop in his tour, unless he was intent on contrasting this kind of frivolous freedom with more serious issues he'd bring up later on the tour.

Most likely, I concluded, Jankowitz was just trying to impress the tourists with edgy American consumerism. We passed a row of high-end stores, each one trying to outdo the other in flashy displays of vulgarity—stores selling leather or jewelry, more antique stores, and new trendy restaurants of every kind. What I cherished were the old rough-hewn mainstays like John's Pizzeria of Woody Allen fame, familiar oily-smelling fish stores, and, of course, native Italian delights like Rocco's Bakery with both young and old waitstaff decked out in striking green aprons and red caps. Tim and I had spent a lot of time together in places like these, gabbing about anything, or playing chess, our Mets and Yankee caps practically touching in such close concentration.

Hank gathered the group together like Napoleon assembling his troops. "We're going across the street for another surprise." We aspirants lingered behind a bit, taking our own bets on what it could be.

"I know, Hank is gonna do a wild, way-out tarantella," Arnold said.

"Yeah, sporting a silver tiara, covering his bald spot," Mindy added.

Their babbling did not dispel my thoughts about Mustache Man and his little note. Should I call Jameson and Gerard to meet me on the tour? No, I didn't need them—not yet. I reached inside for another one of my trusty pills, but Hank beat me to the punch, inadvertently and blessedly stopping me from indulging myself.

On the way, the tour briefly stopped at 337 Bleecker Street, where the brilliant Lorraine Hansberry had written *A Raisin in the Sun* in the mid-1950s. Derek treated the tour to some lovely lines from the play, which made me think how much was lost when she died so young.

"C'mon, Shleppalong, we're on our way to hear some good music at a great shop!" Hank bellowed, bringing me back to the present, now mulling over what was in store for me tonight.

Chapter Eighteen

11:00 a.m.

In the music store, Jankowitz introduced us to his friend Alex, a youthful seventy-year-old black man, who, in due time, informed us that he had played with both Ted Joans, the poet, and the great jazz sax player Charlie "Bird" Parker.

In the late 1950s, after performing at Cafe Bohemia, on Bleecker and Barrow streets, Bird would hang out in his shabby clothes and bedroom slippers at neighborhood antique stores. In winter. A wasted one-time celebrity tragically sliding big time into hellish oblivion.

Alex put on a CD of one of Bird's songs, as Jankowitz asked everyone to focus on Derek, who waved to me from a quiet corner. Donning dark sunglasses and black beret, he instantly became Ted Joans, a colorful '50s self-styled Beatnik character, ready to recite a poem, with Bird's music pulsating in the background. We tour-guide applicants were dutifully able to follow the poem, a copy of which was in our three-ring tour binders:

JAZZ is my religion and it alone do I dig. Yeah, jazz is MY RELIGION.

Jazz is my story, it was my mom's and pop's and their moms' and pops' from the day of Buddy Bolden, who swung them blues to Charlie Parker and Ornette Coleman's extension of BeBop. Yeah, jazz is my religion—a unique musical religion . . .

Some of the tourists, assuming Derek was finished, started to applaud, but Jankowitz, with his diamond-ringed finger on his lips, shushed them instantly. Alex lowered the music, and Derek continued as firebrand Joans.

Jazz is our religion, and it's international all the way. Jazz is an Afro-American music, and JAZZ, like us, is here to stay. So remember that jazz is my religion, but it can be your religion too.

When Jankowitz clapped, of course, everyone joined in. But this time Alex quieted the audience down and got serious. "Met Bird in a bar right here on Bleecker. He was into heavy drinkin' and drugs, bummin' drinks, so I bought him a few. Bird keeled over, his head flopped on the bar, and his horn got knocked over with a terrible clatter. Just terrible. I volunteered to help him. I loved his music, you gotta understand."

Alex turned to Derek and said, "Hey, buddy, how you doin'?"

Derek instantly became Bird, smashed and wobbling around. "Lord, I'm a dyin' drag. Well, like I say, I'm goin' somewhere soon where I won't be able to bother nobody."

The scene being played out was so dramatic, so transfiguring, I couldn't wait to tell Sasha when I got back.

Alex admonished Bird. "C'mon, man—none o' that."

Derek, still standing unsteadily as Bird, responded even more softly than Alex had. "Never thought I'd make it to 1955," and then pantomimed playing his horn, his fingers alighting the ivory buttons, as he recited with grim pleasure: "As my man, Omar Khayyam, usta rap, 'Come fill the cup,' Ol' Bird of Time ain't got far to flutter."

Alex reached out to his friend. "C'mon, Bird, don't talk shit—you ain't dyin', things ain't that bad. You still got your horn."

Bird fingered his instrument, tenderly, sadly belying his next threadbare words. "This beat-up thing? Ain't worth piss—I found it somewhere. My real horn's in hock."

Alex, more upbeat, tried to change the subject. "Hey, how's your woman, Bird? She okay?"

Bird moved away from him. "I wouldn't know," he said. "My woman, Chan, she split. Took all she could—then just spat me out."

Suddenly Derek—still as Bird—started to wince, complaining about his ulcers. "I need to get some radium!"

Jankowitz, on spot, asked one of the tourists why Bird would need radium. "For his illness?" was all the tourist could suggest, averting her eyes from Bird.

Bird turned to her. "Yeah, you tie a string to a piece of radium, and lower it down your stomach." He said it tongue-in-cheek, but none of the tourists laughed. Derek had them in his palm, as he went on. "Hey, I gotta start greasin' the skillet, get together a new band. Yeah, get me a brand new band!"

The tourists, every one of them, started to applaud. So did we applicants.

Jankowitz was silent as a tomb. After a pause, Bird, holding his stomach tight, lunged toward a startled tourist, pouring out his litany of woes: "Here I am—beggin' for pennies and drinks—and maybe, if I'm lucky, a fix. Same old song, puttin' myself down on this here street. And I gotta beg people to let me play? I'm Charlie Parker!" He turned to Alex, paused, and shouted, "Kick me in the ass!" Another pause. "You heard me, brother, kick me in the ass!!"

Alex reluctantly nudged Derek-Bird's backside with his knee.

Derek, as Bird: "You heard me, I want you to *really* kick me in my ass! For lettin' myself come to this. I mean it, man—kick me! Hard!"

Alex continued as himself. "I was reluctant to do it, but I kicked Bird even harder. Then Bird said, and I'll never forget his words, 'Don't ever let this happen to you. You hear? Now leave me.' "

Alex stopped to let Bird say something. Bird closed down.

" 'Leave me, man. I'm busy . . .' is all he said. He walked out of the bar trying to hold his head up. I heard a crash outside and ran out with some others to see him sprawled out, motionless. We got him in a cab to St. Vincent's Hospital. That's how it happened. Not a happy story."

Derek put on his sunglasses and beret again and became Ted Joans. Alex played the CD of Bird a little louder, while Derek soulfully intoned: *Oh, Bird, man . . . JAZZ is a truth that is always black and blue. Hallelujah! I love Jazz so Hallelujah! I dig JAZZ, so yeah, JAZZ IS MY RELIGION.*

Derek paused for a second, then bowed to heartfelt applause. Alex informed us that he had written a book about his association with Bird. (He had also known his wife, Chan, well before she and Parker split up.)

The mention of Bird splitting up with his wife reminded me of Nan, the good times we had before our separation—sharing so much, like hitting all kinds of jams and open-mike poetry sessions. But that was another day.

My thoughts were cut short when Alex announced the price of his book. At first, no one sprung for it. Then a feisty woman, wearing a flowery straw hat, raised her liver-spotted hand, requesting a copy. I figured she was the top honcha of the Japanese tourists. Others quickly followed suit.

While Alex hawked his books, I stole a moment to tell Derek, who was now standing next to me, about Mustache Man's note and our plans to meet later at the Pizza Box. It was a whisper, but Jankowitz's outstretched ears had no trouble picking up our conversation.

"Don't talk," Jankowitz barked at me. "Don't you even *whisper*, Shleppalong, when Alex is talking! You, too, Derek. *You* should know better."

"It wasn't his fault," I said in a faint, but steady, voice. "I asked him something. I'll take the rap." The other applicants, focusing on the scene, like one of those B. F. Hutton ads, were startled by Jankowitz's tirade.

"Oh, you will, will you, Shlepp, take that rap? Okay, tell you what. On tomorrow's tour I'll be expecting a rap from you, okay?" He smiled for a second, then tightened his lips into a leer. Hilda wheeled him away to the other side of the store.

I decided to buy one of Alex's books, but Hank waved me off, shouting, "You don't have to. I got plenty of 'em in my office."

I bought it anyway, a playful challenge to Hank's compulsion to act like a control freak. Jankowitz gave me *his* playful look that said, forget it, let's move on.

I was beginning to actually like him again, even with his annoying need to sit on everyone. I enjoyed taking this tour so far, excited about leading parts of it tomorrow. So I did not want to make any snap judgements about Jankowitz. Why should I?

"Y'know," Alex said, returning my change for the book I bought, "Bird had a way of pullin' cats into his space, like the flow."

"How?" I asked.

"It started with listening," Alex said, "connecting with him, joinin' him in his space, maybe with that generous spirit, if you know what I mean. It's all in my book."

"I'll read it tonight," I said, high-fiving him at the same time. I was about to move over closer to Derek and let him in more on Mustache Man and his scary message, but Jankowitz hyper-motioned for all of us to get a move-on. Turning to me, he uttered, "Oh, what am I gonna do with you?"

Remembering my outburst—real or imagined—with the cops on Friday, I held back challenging him. You can't really know a person until you walk in his sandals, I thought. Or sit in his wheelchair.

* * *

According to the itinerary, the site of Thomas Paine's house was next, just a peek. Then we'd be stopping for lunch, at the Pizza Box, the site where master folk singer, Bob Dylan, got things blowing in the wind, and where I'd up meet up with Mustache Man in just a few hours.

I got this crazy idea that there might be a connection between Mustache Man and hot-headed Donny MacNeil. What got me thinking so was the way Derek fingered those keys all around on his imaginary sax, improvising a song. So far my clues, my keys, were coming up empty, except for these swirling thoughts—was Donny MacNeil, aka Mustache Man, on my trail to strong-arm me to turn over Shady to him? What happened to Antonio? Was he out of the picture? Yeah, maybe this creepy Mustache Man was taking his place. Maybe I should review my insurance policy with Nan.

"Shleppalong!" Jankowitz barked from the door.

"Mr. Jankowitz, I wish you wouldn't address me with that opprobrium."

"What?"

"*Shleppalong*. It doesn't fit me any more, as you can, uh, plainly see."

"Okay, I'll try to remember that . . . Shleppalong!"

After the Tom Paine segment of the tour, we stopped for lunch at the Pizza Box on Bleecker and Sullivan. As we munched our slices, I shared the dream I had last night with Derek. "Heavy, man!" was his response. Things didn't lighten up when I informed him about the mysterious note, but what I said was evidently gripping enough for him to get involved in tonight's encounter with MM.

"I'm with you all the way," Derek said, as he rose for the door. "Beyond! I'm your guy!"

"Where you goin'? "

"Squeezing in an audition for an indie movie."

"Good," I said, as we parted. "Try to make it by 7:45, okay, Derek?"

When I walked into the place, I spotted Hank sitting at one of the tables, with a cellphone in one hand and an iPod in the other. Beckoning the tourists to gather 'round him, he called out, "Have something on us to drink or eat if you'd like—or use the bathroom."

"Meet my friend Julie," Hank said, as he waved us applicants over to the counter. The easy-going, middle-aged Latino owner, decked out in white apron and cap, was kneading a wad of sticky dough. "*Hola*, folks," he said, not bothering to extend his gooey hand to any of us.

"This is where the *real* Villagers like to eat," Hank reveled.

Hilda directed the group's attention to peer at the wooden fence that lined the garden on the right. "This is it, one of our surprises we promised . . . Bob Dylan's garden," she announced proudly. "His home at one time, in the mid '60s. It's called Sullivan—or Bleecker—Gardens, one of 'em. That's where he lived, that brownstone right over there," pointing to a sedate gray building.

"Only way to get in is from the front of the building around the corner on MacDougal Street, a very exclusive entrance," Hank added, pointing to a small open space in the fence. "Take a peek."

The tourists strained their necks to scrutinize the lush "secret" garden, where Dylan had relaxed while he sunned himself and hummed his songs. Tim enjoyed Dylan's early sixties folk-song period more than any other, I vaguely recalled.

Applicant Arnold led the tour group in another rousing rendition of "Blowin' in the Wind." Hilda motioned for me to sing with more spirit. I tried, but it was hard to do, thinking about coming back to the Pizza Box tonight for my meeting with Mustache Man. Why the hell did he want to meet me *here?* The answer, for now at least, forgive me, *was* blowin' in the wind.

Chapter Nineteen

5:00 p.m.

I made it through the first day of Hank Jankowitz's model tour for the applicants. Then I dashed over to Sasha's apartment in the East Village, located in a four-story brownstone between a building of squatters and a trendy sushi restaurant. She couldn't wait to tell me that someone from CWC, Ink called to remind me about my job references. She was steaming.

"Who's CWC? And why did they call you here? What's this about a job? You *have* one already, for chrissakes! Good God, you didn't lose your teaching job, did you? Well . . . ?"

She was so freaked out, I had to calm her down. "CWC is City-Wide Culture, Ink, a tour company, Sash. I applied for a position there as a part-time tour guide." I told her the story: why I was going for this position, why I used her address as my own, why I used bogus references, and how I was being trained now for the new job. Already involved, Sasha had a right to know all this, but I also had to leave out some choice parts—about me being pushed into a car and my meeting with Mustache Man. No need to panic her more.

"Okay, Jeff. I'll go along with it. But I don't like what you're doing. You might get into trouble, get hurt."

I asked her how her day went. "Not well," she confided. "A serious run-in with a dizzy-eyed patient who claimed the technician wrote out a wrong eye-glass prescription. It took a lot out of me to straighten it out."

I couldn't help wincing from my toe flaring up again. It was just like Sash, to forget her own problems in a rush to comfort me.

"You need something for that toe again, Jeff. Let me help you."

Oh, Sasha was heavy into all kinds of stress management techniques. She knew them all—rolfing, meditation, twenty different power yogas, of course, and she couldn't wait to try them all out on me, not to mention trying out her copy of a Tao Sex Manual. For my Yang pleasure," she cooed. "Judas Stalk and Golden Lotus." I stifled a laugh when she claimed there were thirty different sexual positions. Yet, I knew we might only get to first base, yet never hit a home run—because of the separation contract between Nan and me—no fucking anyone else.

"Okay, I have something for you," Sasha said, getting some Epsom salts. "Stick your toe in—careful!" she added, pouring the water into the basin.

"Thanks. My toe's started up again, and I got to go back to CWC, Ink tomorrow, and be able to stand on my feet—"

"Look, what d'you say, after your toe bath, we have a little somethin' to calm you down. I'll give you a real back massage, just learned an awesome new technique."

I didn't say anything.

"Okay, okay, don't get into a snit. What was today's tour about anyway?"

"Bleecker Street and the heroes who lived and worked there. CWC, Ink's owner, Hank Jankowitz, who steered the tour himself today, is a real madcap character. Quite a showman, a speed demon in his whizbang wheelchair." During the soak, I told her all about the Charlie Parker great scene and the moment when Jankowitz paused at the corner of Bleecker and Seventh Avenue, announcing Tom Paine had lived around there in the last years of his life. "Did you know he practically single-handedly started the American Revolution in its darkest hour?"

"I've heard of him," Sasha said. "From England originally?"

"Yeah, he came to Philadelphia in 1774 and two years later convinced the colonies to use *Common Sense*, the name of his pamphlet too, to break away from Great Britain."

"Hey, that's gratitude to the ol' Mother Country." She poured in some more hot water into the bowl after first flicking Raggy, her calico cat, away from it. "Careful with your foot when you pull it out, Jeff."

Cranking up, I went on. "Listen to this, Sash. My silly toe ain't nothing compared to the problem Washington's troops had keeping *their* feet warm in the winter of '76. Pretty awful, huh, using filthy rags for shoes?"

She shrugged. I sat down, trussed to the toilet seat again, as she dried my foot.

"Take a minute to picture this, Sash. Washington reciting the stirring words from Paine's pamphlet. Want to hear a little sample?"

"A *very* little," she said. But I had to continue with the good parts of the story. They got *me* wound up, at least.

"Listen. Paine's words galvanized the troops like a bolt of thunder from the blue. They stopped deserting, sticking it out for a dozen more years until they triumphed in 1783."

"Really *fascinating*, Jeff! Tell me more in the bedroom," she purred, putting away the Epsom salts bowl. "I'll help you there. We can put on the air-conditioning, relax, and—make peace, instead of war. What d'ya say?"

"Wait a minute, hon. Walk me back to the living room. I got the tape right here that Jankowitz played at the site of the Paine home. Put it on, okay?"

Reluctantly, she got me to the couch, tiptoed over to the hutch with the tape recorder, and popped the tape in. Purcell music played in the background while I quoted these timeless words by heart:

These are the times that try men's souls. / The summer soldier and the sunshine patriot / Will in this crisis shrink / From service of their country. / But he that stands it now / Deserves the love and thanks of men and women.

"Those were Paine's words, Sash. Inspiring, huh? Don't deny it now—"

"Well, what happened to him?" she asked.

"Tom Paine died when he was seventy-two. Only six people attended his funeral in New Rochelle."

"Not nice. How come?"

"He got in trouble 'cause he attacked the institution of formal religion. You know what he said? 'The world is my country, all mankind are my brothers. To do good is my religion.' Nice, huh?"

"Yeah, damn straight words, Jeff. Awesome! Fantastic! Good for your man Paine. May he rest in peace! But how 'bout some action—with me!" she said, playfully about to rub my head and dispense some wise Deepak Chopra uplift, when, damn, she noticed my bump.

Pulling down my chin to scrutinize my noggin, her jaw dropped. "Jeez, how did *this* happen?!!"

Here we go again! Was she going to morph into the Capricorn Chronic Complainer, again, when I needed my own space?!

"I don't know, honey. I musta bumped into a wall or somethin'. I . . . I got a lot to do to prepare for tomorrow." I scrambled to her kitchenette—with her right behind me.

"Jeff, why are you doing this tour anyway? I'm concerned that they're going to find you out."

"Who's gonna find out anything? What did I do?"

But she couldn't stop. "I know all this tour nonsense has to do with that rare book. Oh, m'god—stop with it, already, you kook!" she said. "We don't need the trouble it's causing us."

She started brewing a new batch of coffee.

"I don't know. Maybe Tim hid it somewhere."

"I thought you said it was stolen from his apartment."

"Maybe. Or maybe Tim put it somewhere else for safe-keeping."

"But his apartment was ransacked!"

"Yes, but maybe it wasn't there for whoever was looking for it."

"Maybe, maybe, maybe—so, now you have to solve another mystery, Jeff. Hel-lo! Calling Erle Stanley Gardner! Calling Perry Mason! Read all about it in 'The Case of the Stupido Missing Book!' "

"God, it's got to be *somewhere*, Sasha. Maybe Tim left some clues in his personal binder notebook. I'm searching for it."

"*Another* book, you're looking for, Jeff? Come on, give me a *fucking* break! Give *yourself* one too!"

"Not like you, Sasha. Cut that swearing shit out, okay?"

"Okay, okay. But, c'mon, Jeff, get *real*. Tim would've told you if he moved the book somewhere else."

"Hey, *mi querida*, he tried to! His last words, 'Jeff, tour is . . .'"

"So that's why you think the tour has something to do with the book?"

"Yeah, could be some clues on Tim's tour route. I got a hunch I'll pick up some important info on the way."

As I sipped my coffee, I realized why I couldn't involve Sasha too deeply at this point—Antonio. Working the tour was the only way I knew to find him, the key to everything. And now, there's the question about Mustache Man, whoever he is. Too many mysteries—and current risks—to involve her.

Sasha's cat jumped on the counter. She paused to rub Raggy's fluffy nape.

"Sure, thing. Anyway, what're you gonna do with all that money when you find that book? Go back to her, huh? To Nan—!"

"Cut that out. Why do you have to bring *her* up? I can't deal with your constant gloomy suspicions."

"Sure, just like you, Jeff. Don't think about *my* waiting for you for three months—for us to—"

"I keep on reminding you. It's in our separation contract. Nan and I can't go all the way with anyone—at least for now—so forget it. I made a promise."

"To whom, Jeff?"

Rambunctious Raggy jumped off the counter.

"To Nan . . . and myself. I'm sorry."

"You're sorry! So we do the Clinton Thing, everything *but*. You know something? I'm angry! 'Cause you want to go back to her. Admit it!"

"I'm just not sure. I'm being honest. I've got to think about it. Please."

"Just one thing then."

"Yes?"

"Check what's going on with you . . . check your feelings . . . check your . . . oh, God, Jeff, get a hold of yourself. I'm worried about you. Worried sick!"

"Stop! You're talking just like my wife! Always on my case. *That's* why we separated."

"Don't talk about Nan."

"Shuttup! Shut the fuck up, Sash!"

She stared at me, astounded. I said I was sorry. That was the way things stood for now.

Following her into the bedroom, I crawled into bed with her, bringing a smile on her sweet, beautiful face, as if she didn't have a care in the world. For a few moments, the rest of world was gone.

Then my cellphone rang. Sasha's eyes riveted on my hand reaching for the phone. She ducked under the pillow, making sure her ears were fully covered.

"Oh . . . Mrs. MacNeil?"

She apologized for bothering me, said she had gone to Tim's apartment to pick up some things, but couldn't get in. "You know, it's been turned into a homicide investigation scene." Her voice was so soft. "I was wondering if we could get together, just for a short while, until I have to meet my husband. He's working on the Lower East Side today, so I thought I'd join him later."

"Yes, where you now, Mrs. MacNeil?"

"In the Village. At a restaurant on the corner of Third Street and Broadway. You remember The Village Casbah, where you and Tim once met me for a meal? Nice place, Jeff. Quiet. Can you spare any time?"

"Sure, "I'll be there in fifteen minutes. See you soon." Putting the phone down, I recalled the good time we had there. "It's *important*," I told Sasha. "Tim's mother."

I put on my sandals, careful not to let the canvas touch my toe. Sasha, still in bed as I headed for the door, hurled her pillow at me.

"*¡Ay, dios mio!* You *burro!* For a change, think about your *own* book you should be writing. Remember, for Greene Cent?! And think about your daughter, instead of all that Bleecker Street bull! Don't you ever worry that some pimply boy is gonna try something on her like I've been tryin' to do with you for three non-fucking months?

I kicked the door, forgetting about my toe. She saw me wince again and started to cry—or maybe laugh. Maybe both. How many more tears would I be creating for the two ladies I loved? Sasha and Nan were stuck with me like a loose stamp that could fall off if I kept up this unsettling journey to nowhere.

"It may rain, Jeff, honey. Where's your umbrella?"

As I closed the door, I spied Raggy back in Sasha's comfort corner, giving me his evil eye.

Chapter Twenty

Early evening

On my way to West Third Street, I stopped at the building where Charlie Parker once lived, on Avenue B, near Ninth Street, right across from Tompkins Square Park. My aunt lived there in the 1980s. When I was sixteen, I visited her from Milwaukee, and she took me to one of the hottest clubs of the time—8BC—where a lot of sharp bands were playing in the East Village. What I remembered most, though, was walking down Avenue B, witnessing some scary heroin dealing right across the street from where I was now standing in this scrubbed-up Yuppie neighborhood.

Now, with the sun beginning to fade, I looked more closely at Bird's old apartment building. It was well kept up. Near the door was a bronze plaque, with commemorative words celebrating his musical genius. Across the street, kids were playing ball all over the park and yelling, making it hard for me to holler for a cab. I backtracked into the park to ask the kids to tamp the noise down a bit. Then it hit me. Literally. A hard baseball whizzed by, nearly landing on my shoulder. My body started to shake and I began to pant heavily.

A kid behind me caught the ball. "Are you okay, mister?" he shouted. "We didn't do it! Not us! We're not allowed to play hardball in the park!" I couldn't talk with my teeth chattering like a wind-up Halloween skull. I waved to the kids to keep their dumb ball.

Before I climbed into the cab, I saw the back of a man in a raincoat and hood, running away at the other end of the park. It wasn't raining.

* * *

Tim's mother was waiting for me in a booth of The Village Casbah, a cool mixture of Moroccan glitz and funky Village decor, candles, and soft music. On the way in, I greeted the owner, Gloria, wearing her hajib proudly, whom I'd known since her arrival from Tunisia twenty years ago.

I made my way over to a dimly lit corner where Mrs. MacNeil sat. A petite woman with gray hair, she was shrouded in her own thoughts. Her simple spring dress was the only light thing about her. I extended a warm handshake and settled into a leather-cushioned booth. She kept rubbing a silver pendant dangling from her neck, a bird set with a black onyx eye. She had to sense my discomfort.

"Tim gave this bird of peace, a hummingbird, to me for my birthday. He gave Rachel one too."

I held her hand during a long silence.

"Jeff, how are you doing? How's your toe?" I nodded okay. Thank Sasha's good care for that.

We exchanged pleasantries and ordered some soft drinks. Then she got down to it. "It's terrible, how he died."

"Yes, I know."

"They suspect foul play. Why would anyone want to hurt my Tim?" Rachel asked the same question. For both I had no answer.

"I don't know. Mrs. MacNeil, is there anything I can do?"

"I mean, Tim was so good. He was good to everyone. He worked with those high school kids on their living history project and all his college students loved him and—"

She diverted her eyes from me and took a Kleenex from her handbag. I could see Tim in her—the fine cheekbones, the wide, friendly eyes and the always soft, but commanding, voice.

I reached over to her and held her hand. "He was good to everyone, 'specially his sister. I had a brief chat with Rachel on Saturday. I know Tim helped her."

Mrs. MacNeil seemed hesitant. "Helped her?"

"Yes. Rachel told me how Tim really came through for her in her desperate time of need."

I felt foolish bringing the subject up, and was relieved when our drinks arrived. I took a long awkward sip of my Coke.

I understood the pain she felt about the loss of life, in any form, but Mrs. MacNeil herself felt compelled to spill out the so-called sordid facts about her daughter. "The shame of her unwanted pregnancy was too much for her. She was so afraid to tell her father about her condition, and even kept the identity of the baby's father from me. Well, I mean, If it hadn't been for Tim . . . he made sure at least that there was a good doctor to do it."

We just sat there quietly for a minute.

"My husband told me that he and Reverend Johnson visited you. Donny wants to see you again."

Didn't she know that her husband and the reverend had threatened me on that visit?

"Sure. But not tonight, Mrs. MacNeil. Sorry, I have to meet someone later this evening."

"My husband's a very determined man, Jeff. He wants to find whoever . . . did that to Tim. Thinks *you* can help him."

Sure, I thought, stewing over how nasty MacNeil had been to me. Still, I assured her I was on her side. "Well, I've talked with the police already."

"So has Donny. I told him to let them to do their work, but he won't listen. Though they disagreed on many things, there is one thing Tim and my husband did share—a strong belief in justice."

Another pause. She was rubbing the hummingbird pendant again, so gently, as if the spirit of Tim incarnate was in there.

"My husband is a good man, I do believe that. But I wish he'd stop dredging up Tim's past. What he was . . ."

"But you just said that your husband wants me to help him."

"Yes, he does! But at the same time, he constantly blames Tim for his own troubles! As if his 'life style' warranted it! You don't know all the terrible fights I had to endure between Donny and my son over the past few years."

With a pleading look, she took hold of my hand again. I apologized that I would have to go soon.

"No, no. Please, not yet, Jeff. I just wanted to mention, uh, Tim's last call to me. It was on the morning of the day he died. We were making plans to meet him at his building and then go out and celebrate. He said something about what you and he were doing together."

"Yes? Was it about the rare book?"

She nodded. "Yes, and then Donny also mentioned something about helping Tim and the book. He's naturally disturbed to learn that it's missing. It seems so important for the African-American community—and, of course, for Tim's memory. Jeff, my husband wants to join you in finding the book." Just what I needed.

"Also Reverend Johnson would like to help. He's so considerate."

Yeah, I'm thinking—Johnson and Donny, both so nice. Using me, so they can sell the book for their own greedy purpose—to auction it off to the highest bidder.

"My husband can be so angry these days. He yelled at Rachel this morning." Mrs. MacNeil looked so sad, so frail. "I had to call my sister in Atlanta."

Suddenly she brightened. "You know what? Rachel is thinking of moving to Atlanta. But when Donny suggested that Reverend Johnson could give her some good contacts down there, she flatly refused any offers of help from him."

Good! The thought of Johnson connected with Rachel in any way made me sick.

It was seven-thirty, time to go. But I couldn't leave her now without adding something positive about Tim. I told her how Tim had approached me a few years back to join him and some of the university professors to picket the Republican National Convention by holding a rally in Union Square Park. I had sort of hedged, afraid of getting involved because Nellie was having her tonsils out. But Tim put one of his mottoes in full force, "Go for it, or forgo it!" So those rebel professors went for it and wound up in the slammer overnight. The cops claimed the protesters were using a bullhorn in the park that disturbed the peace.

"Oh, Lord, my Tim spent the night in jail?"

"Yes, he believed in what he was doing, Mrs. MacNeil. That took a lot of courage."

"He was always that way. Putting himself at risk for things that he thought were important."

"And that was what made your son so endearing."

"Yes, and so troubling! Thank you." She rose abruptly from the table.

I nodded, contemplating her last words.

"My husband will be along soon. Said he'd pick me up at 7:30 p.m., right outside the door. Like I said, Donny's working on the East Side of Manhattan today. Y'know, he's a maintenance inspector for the City Parks Department."

"Oh?"

"Yes. Today he was checking playground equipment all along the East River and some of the other parks."

Like Tompkins Square Park. Was he the one who tossed that hard ball at me? Jeez, calm down, Jeff. Paranoia acting up again, big time. On the other hand . . .

I took the check and accompanied Mrs. MacNeil outside. There, at the curb, was her husband's car, a forest-green Parks Department sedan. She did say he was a stickler for being on time.

I remembered Tim sharing one story about his stepfather. While on patrol for the First Marine Division in 'Nam, Donny got max pleasure following the advice of his Battalion CO: "Be polite, be professional, but have a plan to kill everybody you meet." I wasn't exactly thrilled about meeting him again so soon.

I promised to stay in touch with her, hoping we'd chat about Tim's memorial at Greene Cent. I waved to her husband as she got into his car, but he seemed to avoid looking at me. It looked like Donny was wearing a raincoat. The sight chilled me. Yes, I did have to calm down—even paranoia has its limits.

Chapter Twenty-One

8:30 p.m.

I hung around the Pizza Box 'til after eight-thirty, looking for Mustache Man. No Derek either. During this time, I asked Julie, a few times, if he had noticed a tall mustached man enter the cafe.

"No, sorry, don't know, Dr. Jeff," he always said, going back to tossing his dough in the air.

I read the note again from MM—"meat you were the wind is blowin' on Bleecker. Food place. Tonite, 8."

That was it. There was another Dylan marker in the neighborhood. Pocketing a can of Coke to drink on the run, I headed two blocks to the corner of Bleecker and LaGuardia Place. On the wall of my own neighborhood supermarket was a glass-paneled mural of Village artists and activists. And there he was, Bob Dylan, along with other notables like James Baldwin, Jackson Pollock, and Edgar Allan Poe. Dylan, squeezed in between Joan Baez and Woody Guthrie, seemed to be leering at me, laughing, as if to say, "Why should we have anything to do with that nut, Jeff?"

Still no trace of Mustache Man. Well, I couldn't blame him for not sticking around. So I got up, spilled out my Coke, went into the supermarket, picked up a six-pack, walked outside, and cracked open a bottle of Bud, right next to the glass panel. I raised my bottle to all of 'em, saluting the folk singers and other artists looking down at me, a dismal foolish failure. The idea that I could ever stay on the wagon for the benefit of my daughter was shrinking like the drink in my hand. I had to go home.

My cellphone rang. Derek.

"Derek, where the hell you been, man!"

"Couldn't help it, Jeff. Been auditioning for a weekend stage gig—just couldn't break away. Good news, I banged it. I'm up for a callback!"

"Congratulations!" I spat out. "You missed all the fun here!"

"What? Tell me."

"Not now. Later." My drinking bout was beginning take its toll.

"Jeff, this is important. Hey, if you're not mad at me, can you come over to my pad sometime tonight? We gotta talk."

"Sure, Derek. Later." If I was up to it.

* * *

Surprise! Jameson and Gerard were waiting for me in my lobby as I sloshed in, clinging to the remaining two bottles from the six-pack I had yet to swig down.

"Sorry to disturb you, Jeff," Gerard said. "We were—"

"Jus' in the 'hood," I slurred.

"No," Gerard said. "We'd like to review some of the events leading up to the death of your colleague. Can we go upstairs? We hope it's not too late for you."

That's right, it was too late for everything. What were they after now?

Jameson added, "Sorry, Jeff. We need to talk with you, uh, if you don't mind."

What the hell, I saw them as old acquaintances by now. I nodded, but still kept my guard up, as much as I could in my glorious condition.

"I think I should have a lawyer with me," I jested, my head spinning around like a washing machine.

"Of course, Jeff," Gerard smirked. "You want to call him—or her? Shouldn't mind a late call, for what they charge these days."

I didn't answer. No more jokes at this late hour, after nine p.m. As soon as I opened my door, I made for the couch, gratefully sinking into its soft cushions.

Finding a nearby chair, Jameson asked if I was okay. "Can we go on?" Without waiting for an answer, she took out her notebook. And, well, yes, chewing gum.

What choice did I have? At least I was comfortable in my own digs.

Gerard walked over to the couch, looking directly into my besotted face. "We've interviewed quite a few people involved with this case. Found a few interesting new twists we'd like to share with you." He grabbed a chair, moving close to my face.

"My sources indicate that you've applied for a part-time job at some tour office. CWC."

"Yes, CWC, Ink."

"What's that mean, Jeff?"

"City-Wide Culture."

"Incorporated?"

"No, *ink,* with a *k,* like what you put into a pen."

Jameson's turn. "City-Wide Culture. I've seen their eight-wheeler busses quite a lot around the city. Good reputation, I hear, with their new improved head-phones for riders. They also handle walking tours, right, Jeff?"

I knew where she was going with this. Maybe.

"And Tim MacNeil was one of their top tour guides on a Village walking tour, right?"

I nodded.

"Funny that you applied for his job. How come? Didn't we tell you to lay off this case? Want to follow in Tim's footsteps, do you?"

"Why not? Don't I have an American right to work where I'm hired?"

"Not in this case," Gerard piped up. "We'd like you to stay out of our way."

Yeah, they were right and I didn't feel like fighting anymore.

So I told them why I wanted the job, to find any tip that'd lead to solving Tim's murder. Why it was important to me that they not know of my connection to Tim, that this might unravel my entire scheme. But there was something I didn't say to them, something I was just finding out for myself. Following Tim's tour was a way of still holding on to him, refusing to let go.

I plotzed my head down on the couch, just wanting to go to sleep. I was in no condition to say anything more. If she just stopped chewing!

Detective Jameson leaned over. I expected the worst, but what came out of her mouth was totally surprising. "Not bad, Jeff. You may be on to something. As a matter of fact, you can do us a big favor to help us crack this case."

I held my breath. Here's a neat switch! They want *me* to help *them?*

"But, listen, Jeff. you got to clean up your act. All those lies! To us, then to CWC, Ink with your job application. Mr. Jankowitz is going to find out about you and then you'll be up Jack-shit's creek in one damn leaky boat. Not a time to lose this job!"

Must be Sasha who snitched on me. Traitor!

"Okay," I said. "Just how can I help you?"

"Keep us informed, if you hear anything that can help us."

"I'll try," I said.

"Call us right away if you see this Antonio. We need to question him."

I told them about meeting—and not meeting—Mustache Man tonight. Then, why I got drunk, as if that was an excuse.

Gerald bent down to my grizzled face. "We 'preciate that, Jeff. Just be careful with him." I told them Mustache Man probably felt the same way about me.

"Thanks." Gerald went on, "Now you can tell us what you know about Derek Molson."

"He works with me at CWC, Ink."

"He was a friend of Timothy Hartknoll. We know all about that."

"All?"

Jameson flipped over to another page. "They were boyfriends, right? Any serious rifts between them two?"

"No, neither Tim nor Derek ever mentioned any."

"You're sure?"

"Yeah, absolutely. No doubt. Hey, you don't suspect—"

"No, we're just checkin' everybody and everything." Her eyes beamed at her partner as she closed her notebook. "Okay, Jeff, we're gonna wrap it up now, but we'd like to ask you a little favor."

"What?"

"We'd like you to come with us to Tim's apartment now."

Jameson tread lightly. "Do you think you could do that for us—and for Tim? Considering you were there on the morning he . . . We know how sensitive this is, but you might catch something that we missed. Just a quick look, I promise."

"Yeah, yeah, yeah." I was okay with it. "But take it easy with my arm! Back up!" They supported me getting up from the couch.

As I got up, I realized the beer was playing funny tricks on me, and the thought of visiting Tim's place was spinning cartwheels in my noggin.

"Don't worry," Gerard said calmly, when we got to Tim's apartment. "Leave this to the pros, no need for you to go backdoor, playing detective. Oh, one thing," he warned, pulling out some latex gloves from his back pocket, "the crime scene investigators are still working in there during the day—very carefully. They'll be back tomorrow. So don't touch a thing. I got some gloves for all of us to wear. Alright, you ready?"

Before I could even get up, it all came pouring out—the beers, the Cokes and pizza from my lunch, my big screw-up to meet Mustache Man, even the hatred for these two cops and myself. All of it, the vomit just poured out. That did it! Who was gonna clean up this dirty mess on the carpet?

Gerard gently put his gloved hand on my shoulder as Jameson gripped my hands. I covered my face to avoid looking at my own vomit. But I could smell it and it just made me want to heave again. All I could do now was dry heave and that made things worse. So much for our first attempt to work together.

They escorted me, if that's the word for it, back to my apartment. Hello! Doree, at my door, with a big heap of papers in her hand, no doubt related to Tim's upcoming memorial.

"Oh, Dr. Gardner . . . I'm sorry," she said, looking her usual concerned self, too embarrassed to see me in this loony condition, flanked by two cops. How did I look to her, with my droopy eyes, my body dripping in stinking sweat? A disjointed Picasso, a splattered Pollock? I couldn't tell if that was a look of concern or or if she was downright laughing at me. Forget about my bum toe and the bump on my head, my grazed left shoulder. When she started to walk away, her look was the unkindest cut of all, if you excuse me, Master Bard.

As Doree turned to head down the hall, she called out some kind of date for the memorial that I couldn't make out.

"Sorry," she said again, even more quietly, as she stole a final pathetic glance back at me.

"So am I!" I yelled, as she disappeared into the elevator.

I had every reason to slink into my bed and cover my shameful head under a sea of pillows. But, something was nagging at me. Then I remembered, I had to get over to Derek's place.

Chapter Twenty-Two

10:00 p.m.

Derek's building was an old tenement on Christopher and Hudson, squeezed in between a gay bookstore and a small restaurant called Braising Saddles, festooned with purple Western-style lights. Derek buzzed me in and, as a precaution, I maneuvered the six-floor walk-up with my right heel doing all the work.

"You look a mess, Jeff. Take a load off," Derek said, greeting me with a warm embrace.

"Thanks, Derek. You don't look so hot yourself."

"What you say? I'm not so *hot?*" In his tight jeans and torn T-shirt, he came off seductive enough.

"Cut it out. I didn't mean it *that* way," I lamely joked. He laughed anyway.

Since he was humming an up-tempo version of John Coltrane's "My Favorite Things," I mentioned that I knew one of 'Trane's former drummers. "Rashid Ali, who lived in Soho, once took part in a dynamite jam session in a class Tim and I taught. A couple years later, Ali's daughter baby-sat for Nellie. Small world."

"Yeah? Well, I gotta tell you, Jeff. Tim thought your Nellie a real charmer."

He gave me the cook's tour around his cramped but super-neat studio space. CDs were stacked high in two corners and one wall was covered by large posters of his fave C-jazz musicians: Coleman Hawkins, Charlie Barnett, Charlie Parker, and Charlie Mingus. Then he went on about the musical tastes he shared with Tim—all kinds, from folk to Afro-Cuban, and, of course, soul. Curious he didn't mention Sam Cooke, whose song "A Change Is Gonna Come" the gospel choir sang so passionately at Tim's funeral.

"I guess I been runnin' at the mouth. Do you smoke?"

Derek gingerly picked up a guitar resting in the corner, and, waiting for my answer, strummed a few chords.

I told him no, not for a while, neither regular nor weed.

"Yeah, me, neither. Been months since I rolled a J. Have a couch, man. Relax. I'll fix us up some hot java."

I shared what I had just gone through with the cops. He took it all in from his little kitchenette, which was actually one-half of the tidy living room.

"They been on my case, too. A white man and a black woman cop. Jamie—or somethin'. Early this morning. Woke me up. Askin' about a book. I told 'em, like I told you, like I told everybody . . . I don't know nothin' about a book on Frederick Douglass."

So, they were here already. Cops never even mentioned it to me.

"You believe me, don't you, Jeff?"

"Sure."

I looked around. There was a famous sculpture of the great Paul Robeson on a stand underneath a familiar portrait of Malcolm X, jabbing his finger at someone. Next to that, a poster of a sultry Josephine Baker complemented Paul and Malcolm's fiery presence with her splendid saucy nakedness. No pictures of Frederick Douglass anywhere, though. Curious.

"Dig this, Jeff. After I just said that, the fuzz turn around and want to know if I copped the damn thing with—are you ready for this—*you!* Holy shit, man! Get 'em off my raggedy black back!"

I laughed with him, but he was just getting warmed up. "Then they give me the whole spiel, askin' me where I was on Thursday, last week. How the hell should I remember? I don't have one o' them fancy iPalms, or whatever, y'know. Oh yeah, I tell 'em, of course, I was workin' on one of the scenes on Shakespeare for the old man, Jankowitz."

"Shakespeare?"

"Sure, scoutin' out the site of the old Winter Garden Theatre, a bunch of stores, on Bleecker and Broadway, where the three Booth brothers—Edwin, Junius Jr., and John Wilkes—performed *Julius Caesar,* six months before Abraham Lincoln was plugged by John Wilkes. Imagine, those cats were playin' that whole conspiracy thing out at the Winter Garden in 1864."

"Wow!" I had no idea.

"That's what I said to Jankowitz, 'Like, wow, you got the whole conspiracy scene played out way before Wilkes iced Lincoln!"

"Wow!"

"You said it again, brother!" Derek said. "So that's it. The cops split, satisfied that I didn't do my friend in. Still don't like 'em."

I could see why Tim loved him. A really sweet guy.

Close up, I spotted a little zigzaggy scar below his chin, partially hidden behind a fold of discolored skin. Derek picked up on my curiosity about his scar.

"That? Sorry to let you down, Jeff. I ain't never been in a gang, or been sliced up—"

"Wait, I never—"

"Got it from diving, like, you know, into water, doin' an inward dive, tucked position. I untucked in the air, my chin *hit* the board—and my posse at the settlement house in the Bronx hit the shit. An ambulance toted me—the Black Wave—away 'n' gone!"

Laughter rolled out of us, easy.

"Hey, I got an idea," Derek flashed. "You know that flick about that bird—that's what Sam, the Spade dude, called it, right?"

"Oh, you mean the bird statue in *The Maltese Falcon*? Yep."

"Yeah, Jeff, that could be our code name—Black Falcon."

"Nah. Sounds corny. Mind if I simply call you *D?*"

"I like that, man."

"Okay, D. Now get back to your story about the Winter Garden."

"Gerard and Ms. Whatever drilled me good 'bout where I was last Thursday, but I wasn't worried, 'cause I had a witness—yeah, old man Hank himself—at the old Winter Garden. We were there tryin' to tie it all together, and—plum dang it, if we didn't get it right on, thanks to Tim's great work on the script!"

"Tell me—if you can—how'd Tim get along with Hank?"

"Great. Why not? Tim loved his job and in turn helped the company, y'know, prosper. There was only one time I ever heard 'em argue."

"Oh, yeah? What about?"

"Ah, never mind, it was nothin' really."

I didn't press him on it, but made a mental note. As he picked up his guitar, I refilled my cup, waiting for him to continue. "But on Thursday morning, Tim wasn't with us at the Winter Garden site 'cause he was with you doing your class, and then—"

Derek plucked his fingers across the guitar strings and stopped, waiting for me, I guess, to finish his sentence.

I got the words out. "He died of an overdose . . . of sleeping pills."

"I should've been there with him, at his side," he said.

I was by his side . . . I thought. Yeah.

Derek closed his eyes. "God! Sleeping pills? How can that be? I know that he had trouble sleeping lately—he was often up half the night. But, man, he was always so careful about what stuff he put into his mouth. He would never have accidentally OD'd on sleepin' pills— My God, do you think he intended—"

"No, D, not a chance. He had every reason to live—what with his promotion and the rare book—"

"So then you're sayin' he was . . . murdered?"

"Yeah. And you know what we gotta do? Find out how he was poisoned with all those sleeping pills."

"Tough call. With so many of those students givin' him drinks that terrible day."

"Yes, who knows where to begin?"

"Well, the cops are already starting on any leads at your school. That'll take time."

"Okay, so in the meantime, what can we do ourselves about Tim? We have to brainstorm, think outside the box. Remember Tim's last words—'Tour is—' ?"

"Sure."

"I mean, well, maybe someone in your tour office could've done it."

"Hold on, man!! That's freakin' heavy! You're not thinkin' I had anything to—"

"No, no, of course not. All I know is that there has to be some connection between Tim's murder and the tour. I told you what his last words to me were."

He nodded and picked up his guitar again.

"D, he told me something else after our class, that in the school he had just run into someone from the tour—"

"Who?"

"He didn't say—damn, I don't know!"

"Okay, okay, take it easy, Jeff."

"We gotta make a list, buddy, a list of everyone from your office, even those who took tours with him."

"You jokin'? Calm down, bro. We can't go checkin' out all those peeps who took the tours."

"Well, why the hell not? Jameson and Girard are checkin' out all Tim's students. Remember when I asked to see Tim's notes, from his Bleecker Blues personal binder? They could also help us track down—"

"Yeah, who killed our friend." He strummed some twangy arpeggio chords and then laid down guitar to grasp my hands. "I'm with you, brother. No matter. Tim left his binder here when he last stayed over. Let me get it."

A minute later he returned with the binder tucked under his arm. He casually flipped through it, one page at a time, but suddenly stopped.

"What are we really lookin' for, Jeff?"

"I'm not sure."

"So we're clueless?"

"Let's rewind, page by page, D, and see if we can connect anything with Shady Lady or what happened to Tim."

Silence. The flickering purplish light from the neighborhood cafe danced up and down on Tim's Bleecker Blues binder cover, casting an eerie radiance.

"Okay, Jeff, let's act on it." He adjusted the window shades to shut out the flickering light.

We slowly went through Tim's personal binder notes, starting from the beginning of his scribbles in the margins. On page three there was a little hand-made map with some notes Tim had made. One was labeled "The Bitter End," the night club where Woody Allen had gotten his start and Bill Cosby had also performed. In the left-side margin, scrawled in big letters, was the word *MORE*, or was it *MOR!* with a big exclamation point? Derek and I exchanged a quick questioning glance.

"But I still have no clue," he said. The buzzer interrupted our shared concentration.

"Hey, Derek, Look, If you have company, I could split."

"No, man. This won't take long. Important that we hang together on this. I mean—"

"I know, I know . . ."

Chapter Twenty-Three

Immediately following

Derek unchained the lock, and let a kid in. Black. Maybe fifteen. Baggy shorts, rose-colored T-shirt. Afro haircut. Kind of small, but not his voice.

"C'mon, Mr. M., all the kids be waitin' for you!"

"Sorry, Lazon, got me some work to do here with Dr. Gardner, a friend of Tim's. I'll see you later, at the pier. Okay?"

"Okay. One—" Lazon said. But when he turned to me, his face was a washcloth full of scorn. I sensed that to him I was some kind of interloper at best, an annoying enemy at worst. I waited a minute to make sure he was out.

"One?" I asked. "Some kind of Metallica reference?"

"Their way of saying good-bye. Tim and I were workin' with a whole bunch of these kids. High school drop-outs, gay kids who hang 'round here on Christopher Street at night, And when, y'know, the neighborhood, already with a lotta crime, starts complainin' 'bout the outside noise, the kids drift over to the piers. That's their home."

"What's his story?" I started on my second cup.

"Whose—Lazon's? "He was one of the stars of Tim's Living History program at Washington Irving High School. A whiz! Knew all about history, loved actin' it out."

He paused, waiting for me to pepper him with questions. I nodded for him to go on. He plopped down on the couch again, his head down, eyes half shut, but suddenly sprang up like a frisky jack rabbit.

"Then—boom!—Lazon drops out. There was an incident, a fight. Huge. Tim tried to intercede, but the principal's a hard-ass, and the suspension held. Lazon's mother beat him up. That was it. Lazon never returned to school or to her. A couple months ago, Tim saw him hangin' out in front of this building. Got him away from some of those kids who were pissing on the street, doin' the kind of stuff late at night that really bugs the people who live 'round here—can't blame 'em."

"I see—trouble all around."

"More than that. Tragic. When I first met that kid, y' know what he told me about his troubled life? Are you ready for this? 'Nobody's perfect.' "

"Of course . . ." I knew there was worse, like scoring drugs late at night, or sellin' their bodies. The old story.

"Tim and I hooked up with The Door, a fly organization. Been working with 'em to get these kids back to school, some to the Harvey Milk School in the Village. There's also a mad cool summer program in the works we'd been talkin' about."

"Sounds wonderful."

"These kids really loved Tim."

"I know."

"Hold on. I want to show you something." He retrieved a DVD disc from his drawer.

It showed Tim and Derek, and about fifteen of these homeless kids on the Circle Line, gabbing about Robert Fulton, the inventor of the first steam-propelled ship, which sailed from the Christopher Street Pier 45 in 1807.

"The same pier you rascals hang out on. What d'you think of them beans, kids?" Tim was saying on the video screen.

They plied Derek and Tim with questions flying in from all directions. Lazon, leaning against the boat's railing, asked, "This Fulton—was he a young punk like us?" The kids roared.

On the video, Tim breezed with the kids gathered around him. "And to think, Fulton was only thirteen when he started thinkin' about his steam-driven ship. Driven by his imagination, he attached home-made wooden paddles onto a fishing boat and sailed it down a nearby river in his home state of Pennsylvania. Can you picture him—at that age—picking out the right tree in the forest, cutting it down, forming and shaping the wood, planing it, sanding it, shellacking it, and finally fastening it to the boat?"

Derek pulled from his pocket a small wooden model of Fulton's boat. The kids were blown over by it, but even more so by the knowledge that Derek had carved it with his little penknife.

"Was he black?" a kid next to Lazon asked, spilling out laughter from the other kids.

"No. But, like you, Fulton had a dream, Derek told you, inventing a really cool steam-driven ship. Lotta people made fun of him, put him and his invention down, calling it 'Fulton's Folly.' "

The kids in the video were transfixed, most of them rolling their heads in wonder.

"Yeah, but who's laughing at Fulton now, when his steamboat up the Hudson opened up commerce and helped to make this country so great?" Tim concluded, "So, let me ask you, what did you get outta this?"

Lazon shot up his hand. "I think I know. That white dude Robert Fulton sure was a big wheel!" A lot of laughter and good cheer.

They finished up, telling the kids to stick with things, to steam on ahead, but get grounded with education, the key to the whole thing. By now, all kinds of questions were buzzing around, about New York history, about Fulton, about their lives—what they, the suspended kids from school, got from these educational and counseling services. No metal detectors, no gangs—but lots of help and hope.

Derek turned off the DVD. "Yeah, who's laughin' now? You saw that kid Lazon? That was me . . . seven years ago. The same place. I almost didn't graduate. Gonna drop out too. Holin' up in a shelter in Queens with my aunt. She tried, but life was a downer. But then I got lucky, got a theater scholarship to SUNY Binghamton upstate. To get it, I had to pass an audition. From then on, a lotta good people were lookin' after me—makin' sure I was doin' all my studies, not just actin', you know, but learnin' things I could use later."

Derek picked up the binder, motioning for me do the same. "Take it home, go over it."

"Not now?"

"No, Jeff. I promised the kids I'd meet 'em soon. I gotta split, man."

"One, huh? Thanks, D. I'll see you on the tour tomorrow."

"Great, J-Bird." He grinned, throwing up his hands in mock surrender.

I groaned. "Stop, enough with the birds already!"

"Good, man, thanks for hangin' out t'night. Gotta bounce—let's get outta here."

Derek planned to head over to the pier to talk with the kids about Tim. I had to go home, dig into Tim's personal binder notes, and get some rest for a big day on the tour tomorrow.

We took the stairs together, humming a snappy Broadway tune in unison. It was past twelve a.m., the street swarming with people of every color and size, gays, straights, and some in-betweens. The air was warm, and on this evening, most of the folks seemed to be having a good time, whether high on drugs or just on life.

I looked across the highway to the Hudson River, noticing some little boats still lit up at this late hour. Pointing to them, I said, "Robert Fulton has nothin' on them." Derek agreed.

We turned the corner on Hudson Street to wave down a for a cab for me. Neither of us spotted the car zooming down behind us, aiming for a direct hit. Derek shoved me hard to the side as the car barely swiped us and sped on along Hudson.

"Holy Crapola, what was that!" cried Derek, shouting for the "hit-and-run low-down fucking bastard" to stop.

Could he stomach more bad news? I told him the story of how I was pushed into a car, almost hit by a hardball, blah, blah, blah. He listened intently, smiling in sympathy.

I hailed a cab quick. Not to follow the crazy car, but to get home, thankful I was still alive. Sensing that I was an emotional wreck from the near-collision, Derek insisted on accompanying me home.

Yep. The Law of Unintended Consequences: looked like whoever was trying to knock me off, only succeeded in bringing me and Derek closer. "No, thanks, you don't have to do that, D. You said you had to meet those kids."

"I can, uh, later."

"Better be careful," I said. "Sam Spade's sidekick, Archer, was a goner five minutes into the movie.

"Right. Dig."

"Oh, I meant to ask you, D. Your week-end movie audition went well, I take it."

"Super! Indie flick. It's set in Washington Square Park, 'bout a drug pusher who cleans up his act. If I'm cast, I'll play—you'll never guess—a cop!"

"Yeah? Wild."

"Yes! And I got plenty experience doin' that," he said proudly, tugging on his CWC, Ink T-shirt. "I mean, playin' a cop on the Bleecker Blues tour. You'll see, man."

When we got to my apartment building, Derek sat tight when I got out.

"Do you want to come up?"

"No, Jeff, you're right. I gotta go back to amp up those kids."

"Amp? You mean ramp."

"No. Amp 'em up, man, pump 'em up," he sang, swinging his arm like an airplane propeller. "As long as we don't *puff* 'em up, 'cause it'll take an awful lot of work for them—for us, too!"

We bumped fists.

"Go, man! Hold onto that binder as long as you need it. Like I said, I gotta get back to those kids on Pier 45. They 'specially need me when the pier shuts down at one a.m. I prod 'em to get their big butts over to The Door—or to another safe shelter. Got a whole list of 'em."

He calmly directed the cabbie to head over to Houston Street and turn left. We knocked fists again, looking forward to tomorrow. On the sidewalk entrance to my building, even at this late hour, Greene Cent students were chalking out messages to Tim. Some were from Tennessee Williams's play, *A Streetcar Named Desire*: "Our prince from Arabian Nights . . . with the beautiful mind . . . we were not strangers when we depended on your kindness."

I made it upstairs and immediately read through Tim's personal binder for a couple of hours, fell into bed, and nodded off for three blessed hours.

Chapter Twenty-Four

As I shaved that morning, I wondered what Jankowitz made of me. Did he see me as just another candidate for a job that needed to be filled? Or, more troubling, did he suspect why I was really hanging on—to search for clues to Tim's death? In either case, I was still game to get to Abingdon Square for the second day of the tour guide trials. And, to hold down the gig, I felt I needed to make a solid impression on the boss.

In a couple of neat strokes, I shaved off my goatee and mustache. Smooth as plain yogurt! Hey, this Friday the Division Tenure Review Committee might be tickled pink by my exquisitely neat way of showing my new face. I made sure my interview clothes were neat and trim, from my cleaned-up baseball cap right down to my newly scrubbed sandals. By now I had fully recovered from my toe injury, so that was one worry I didn't have any more. I was ready to shine.

Turning the corner on Bleecker to LaGuardia Place in search of a cab, I ran into Barbados-born Sandy, one of the crew who ran the little post office on LaGuardia. "Where you been, guy?" he asked, clasping my hands.

True, I missed—which seemed like an eternity—hanging out at my favorite haunts on the block: occasional mornings at Moxa's Coffee Shop, owned by a perky young Indian couple, or the wee hours spent in arguing politics with the Albanian manager of Tres Giovanni's, Nellie's fave pizza place. I passed by Marumi Sushi, which Sasha adored, and the new kid on the block—Favela Cubana—which sported Conga drums for seats.

We were all global Villagers, one of the reasons I loved it here. I looked forward to being a part of the tour was to catch up on some forgotten history.

Once in the cab, I called Nellie, figuring she was just about leaving for school.

"Hi, Pops," she said cheerfully. "How ya doin'?"

I said okay. She reminded me of my birthday coming up. Number forty. She always celebrated it with me a week or so early, before she departed for summer camp.

"Gotta hang up," I said. "It'll be hard to reach me during your lunch hour at school, so I'll call you tonight."

"Cool, Dad. Chat with you tonight—live!"

I kissed her into the cellphone. To be on the safe side, if Nan was right, I needed to have a straight talk, embarrassing enough, with Nellie about boys—and their screwy hormones—before she headed for camp and *they* taught her. The tour would be passing by her school in two hours. I hoped we wouldn't bump into each other, sending her into shock about my facial makeover.

As soon as I got to the park in the West Village, Hank Jankowitz complimented me on my new look, how it made me look ten years younger. Okay, that went along with Mark Twain's observation that you're middle-aged when friends start telling you how young you look.

In his omnipresent wheelchair, the boss huddled in a shady spot with the other applicants, doling out select tour information bits to us. "I got some meetings to go to, so you'll take turns leading segments," he said. "Hilda will be right with you all the way, taking notes. Jeff, you'll start here with Abingdon Square, covering the early Dutch and English history of the area, then take 'em over to Alex's music store. I'll be back for lunch, at the Pizza Box, where we were yesterday, to see how everything's goin'. I hope, people, you have your various assignments down pat."

The other applicants—Arnold, Francesca, and Mindy—mumbled some words of encouragement to each other and spent a few minutes straightening out their attire, filling their water bottles, and making sure their tour-guide binders were set up properly.

Mindy was impressing Fran with how she took care of her little brother while their mother was out of town.

"I think he'd love this tour," Mindy said.

"Better make sure he's over twenty-one," Fran winked.

With his usual bravado, Jankowitz announced to the tourist group that this particular tour was on him, *gratis,* since only we lowly applicants would be leading it. He also hoped that no one would be embarrassed by some frankly adult content. He reminded them that they had all been tipped off earlier about this when they signed up for the tour. Some blushed, some jostled each other, while others looked dog-tired and bored.

I sneaked a few glances at a pert blonde woman, who reminded me of Nan. Did I miss her still? Of course, I did, especially with my birthday looming up next week. There was a time when celebrating it was a big deal in our lives.

Jankowitz turned to the tour group, addressing them with his trademarked air of confidence. "You know, folks, I caught the Amazing Race on the tube last night. They travel around the world, 14,000 miles, eleven teams. Right here we got *one* beautiful group, from all around the country, visiting Greenwich Village—Home of Liberty, Cultural Revolution, and Free Love. This is the *real* deal, not a show. So, enjoy!" He whispered something to Hilda and rolled off.

Basically, I was going to go over the same things Hank did the day before. I would add a few words about the English explorer, Henry Hudson, whose sailors on the Half Moon referred to the natives of Manhatta ("hilly land") as "good and loving people," which I decided to call this new group. And did they eat it up! Then I casually mentioned the Dutch West Indies Company pulling off one of the greatest real estate deals of all times when they ripped off from those trusting and loving Indians the island of Manhattan for $24.00 worth of colorful blankets, beads, and other cheap dreck.

A timid-looking black man with wide-rimmed glasses, spoke up. "This is all supposed to be about freedom, right, sir?" I nodded, and he went on. "Then, can you say something about the slave revolts in New Netherlands during the Dutch period? Maybe you know something about Peter d'Angola?"

"Well," I said, flipping hurriedly through my binder notes, " know eleven black male bondsmen and three female slaves, uh, arrived from Angola." That gem depleted my great storehouse of knowledge on the subject.

Hilda turned to me, raising her voice. "Do you know what happened to Peter d'Angola? Didn't you read *all* the notes you were given yesterday?"

Then, thankfully, she grilled the other applicants. "Do *any* of you know?" she inquired impatiently. Ever reliable Mindy spoke up in a steady stream, what must have been memorized: "In 1641 nine slaves or bondsmen, as they were called, including Peter d'Angolo, confessed to murdering a tenth bondsman. They protested that it was an accident, and no one was really guilty. Furthermore, they objected to all being tried for the same crime."

Man, Mindy really had sucked up the notes like a vacuum cleaner. She reminded me of some of my sharper spot-on graduate students.

"Do *you* know what happened afterwards?" Hilda ventured, facing me again. I coughed, long enough to cover up my transparent ignorance.

Mindy Whiz, spoke up again. "The nine men were acquitted provided they pay an annual tribute of farm produce, including one fat hog."

When everyone laughed, Mindy's crinkled grin turned into a cheery smile.

Hilda was on fire now. "Good, Mindy." But not to be outdone by Mindy's contribution, she just had to berate us further. "None of you mentioned the insurrection of the slaves in 1744 who were whipped and lashed to death. Jeff, c'mon, didn't you go over *any* of your notes last night?"

Silence, as I made a mental note—to fix it tonight.

We continued along Antique Row. By this time, judging from the enthusiasm of the tourists, I thought I was doing fairly well with my comments. From time to time, the other applicants added their own to bolster mine. But again, Hilda found a moment to pull us aside and comment on our grave sins of omission.

"When we passed by Peter Warren's big telescope, not even *one* of you mentioned what Mr. Jankowitz told us yesterday—that Warren's mansion on Bleecker and West Fourth was burned down as part of the insurrection. Look sharp, people. If you want to be hired, Mr. Jankowitz wants you t'know those notes cold!!"

She was right. I felt foolish not having digested Tim's research. But, give me a break, I had been up half the night, with his notebook, focusing on his personal comments. Unfortunately, that left me zero time to crib on the facts for today's itinerary.

After Arnold conducted the Tom Paine segment on Seventh Avenue, it was my turn again to lead. My part included Abbie Hoffman's Free Store, a place that raised money during the Civil Rights Movement in the '60s. The group seemed to like hearing this, especially those who were originally from New York but had retired now to far-off places in the West. One lady gleefully burst out that she once had even bought some vintage clothes at Abbie's store.

"Any furniture?"

When she shook her head, I mentioned that Abbie and his merry band of volunteers raided the back lot of Macy's for furniture—and I added they then lived right in the store, which he called "Liberty House."

I was going to divulge that Abbie Hoffman, one of the leaders of the YIPPIE movement, had committed suicide after running for years as a fugitive on a drug dealer charge, but I decided, with their mood now so breezy, to cut out the death stuff. Just too downbeat.

Hilda was just about to start moving along, when literally out of the blue—from behind a dark blue sheet—Derek stepped out, flanked by two white guys, all accomplished actors. They took turns telling about Freedom Summer, how SNCC (Student Non-violent Coordinating Committee), along with other civil rights groups, inspired young people from all around the country to go Down South and help black residents register to vote. "Freedom riders risking their lives, getting beaten up and jailed," one of the actors said in a subdued tone.

Derek thrust his hands toward me, saying in effect, *dig this, pal.* The three actors eagerly led the tourists to sing some freedom songs like "Everybody Sing Freedom" and "We Shall Not Be Moved," ending with some Parchman Parodies, like this one Freedom Riders sang to the tune of "Yankee Doodle ":

Freedom Riders come to town
Riding on the railway,
Mississippi locked 'em up,
Said you can't use Trailways.
Mississippi, you are wrong,
You've gone against the nation,
We'll keep comin'—big and strong
And we'll end segregation.

I marveled how the three, without a trace of costumes or props, transformed themselves into James Cheney, a young black Mississippian, played by Derek, and two white volunteers from New York, Andrew Goodman and Michael Schwerner.

Everyone was blown away by the actors staying in character to answer questions about how they were arrested in Philadelphia, Mississippi, then suspiciously sprung from jail. Very late at night, they were ambushed on the road by a sheriff and his deputy and other white terrorists. Beaten with heavy chains and "shot . . . to death," the trio said together, still holding hands. Slowly they moved behind the large blue cloth. No applause, the onlookers completely caught up in the emotional residue of what had happened in the hard-fought struggle for justice and equality.

I waved "nice job" to Derek, looking at Hilda for her approval. But she only scowled at us again.

Later, on a break, I mentioned Hilda's attitude. Derek laughed and said she was all right. She'd been with him and Jankowitz when they cased out the location of the old Winter Garden Theatre for a possible tour scene, and she had been quite critical—but totally supportive too. As always, she just wanted to make sure everything involved with a CWC, Ink tour was as good as it could be, including its itineraries and staff. So, no good accusing Hilda of intimidating the applicants. She was just doing her job.

"Okay, D," I said. "Well, what about Hank? Last night you said something about an argument he had with Tim—that you over-heard."

"Oh, yeah, a couple weeks back, I was standin' next to Hank's office, goin' over my script, when I heard him screamin' at Tim. It knocked me outta my smelly socks . . . somethin' to do with the tour. Then Tim ran out of the room, running past me, blubbering, 'Damn it, Derek, Jankowitz's accusing me of takin' over his business!' That's all I know, Jeff."

"Listen, D, when the cops visited you, did you tell 'em what you just told me?"

"No, like I said, they only asked me about the book. Nothin' about what happened between Tim and Hank. It really didn't seem that important."

"I don't know. I just don't know, Derek. Frankly, I'm confused. But I'm not pointing a finger at anyone—yet."

Any snap judgement about either Hilda or Hank fell flat in the face of what I had learned from Max Raben and his mentor Isaiah Berlin about the fickle nature of history—that it does not reveal any causes. Only foreshadows a "blank succession" of unexplained events. Here I was almost making an accusation against them, just like those Dutch judges had, without any substantial evidence, against those nine black slaves. At least Jameson and Gerard were chasing after a suspicious circle who had been close to Tim that fateful Thursday morning. I better be more careful about my own finger-pointing. Max always said solid evidence was the doorstep to opening history's truths. I'd try to remember that and not get stuck in the door.

Chapter Twenty-Five

10 a.m.

When we got to Bleecker and Sixth Avenue, the part of the tour I led was over, and we approached the Little Red School House, which my daughter attended. The school fostered the educational principles of John Dewey, "learning through doing." A lot of hands-on experiences and across-the-curriculum projects. And, I might add, a bushelful of money for parents to pay to savor this "feel-good" but solid education.

My luck! Hilda informed the group we'd now be actually going into the school for a short tour. "No, I can't go in there, Hilda," I whispered into her obliging ear. "My daughter goes there, and she doesn't know—"

"Know what?" Hilda snapped. "Like, that you're leading a tour—or tryin' to?" She paused. "Okay, I can see you're a *little* embarrassed. You can wait here *a little*, while we have a quick look at the school, coward!"

I nodded feebly, feeling for my mustache and goatee, now gone.

"Don't worry," Hilda said, collaring me before joining the others. "If you think you screwed up, don't worry, 'cause Mr. Jankowitz thinks you still have a chance. So I'll let this little problem pass. But be careful next time!" Oh, bless you, most bountiful Hilda!

The tourists jammed through the school's red door, but I lingered a few minutes outside, before I mosied next door to the Russian pierogi place for a quick Coke. Bleecker Street, the tourists were finding out, still had a fine diversity of restaurants—an Indian spot across the street, the famous Borgia Coffee Shop at the corner of MacDougal Street, and a whole bunch of crammed pizzerias and sweaty falafel cafes. But did they also notice the *missing* historic sites, like the Figaro, replaced now by ugly condos or fast-food joints? *Erasing history,* I lamented, too bad.

In fifteen minutes, I rejoined the group, observing the tourists tumbling *en masse* down the stairs from the Little Red Schoolhouse, heading for the Pizza Box. Once we arrived, one of them, a Southern gentleman named Harvey, asked Hilda, "Is this where that great surprise is, you were talkin' about?"

Suddenly You-Guessed-It swooped in.

"Hey, Pops, Pops! Omigod, what happened to your beard?"

I shushed her, waited a second or two, and ushered her out of the restaurant while Hilda led the other applicants to the garden in the back to peer at the surprise, Bob Dylan's lush Sullivan Street Garden retreat.

"Hi, honey, what's happenin'?" I breezed, attempting to appear nonchalant.

"I don't know. Some of my friends said they saw you outside of the Little Red, waiting . . . waiting for, uh, those people who went into the school. That's your tour thing, right? Then they saw all of you stopping here. It's lunch time now, so I sorta cut outta school for a sec."

Like father—like daughter. She had to do her own thing. Even when she was three, or so, Nan and I had to keep close tabs on her, or she would wander off without our permission, not too far, but enough to scare us.

Nellie's braces were glistening in the sun, pigtails wafting in the gentle breeze, her little hands gesturing in the direction of the school. I should be spending more time with her. Wasn't that the reason I worked my *tuchus* off at Greene Cent, with all those extra projects, to support this delicious creature in front of me?

"Pops, I gotta run! Andy, the security guard, told me to shoot right back. Mom's real mad at you."

"You mean *very* angry. About what?"

"A *lotta* things. Like you leading tours and stuff. You better call her."

"Okay, honey. You alright?"

"Yeah, working on my exit project for graduation. Civil War stuff. Two teachers, Wayne and Abby, got together and we used these neat Quaker Oats boxes, I told you about, 'member, for two different projects—a pinhole camera for social studies and the cereal stuff for a papier mâché art project. And oh, yeah—"

She started giggling. I was getting antsy about returning to the group, when she floored me with her next comment.

"He asked me, Pops! This cool guy finally asked me to the big graduation dance next week!"

"Which cool guy? Not that thirteen-year-old geek, Albert, who imitates Hi Jinx and those other insidious rappers?"

My thirteen-year-old daughter—already going to dances—nodded sheepishly.

"C'mon, get rid of Albert!"

"Why? His lyrics ain't bad. He writes cool stuff like the Dead Heads."

"That stuff is nasty and homophobic, but I'm not gonna argue with you here! I want to talk with you, soon."

" 'Bout what?"

"Boys."

"What about 'em?"

"You'll find out."

"About *them*?"

"Whoa, now. Don't get smart."

"Don't get mad . . . angry . . . with me, Pops!"

"Okay, okay. You'd better get back to school, Nel."

"Don't forget to call Moms," she tossed to me as she headed back.

"Nellie?"

She stopped and turned around.

"I love you."

She blew me an air-kiss just as bug-eyed Hilda came out and saw me throwing a kiss back to Nellie.

"Who's that?" Hilda asked, with more scoff than smile. The other applicants and tourists hurried to wolf down their pizza slices and drinks at the counter. Hilda stayed at the door to keep an eye on lucky me.

"My daughter. I told you."

Her lips puckered, like a limp tulip, and she continued to glare at me as we made our way to the garden in the back, where everyone joined us in a few minutes. Everybody seemed to be having a good time. Hilda corralled us applicants to a corner to let us know who would be leading the rest of the segments this afternoon and tomorrow—each day with a different tour group.

My cell rang just as Jankowitz rolled in, bulky master binder in hand. He nabbed Hilda on the fly. Glancing at me now and then, they had a fantastic conference of two whole minutes.

"Hi, Nan! Okay . . . okay . . . okay. I'm working now . . . I know it's important . . . Yes, I'll meet you. I'll see if I can get off for a few minutes. But you gotta meet me down here, in the Village. Café Español . . . on Bleecker. I'll see you in ten minutes. Bye."

I put the cell away, calling it was a no-no on the job. But, even at lunch? I guessed so, because I spotted Jankowitz glowering over my shoulder. He motioned me to step up to the food counter, far away from the tourists chatting like magpies in the garden.

"Are you done with that call? Because you're *done*, Shlepp!"

"My wife. Important."

"I don't care if it was Hilary Rodman Clinton! You *lied* to me, Shlepp!"

He pulled out a picture from his master binder. It was of Tim and me, with some students, in front of the Nathaniel Greene statue at Greene Cent.

"You fooled me!" Hank growled. "You never said you knew Tim. I thought you looked familiar. Tim gave me this when he submitted his résumé last year."

"I—"

"What's going on with you, anyway? So, you were friends with him, huh?"

I nodded. "Yes, he was my friend and colleague."

"Why didn't you tell me when you applied for this job? What was the purpose of leaving that out? We gotta work with trust in my company."

Quickly stretching his hands out from his wheelchair, Hank pulled me down to his face. "Oh, and while I'm at it, there's a couple of other things. Hilda said you weren't up on your facts today. And you're always on that damn cellphone. I thought I made it clear, no cellphones when trying out—"

"I'm sorry. It's my wife. We're separated. She wants to talk to me about our daughter. I gotta meet her in a few minutes. Just a quickie. It's near here, only a block away. Can I go?"

" 'A quickie'? Sounds salacious."

"No, just have to talk with her about our daughter."

"Oh, that's another thing. Gabbin' with your daughter on my tour! Incredible! This is a job, not a family reunion. What's with you?!"

Why didn't he boot me out right there? Well, maybe I was right. Maybe he did need me for some purpose, not just the tour.

He gave me twenty minutes to get back, or I "was history."

I met Derek outside. "We gotta check Hank out," I said. "Before the hell he lets me go. He may have hid the book in his office or somewhere."

"I don't know, Jeff. He works late—'til eleven a lotta times."

"Then we'll get in there after that."

Derek just kept repeating, "I don't know, Jeff, I don't know."

"Yeah, okay, D—I gotta run—see my wife. We'll talk about it later."

"*Anytime*, bro."

Chapter Twenty-Six

11 a.m.

Nan and I hooked up at Cafe Español, a cozy restaurant on Bleecker and Sullivan, with the best paella in the Village—Nan's suggestion. She knew I liked the author James Agee, who once lived in the same old red-brick building above the restaurant. We chose a sunny table near the window, adding a little cheer to this otherwise morose reunion.

"You used to tease me about it, Nan. Remember your, uh, untoward remark when I told you Agee wrote *The African Queen* film script upstairs? You said that Tim sometimes came on like an African queen. You *did* say it, right?"

"You know I didn't come down here to insult him, Jeff. I'm so sorry about Tim," she said softly.

"I read the account of him in The New York Times—and your quote was beautiful. You do write well— 'beloved colleague and co-worker and—' "

"Thanks, Nan. But I just said it while the reporter took the words down."

"In any case, I felt your pain. And I still do."

"I have to tell you that everyone who had been with Tim the day he died is being investigated."

"You too?"

"Of course. I already had a long talk with two detectives."

"Well, I suppose it's necessary, Jeff. But I'm not worried about you. You'll come through this ordeal with high-flying colors."

I wasn't quite reassured, despite her chummy tone.

"I cabbed down. I only have fifteen minutes, Jeff."

"Me, too."

"How's the book cover design business?" I inquired, sipping on my second Coke. She nursed her Chardonnay, daintily, reminding me of the good old days.

"The same. Vain authors always trying to change the cover before their baby is published. How's *your* book coming along? The one you're writing for your tenure at Greene Cent?"

A hefty silence, almost as long as the time I was not spending writing the book.

"That's the trouble, Jeff. You should be working on it, instead of—"

"Instead of what?"

"You know very well what I'm talking about. Instead of playin' around with the tour! Do I have to remind you that your tenure review is in three days . . . and you don't even have a book idea yet!"

If I could find Shady Lady, I might.

"Look at yourself. I'm not exactly inspired about your new squeaky-clean look. Where'd that come from? You're really scaring Nellie. She called me . . . didn't know what to make of you when she saw you fifteen minutes ago. That's why I cabbed down here right away. You've got to pay attention more to Nellie's feelings, Jeff."

"Nan, I do that whenever I see Nel. I asked her how she felt today. She said she's doin' good."

"Oh, yeah? She didn't know whether to laugh or cry when she saw your new look."

"Huh? No way! Nellie actually laughed when she saw me. I must've made her feel good."

"God, Jeff, she cried to *me*. A mom always gets the real news. And I don't like it. What you do with your life is, of course, your business. But not the way you choose to overlook her needs!"

"Overlook what?" I had to ask, getting annoyed.

"Come on. You did promise to pay for her camping."

"Oh, is *that* due already?"

Averting her accusing gaze, my eyes wandered out the window to a couple of skate boarders zooming by. Lucky souls.

"Yes, Jeff, it was due two days ago—and your share of her graduation party."

"I—"

"And you promised to have a talk with her—"

"Talk?"

"Yes, about creepy camp boys who might tempt her."

"I did already."

"Well, what did you tell her?"

"I told her that I'd talk to her later about those creepy camp boys."

"Better make it sooner, than later. Do you know anything that's going on? That kids in her school are posting semi-nude photos of themselves on line?"

"But not our Nellie! No!"

"I don't know——but my friend Helen says it's going 'round."

"Tell Helen to take her fat butt out of our business."

"Jeff—be serious. These so-called cybersnaps are nothing to laugh at. The boys call them 'sex-ting'—it was in the papers."

"I'll check it out, Nan. I'll go to the school. I will."

"Well, don't wait 'til Christmas. Follow through on what you say for a change."

"Frankly m'love, I will remember because I *do* give a damn."

"You should get an Oscar. Well, how could you remember *anything* when you're somixed up with this tour-guide stuff?"

"I'll talk to her and send you a check tonight. I swear—"

"Tonight? How about *now*?"

"I can't. Gotta get back to Hank."

"Hank? Who's he?"

"He runs the company—owns it."

"The *tour de farce* you're clowning 'round with?"

Well, that was it, her making fun of the tour. And me. And Tim. No way was I going to let her get away with it.

"I gotta get back, Nan. But let me tell you something first."

"What?"

"Tim did a great job working this tour out. See, he's designed it like a play. Beginning stuff, all dark, and sad, with Charlie Parker, Thomas Paine, Abbie Hoffman, Lenny Bruce scenes—all downers, drugs, drinking, depression, suicide. Still, ennobled by their stubborn principles! Then, as the tour goes on, things begin to brighten up, with Frederick Douglass escaping to freedom, Walt Whitman fighting for freedom of expression, Margaret Sanger, for women's rights. The search! Isn't this important?"

"I gotta hand it to you, Jeff. For a man who can't act in life, you're sure doin' a lot of it in Fantasyland."

"Just a minute, Nan. Hold on! I like the acting part of it, something I miss from my past. And what's more crucial is what I'm doing now just might save the day. You see, there's this book—"

"Save the speeches for your tour groups. One request, okay? Don't scare Nellie anymore."

Jeezus! Across the street, leaning against a mailbox, so casual, there he was! The guy I'd been trying to catch up with all day yesterday. Waiting for me? I dropped some dollar bills on the table and ran out.

Nan yelled at me as I flew out the door, "HEY, WHERE Y'GO-ING, YOU CRAZY SON OF A BITCH!!"

Spotting me cross the street, Mustache Man waved for me to follow him. We scooted a block over to a small triangular park at Sixth Avenue and Carmine, a quiet place where we could talk—if the outdoor piano man wasn't playing. Okay with me, thankful to be in a public space, because looking at this gorilla-Hulk creep made me want to just pick myself up and take off. But I couldn't do that—too much at stake now. For a moment we just sat there, glaring at each other, waiting . . . .

Someone had to start the ball rolling, so I dove in. "Who are you? That message you gave me yesterday— to meet to you . . . then you didn't even show up. What the fuck's going on?"

He spoke softly, yet forceful. Scary shit combination.

"I know 'bout your friend, the black man who got iced. An' I know my friend give him somethin', somethin' big. Very big."

"Your friend? Hey, you mean the guy who calls himself Antonio? Where the hell is he, anyhow?"

"Outta country. Immigration problems. Told me t'finish matters for him. I promise him I would. He trusts me. Good friend." He grinned, revealing a large gold crown in the corner of his mouth. Okay, had to stall him so I could think.

"Look, I gotta get back to the tour now, or I'll get canned. We'll be through in an hour or so. Can we meet later?"

"*Sí*, we talk later. I gotta get back to work m'self. On a crew, see, fixin' up a building near here. You an' me, we meet tonight."

Where? Alone?

"How 'bout Kenny's Castaways, jus' down the block, y'know. "Five-thirty, *sí* ?"

So far, so good, but don't overplay the ethnic, I told myself.

"Right, I be there. But you, too. Hear me? Show up! Gotta tell you, I saw you before, with that cute little girl with—how you say— braids? Your daughter, huh, *amigo*?"

I bolted off the bench towards him, sending the pigeons in a panic. "You bastard! Leave her alone!" Some sunbathers on benches turned to me. Screw 'em! I didn't care who heard my scream—or his. I inched toward him, turning up my fist at him, feet planted squarely on the concrete. I was ready.

"Just kidding! Wanted to see, uh, if you have *cajones*!" he said, backing away from me and laughing idiotically. "See ya later—five-thirty."

Just kidding huh? I called the cops. *Pronto*.

Chapter Twenty-Seven

12:30 p.m.

Gerard said he and Jameson would meet me at the Underdog, our next stop on the tour. They knew I was anxious to speak to them.

I made it to LaGuardia Place, just as the whole tour melange was descending the steps of the Underdog. With only three or four tables, everyone squeezed together like a box of toothpicks. The owners were happy to get the free publicity, along with hot dog sales.

Hilda, was already smirking. "So pleased you could finally make it, mister." Hank motioned for me to get on with it. I glanced at my binder, reminding myself what to do, since I was leading this segment.

I announced that CWC, Ink would provide a free drink for anyone in the tour group who wanted to buy a hot dog or hamburger, which seemed to tickle some of the tourists to no end. An energetic-looking nun, Sister Veronica, dressed in regular clothes topped by a little white cross, paused from chatting with the other tourists to greet me. She told me she belonged to the same order as Dorothy Day, the social-activist nun, who founded the newspaper The Catholic Worker in the 1930s.

With flair to spare, Hilda pointed to Francesca, who took a plastic cup off the counter and, using it as a filter, cried out in a big, booming voice: "Ladies and gentlemen, live from Cafe Au-Go-Go—Mr. Lenny Bruce!"

At that precise moment, two things happened simultaneously. In walked John, the young actor, who yesterday had played Andrew Goodman. Now he was wearing a blue serge suit and toting a microphone. At the very same moment, a tremendous crack of thunder rocked the room. What was that, another one of Jankowitz's unbeatable theatrical showman surprises?

"Glad I brought my umbrella. I'm off to my Brooklyn sites. Watch the store, Schlepp," Hank, with an impish smile, whispered to me as shoved off in his wheelchair.

John actually looked a lot like Lenny Bruce, with his deep-set eyes, sunken cheekbones, and wavy black hair. He gazed around the group, making eye contact with almost each tourist, and then zeroed into his act.

"Hey, why am I in such a dumb, good mood, huh? I feel lousy. Yeah, guess we all do, thinking of what happened to poor old Jack down in Dallas. Y'know, it all happened so fast—Jackie turned around, she saw Jack, so she hauled ass to save ass. Well, she was human, wasn't she?"

I looked around. Everyone was clearly uncomfortable, even me. Sister Veronica crossed herself. In turn, Lenny genuflected sincerely when he noticed her.

Still, no sign of Gerard or Jameson. I forgot to tell them whether to meet me inside or outside.

"Aah, let's rap about somethin' more pleasant. Yeah, like uh . . . performing an unnatural act, *fressing*. How 'bout that? Y'know, evil oral sex? So, anyone here been slushing around in that?"

Some muted, uncomfortable laughter rippled throughout the room. A heavy-set, giggling tourist raised his hand, as the woman next to him, most likely his wife, slapped his wrist in good fun.

Lenny continued: "Yeah? How often? Before meals? Good show! I got to dig up some prizes. So what's wrong with the rest of you? Come on, nowadays everyone's a *fresser*."

Some closeted vampires might've objected if he'd gone on about kids today *fressing,* but he didn't. He seemed to be doing the actual monologue that Lenny had delivered back in the '60s.

"The old *shtuppo*'s never enough anymore. Harry—" He turned to the gentleman who had just volunteered that he *fressed.* "You're not Harry, are you?"

"I don't think so," the man said. This landed a good laugh, and Lenny went on.

Suddenly, Derek and the actor who had earlier been serving the hot dogs came through the door, just like I had seen them do the day before. And just like yesterday, with their Underdog server hats off, you could see their short haircuts. They made a big deal of taking out their dinky miniature tape recorders, turning them on, and slipping them into their pockets. Then they took out their spiral notebooks and started writing like speed demons, reminding me a little of Jameson. God, I could use her now. Lenny had no trouble snaring the audience's attention again.

I knew that this was part of his act, Lenny suddenly doubling up in pain. One of the tourists made a move to help him, but I motioned "he's okay," even as he groaned deeply. "Oy!" Lenny gasped, followed by some startled murmurs from the tourists.

It was time for me to say my first line: "Lenny, what's wrong?" And now began our shtick.

He winces and says: "Goddamn pleurisy." No genuflection to the nun this time. He *was* Lenny now, all the way. He straightens up and gives the two servers playing plainclothesmen a quizzical, pathetic look.

"Now dig how paranoid I get. These two poor *zhlubbos* over there—I don't think they're writing home—"

He faces the detectives squarely and continues: "But you wouldn't be that blatant, would you?"

Derek walks over to Lenny and says, in his best dumbo detective voice: "Lenny Bruce, you're under arrest." Overacting, but it fit.

"What's the charge?" Lenny asks.

The other cop: "Section 1040 New York Penal Code."

"What kind of charge is that?"

"Enough to put you away!"

"He's getting technical on us," Cop Two adds.

The cops brusquely handcuff Lenny and haul him over to the corner of the Underdog, while a gal, dressed all in black, wielding an oversized gavel in a lordly manner, seats herself in the other corner. It was Renee Alvarez, the graduate student Tim had flunked for plagiarizing a term paper. Well, you live and learn.

It's my turn to say another line, this time delivered as a firebrand newsboy: "Extra! Extra! Read all about it!! Lenny Bruce busted on Bleecker Street in the Village!"

On the spot, I tell the tourists, who would act as the jury, led by Francesca, "Kindly pay close attention to the proceedings."

The judge bangs her gavel and starts the trial: "This court will come to order! Order! The People of New York versus Lenny Bruce."

Lenny: (wryly) "My day."

Judge Renee: "Read the charges."

I read them, loud, as the District Attorney: "Under Section 1040 of the State Penal Code—"

Lenny interrupts: "Wait a minute—isn't that prostitution?!?"

Cop One: "Shut up, Lenny—don't get so technical."

Judge: "Siddown!"

Sternly, the judge continues: "The defendant must must restrain himself. Take heed, Mr. Bruce. Mr. Prosecutor, proceed."

I continue reading: "Your Honor, the defendant seems quite uncouth, but we will let that go—for now."

Judge: "Proceed. We don't have all that much time, sir."

Me: "Yes, Your honor. We charge him first with putting on a spectacle, obscene, indecent, immoral, and impure, which could corrupt the innocence of youth, and no less countless others, to be sure!"

With a ferocity that startles even me, Lenny jumps up and bursts out: "Hold it! Wait a minute! What is this? A fair trial, that's all I want—don't treat me like a hood! Oh, you'd love to see me locked away and shut my mouth for good!"

Renee bangs her gavel louder, but Lenny persists: "You toss me like a yo-yo, you howl when I react. You sound like you just want my blood, some downtown devil's pact! Listen—an ol' legal screwin's what you're doin! You're screwin' up my act!"

One of the cops growls: "Shut up, Lenny! Watch your language!"

The other repeats his mantra: "Yeah, and don't get so technical."

The judge commands: "Siddown!"

The cop steps forward and holds up a little spool of audiotape, proudly showing it to the jury of tourists. He turns back to Lenny and spits out the words: "Look, we got your act—all your words, here on our tape!" He hands the sheet to me.

Me: "We offer this in evidence, Your honor, and I quote: 'And here I went for my academy award with some cloddy cop dialect dug up from an old Dead End Kids movie: 'With a shit three sizes too big—!' "

Lenny: "I said, 'With a *suit* three sizes too big!' "

Judge: "Siddown!"

Me: "I quote again: 'The lowest tit can . . . the sight of an—indistinguishable—big ass.' "

Lenny: "No, that's 'Pitkin,' ha-ha, 'five vaudeville, five big acts!' "

Other Cop: "C'mon, Lenny, quit nit-pickin', don't be so technical. That's evidence."

Lenny steps forward and turns full force to face the tourists. Some of them back away in self-defense. Others take a few steps toward Lenny to better hear his plea: "Technical, huh? 1,237 words of my act were omitted on your *facacta* taped transcript. 857 words on your fudged tape, I *didn't* say. You guys make me say more dirty words per minute than I could come up with in twenty-five fuckin' performances!"

Judge Renee gets off her high stool, walks over to Lenny, and hisses: "Shush your mouth. I've seen enough of your act, Leonard Bruce. I sentence you to four months in the workhouse." She bangs her gavel hard. "Next case!"

Lenny gasps for breath and says more to himself than to anyone else: "I'm innocent."

Derek sputters: "Sure," and grabs Lenny's arm. "C'mon, will yuh?" he barks.

Recoiling, Lenny suddenly collapses, knocking over a chair. After a slight pause, he mumbles: "Rotten fascists!"

The cop looks down at him, and whispers disgustedly: "Scum." He hoists Lenny roughly to his feet, his voice normal now. "C'mon."

Lenny, facing the tourists, squeezes out the words with poignant bluntness: "I'm innocent—"

His eyes blink a few times, then turn lifeless. He is supported limply by the cop's arm as the other actors join them for a bow.

* * *

The tourists stood in silence, not knowing at first whether to applaud or not. I'm not a critic, but that Lenny act was one of the best—and most disturbing—performances I'd ever seen. I was about to pass that on to the tourists, when from the corner close to the door, who stood up but Officers Jameson and Gerard! Damn it, how long had they been here? Enough to see that unflattering portrayal of the cops busting Lenny? They shot a dim glance at Derek and me.

But I soon learned that they were not after us, as they brushed by, heading straight for Renee Alvarez, who was in the middle of removing her judge's robe.

Jameson flashed her badge at her. No doubt, some in the audience thought it was part of the act they had just seen, while others were oblivious to what was going on. Hilda just looked confused.

Jameson smiled faintly at Renee when Nice Guy Gerard whispered something in her ear—not to compliment her performance, I was certain. Then Jameson turned to me. I only heard, "Meet you outside," before she squeezed past the tour group to the entrance.

A dazed Renee gathered up her costume and stuffed it and her judge's gavel inside a small bag. Ignoring an appreciative audience thrusting their hands out at her, she headed for the door, with Hilda smack behind her. Derek caught up with them just as they reached the exit. I made a move, but Hilda blocked me, telling me to stay put and finish up with the tourists. Sensing that I needed him, Derek offered to take care of this, and without any explanation, I flew out of the premises. Hilda would just have to get used to living with my, oh, so quirky impulsiveness. So would I.

Chapter Twenty-Eight

Immediately after

What the cops wanted from Renee, I didn't know, but Derek would. Now, they were focusing on why I called them.

Gerard coaxed me to a quiet spot across the street, Jameson, at his side, taking out her trusty notebook. "Jeff, I'm happy to see that you're on our team. What's up?"

"You're not annoyed how we portrayed the cops in that scene?"

He laughed. "No, I'm a big fan of Lenny. He's from Brooklyn, you know. So let's move on."

I came to the point about my contacts with Mustache Man today and our planned meeting later on tonight. Worst of all, his not so veiled threats toward my daughter, which scared the hell out of me.

"It's about time we stepped in," Gerard said. "Don't worry. Listen, go ahead, meet him as scheduled. We'll be standing close by, and when the time is right, we'll nab him."

"Then you're going to arrest him?"

"We can't really. No real charges . . . yet."

Jameson interrupted, barely smiling. "Of course, we'll make sure he comes with us to the station for a few questions. Go back to your business, Jeff. Don't worry. It'll all be taken care of. We're on top of it. We'll catch you later."

Catch me?

Relieved that they knew what they were doing, I went back inside the Underdog, hoping to wind things up.

Just as Hilda wanted me to do, I asked if there were any brief comments or questions. One woman, who said she enjoyed the show, wanted to know if it was *real*. John, who had played Lenny, replied that the monologue was, and so were the words from the trial Lenny used in his nightclub act.

"But his other words, and those of the cops and judge and district attorney, were made up by us," John explained.

"But isn't that . . . uh, playing with history?" another tourist drawled. He was a thin elderly man who resembled a yellow-haired silly scarecrow.

"It's making history come alive," I said. "There's nothing we said or did in the scene that contradicts what, in essence, really happened to Lenny back in the '60s."

My mind, far removed from the '60s, was now on Nellie. I had to make sure she would be okay for the rest of the day—'til Mustache Man was totally out of the picture. And I knew what I had to do for her and Nan.

"Any more comments or questions?" I asked, hoping that would be the last one, so I could get right out of there.

"Yeah," another tourist piped up. "What happened to Lenny? I mean, after what we just saw?"

I tried to say it carefully—but fast. "Here's some good news. Lenny Bruce, thirty-nine years after being convicted of obscenity for using some bad words, was posthumously pardoned by New York Governor Pataki. A fantastically huge victory for the First Amendment!"

Cheers! Hilda, coming through the door, motioned that we could exit now.

"Bless you," Sister Veronica intoned, almost in prayer, "and Lenny."

"Thanks, John," I said. "Let's keep moving, everyone. Rock on! Let's go!"

When we got out, I saw Derek with Renee, looking so forlorn. Her eyes met mine for a second when she saw me leave the Underdog. She looked so lost, first hesitating a bit, then running toward La-Guardia Place—out of sight in a matter of seconds.

"D, I gotta talk with you," I whispered, as the tourists finished streaming out of the Underdog. "What was that all about with Renee? They sure caught her by surprise."

"Here's what I know. Renee told the cops last week about Tim's flunkin' her for the term paper she copied from somewhere. What a dumb thing to do! To shell out forty-seven bucks to produce a badly-written term paper, y'know, riddled with misinformation and typos. They were following their lead, checkin' out her alibi for last Thursday morning."

"Why now, D?"

"I don't know. Maybe they think she unloaded on Tim for flunkin' her."

"Whoa, wait a minute, Derek! You don't think that Renee—"

"No way, bro! Renee is cool. 'Member I told you on the day Tim was murdered, that I was with Hilda and Hank, checkin' out the old Winter Garden Theatre site on Broadway and Bleecker? Renee was with us too. Easy for the cops to verify. Besides, Renee made a deal with Tim. She was gonna make up that failin' term paper by writin' one on how to teach Shakespeare. Y'know, in the community—usin' our tour as a cool model. Anyway you slice it, it's a great second chance for her."

"Really? What else she gonna do?"

"I don't know, Jeff. She's still workin' on it."

I wanted to know more about how Renee got into acting in the tour, but I had to take care of Nellie now, to make sure she was absolutely secure.

"Look, D, I'm meeting Mustache Man today at 5:30. Can you join me?"

"Today? Wow! You know I'll be with you, Jeff."

"Derek, there's somethin' else I have to tell you. This slick guy might be really dangerous. Seemed like he was threatening Nellie when we met today. Scared the stuff out of me. We'll be okay, right?"

"Damn it, Jeff, I won't miss this for anything! I'll be there. Count on it!"

I told him to meet me first at a neighborhood bar later, where I'd clue him in on the plan.

"Just one more little nagging question. Are you sure you want to come? Didn't you make a commitment for that indie film? Tonight?"

"Yeah, but the heck with it. It's only a student film. What we're doin' is a whole more important! I'll call 'em up and explain. Look, Jeff, sorry. We gotta fly to the next spot now. I hate to be late. You know Jankowitz 'bout bein' on time."

I was so glad to have Derek along, I could've hugged him. It looked like rain again, so we had to hurry to finish this segment of the tour.

* * *

On the sidewalk, some of the tourists were still arguing about Lenny—specifically about his creative use of dirty words. I could see why Jankowitz had advertised the tour as "off the beaten track and off-beat." One relatively younger tourist, thirty or so, approached me and asked how old Lenny was when he died. "Forty," I told her.

My age in a week.

Hilda waved to me and came over. "Your tour guiding today was—"

I waited for the ax to fall. "Good job, Jeff," she continued, sidling up to me. "Thanks for helping me out. I know you'll do great at the Shakespeare segment tomorrow. See you in the a.m."

Shakespeare segment? I paged through my own binder. Yes, tomorrow's tour included something about the pre-Civil War African Grove Theatre doing *Macbeth.* Renee's chance to "redeem" herself. Unless my rendezvous tonight with Mustache Man, well, interfered, I looked forward to the part I would play in it and the Sanger and Whitman scenes.

" 'Let the kettle to the trumpet speak,' " I said, saluting Hilda when I left. I couldn't help wondering if she was hooked up with Derek in a good way, doing their own little investigation.

On my way home, I greeted some people I knew from the building. Not a word from any of 'em about my appearance. So much for my paranoiac fantasies.

Chapter Twenty-Nine

2 p.m.

But when I entered the lobby of my building, Dave looked at me in a funny way. I guess word had already gotten out I had been visited by detectives last evening.

A small envelope was waiting for me at my door. My heart did a tap dance in double time. No return address. Another threat from Donny MacNeil? Mustache Man postponing our meeting tonight? Renee with whatever on her upcoming scene? I ripped it open, an eager hungry dog with his bone.

A note from Doree. "Been trying to reach you, Dr. Gardner. I found Mr. Hartknoll's course notes. Thought you might be interested."

I was, of course. But I also wanted to thank Doree for word processing some additional notes for me to look over before Friday's tenure meeting. *This Friday?* Only three days hence?

I rode up to Doree's apartment to thank her personally. I knocked a couple of times, but no answer. Maybe working late at Greene Cent. Then a mumbled voice filtered through the door. I could barely make out a word.

I called out, "Doree? That you? It's Jeff Gardner."

"Go away—she's at work!" The voice of Doree's mother came through now, stronger.

"Sorry. Tell her that Dr. Gardner called, thanking her."

"For what? Get the *ef* away! Go away!" She sounded so weird, like the Wizard of Oz himself on speed.

Doree had mentioned several times in casual conversations that things had gotten worse for her mother when the anniversary of her husband's death, years ago, drew near. His horrible fatal accident took such an emotional toll on Doree's mom that she never budged from her apartment. A recent slip on the kitchen floor, leaving her with a bad back, just worsened her overall mental condition. It was amazing to me how Doree carried on so resolutely.

Back in my own apartment, I pressed the cellphone buttons and found a load of messages. Nan's was a steady stream of reminders for me to cough up Nellie's overdue camp balance, with even a vexing threat to bring up the matter of my recklessness at our next group "separatees" meeting. I made sure I put a check into my wallet. Didn't want to face that whiplash again.

Donny MacNeil, bless his cold, cold heart, called to volunteer to assist me in finding the monster who took away his son—and the rare book.

Rachel had a request too— "to see me asap." She had some "awesome" news about the rare book she had to share—"ultra-important!" I'd take care of that too, right after my business with MM tonight.

And Renee called to thank me—for what, I had not the foggiest idea. She was looking forward to me seeing her in her "boss" role of Lady Macbeth on the tour tomorrow and tomorrow and tomorrow.

Max Raben's call said: *"Make sure!"* meaning, make sure I gathered all my materials together for the tenure meeting this Friday, including any additional letters and recommendations—true, this time—supporting why I deserved tenure this time around.

Sasha's message was replete with tips on how to approach the tenure interview stress-free. Her holistic advice: "Stay cool. Breathe. Stay calm. Place your hand on your chest and pat gently. Feel your abdomen expand as you breathe. Calm down that tense energy. Release and relax. Love you."

Instead of doing all of that, I went to my bedroom and called her about my meeting with MM and for her to stay tight in her apartment. She seemed assured once I told her the cops were on my back. Then I made additions to the wall chart of all the things I was keeping track of:

o General Bleecker Blues binder—my own copy—ok.

o Tim's personal tour guide notes in his binder—finish reading it!!
o MM!!—Hook-up 3 hours away!

Whatever I had to do, I had to be super-cautious about Nellie today. That meant going to her school and picking her up. I stared at the clock. Still about an hour before school let out.

So I spent some time rummaging through the papers Doree had given me. First, I sorted through the Shakespearean notes. Oh, Tim, you are amazing. Realizing that *Julius Caesar* was a ninth-grade English class staple, he had a whole raft of notes justifying why the play should be taught in grad school, with three pages, alone, of notes on the pros and cons of personal and social rebelliousness.

Doree's note also said there was a "lot of other stuff" the cops had overlooked in a corner closet of Tim's cubicle. Yeah, a mother lode of good stuff for Jeff Gardner, Private Eye, to mull over! That, too, I'd take care of later.

By 3:00, I was mingling with a few other parents outside Little Red, trying to keep my cool. They chattered mostly about our kids and all the pollution that the monster double-decker tourist busses caused as they zoomed down Bleecker Street. That made me feel proud of Hank's tour—covering everything on foot.

And one other thing. NYU, which owned the building I live in, was starting plans to put up new huge towers all around us, taking away our open green spaces and causing massive construction health hazards. I looked forward later to fighting the mega corporation posing as a university.

When kids started charging down the steps, I had a moment to think about what I would say to Nellie, who might be wondering why I came to pick her up.

"Hey, Pops, hi!" she called out, running toward me. "How come you're here?"

"Well, you know, just finished giving a tour of the Village, and thought I'd take you to your mom's." We began walking, with Nellie's excitement spilling out.

"Cool! Guess what! We get a half-day off from school tomorrow. The teachers have to work on their records and stuff and I'd give chocolate chip cookies away to be on that tour of yours! I'm dyin' to see you lead it tomorrow!"

"We'll see, honey. I don't think Mom'd want you to see *some* of it, okay? Just check it out with her first, okay?"

I knew there was no way that she was going to tag along until MM was totally out of the picture.

When we arrived at Nan's building, Nellie helped me up the steps, like I was an old man or something. "Everything good with you, Dad? The toe still bothering you, huh? Bad?"

The least of my worries at this point.

"No, I'm fine, just tired. But thanks for your concern, honey."

"Yeah, sure, Dad."

We entered the apartment with Nellie's key, as I forgot mine. I made straight for the couch.

"As a matter of fact, I think I'll lie down for a while, 'til your mother gets back from work. She won't mind."

"Great! Hey, I almost forgot to tell you. I'm taking awesome pictures of my classmates."

"Huh? What kind of pictures?"

"For my Facebook. Really funny. Took 'em in the park yesterday. sent them to your computer. Take a look! They're somethin' else!"

When we got to her room, she switched on the computer and logged onto her Facebook pages. Cute pictures of Nellie and her friends horsing around in Washington Square Park. I felt a touch of nostalgia for my little girl, growing up so fast. Becoming quite lovely, really. Then I noticed him, sitting alone on a bench, barely noticeable at the edge of the park, his ugly smile, those dark eyes—Mustache Man!

Kill him, kill him, kill him! my voice screamed over and over inside me.

Chapter Thirty

4 p.m.

"Hey, you, wake up!" I felt my shoulders shake. It was Nan. Not in a very pleasant mood, of course. I left her high and dry in the restaurant when I sprinted out to catch MM. I must've looked like a jerk then, and now also, snoozing on her living room couch.

"Get up. You got a little explaining to do, mister. Like, why did you run out on me today? It upset me so much, I just couldn't finish working—had to leave early. So, what's goin' on? Explain."

"You know I had to get back to work, Nan. The group was moving on, and I had to hightail back—"

"Now I really know what's important in your life!"

I was not lost in the irony of her statement, especially since all I was thinking about now was Nellie's safety.

"Well, did you bring it?"

"The check?" I feigned a "who, me?" gasp.

"For a historian, you sure have a short memory, Jeff."

I took the check out of my wallet and gallantly placed it in her hands. "Here, madam. Satisfied now?"

She looked it over carefully, like she was checking for counterfeit bills. Finally, Nan relaxed and smiled. "Looks real, alright. You want some coffee? I made the kind you like."

Nellie crept into the room and chuckled as she witnessed the quiet, domestic bliss of her parents.

"Hey, Mom, I have a half-day off tomorrow. Can we see some of Pop's tour? He says it's okay."

"If your father says it's fine, then, I'll go along with it. But," she said, looking at me rightfully concerned, "it depends on the topic. Dad, what do you think?"

"Can I call you later on tonight? Gotta review tomorrow's itinerary. I'll let you know if it's PG. Fair enough?"

Nan looked at me relieved. "Yes. Fair enough. And I'd be happy, guess, to accompany her. Excuse me for a moment. Been a while ince I last checked my phone messages."

Good time for Nellie to wend her way to me and snuggle close. We talked about this and that, our cozy conversation finally leading p to her big "surprise."

"I bought you something, Popster. For your birthday. Just can't rait to tell you. A new scarf from Paul Smith on Greene and Houson—"

"No, you didn't, Nell! That place is more expensive than Armani's. Do I look like some Upper East Side fashion plate? I thought I taught ou values," I said, smiling weakly.

"Just kiddin', Dad. I really got it at a cute little thrift store on hompson."

Nan returned, not in a pleasant mood. "Nellie, go to your room! Jow!" she ordered.

Nellie stood her ground, preferring to simply stare at me with her ovely brown eyes. I sank back onto the couch, another stupor of eariness catching up with me. But I felt good, giving myself some redit for coming through for my family tonight.

"Jeffrey, we gotta talk."

"Yes, dear," I said, my eyes studiously avoiding hers.

"I don't know why you couldn't make this your home, Dad."

"Nellie!" her mom burst out. "Why are you still here?"

I saw that Nan meant business, so I coaxed Nellie to leave for a w minutes. She bent down and smacked a big kiss on my cheek, hen made a baleful bee-line for her chat-room fortress, where she ould lock herself into a snug world of super Blogway and Friendster ossip.

Nan paused until Nellie was out of hearing range. "Smart girl," he said.

"Must take after her momster," I joked. Feebly.

"No, I think she senses I want to talk with you about somethin important."

"Listen, Jeff." Sounds cheesy, but her caring look reminded me c the Nan I once knew. "I'm really worried about you. I'm getting a these calls because it appears no one can reach you. You don't liv here, so why are they calling *me*? Why did you give my number out I thought that when Nellie and I moved out of the Bleecker Stree apartment, we wouldn't be bothered anymore by all your kook friends and acquaintances. So why am I still getting those calls?"

"Force of habit. Who called anyway?"

She rattled off a list: "Those detectives again; a reporter from *Th Villager*; Dr. Raben, about your upcoming tenure meeting wit Greene Cent big-wigs; and a Derek Molson. He called a couple c times. Who the hell is Derek Molson?"

"From the tour—"

"I would've figured. This Derek . . . is he black?"

"So what?" Petulant silence.

"How close are you to him?"

"Fellow worker. Nice guy."

"You seem to have an affinity for—"

Disconnect. Her earlier suspicion of me carrying on with Tim wa coming to the fore like Ahab's whale rising in the mist. "You seem t have no limit for bringing that subject up, Nan. Maybe we ca arrange for a mènage á—"

She slapped me hard. A real zinger.

I belted out a sassy J-Z lyric, "I wanna do something to you . . .'

Then ever so softly she rubbed my beardless chin . . . and kisse it. And, like a fatal distraction movie, we were smooching soulfull blissfully, ceaselessly.

She broke away.

"God, your breath, Jeff. Ugh."

" 'Only breath I got,' " I warbled. We both laughed, as I struggled to sing some more from The Police song.

But I like your new look, handsome. Watch yourself. Don't get any ideas."

"Hard to do, Nan, when it's getting hard."

"Some day . . . " she teased.

She must've been thinking the same thing as she kissed me hard.

"Wait a cotton-pickin' minute! What about our separation contract—no sex—all the way, all that good stuff?"

"Fuck the contract, Jeff!"

"That might be a little hard to do, Nan. How about you instead?"

"Game, if you are, big boy!"

Sure, I wanted it so bad. I started humming the Sam Cooke oldie, "You Send Me"—"honest you do, I know, I know, I know when you kiss me—" and the next thing we knew we were in bed, hugging, cuddling, kissing and then, bang, paradise regained, up and down. She was right. Yeah, fuck the contract, we were still married. I could've danced with her all night.

We helped each other dress, like in the good old days—and nights. There was no question that I wanted to be with this woman for more than just a fleeting moment. The sex was just the frosting, the release. Inside me, I sensed my soul finding hers, begging to reunite. But when? How?

"Don't tell your brother Hiram what we just did," I said.

"Don't tell your girlfriend Sasha either—"

We returned to the living room—and to the samo, samo Nan's bickering again. Too much on my mind—like meeting MM tonight.

"Jeff, be responsible! I'm really concerned about you. So is Hiram."

"I hear, I hear!" But, the truth is, I didn't feel like hearing it again and again.

"Think of other people," she said.

"I am," I said. If she only knew how much I really did care.

"Oh, there was another call—from a Mr., uh . . . *Major* MacNeil. Tim's dad."

"Stepdad."

"Well, he seemed very nice. Said he's been trying to reach you. Got my number from Rachel. We talked a little . . . said a lot of nice things about you."

"I'll bet. What did he want?"

"Just said you're working on a book together—something that—that would bring a lot of pride for African-Americans in this country—all over—said he's forming a committee."

Sure, a nice little committee of cutthroats.

"A committee to sponsor it. Sounds good. What's going on, Jeff?"

I assured her I'd tell her the whole story—soon. Maybe she'd be proud of me too.

She smiled, tightening her lips. "Jeff, do me a favor."

"Yeah?"

"Stay alive. Because Nellie needs you, okay?"

Right on cue, Little Nellie Sunshine returned, school notebook in hand.

"Are you two fighting again? Please don't!" she stammered.

"No, no, Nel, things are actually cool between us." Dependin'.

"Awesome!" she cried. "Now, Dad, kiss Mom!"

Nan and I just looked at each other and laughed.

"Popster," Nellie said, "I need help. What's ante-bellum? Somethin' like my Auntie Esther?"

My daughter's a punster like her dad, and she has beautiful soft eyes like her mom.

"Remember the oatmeal box I showed you yesterday? Wait. Gotta get something. Don't leave!" She ran to her room.

Nan rolled up her shoulders and smiled. I gloated. Our daughter returned in seconds, with the refurbished oatmeal box in her hands. "Look into the pinhole, Dad. See?"

I loved it when she called me *Dad*. I *never* even called my own father that. Never.

"Looks just like a camera, right, Dad?"

A fatherly encouraging nod from me. Like a little Houdini, she zipped out her hand from behind her back.

"And, see, this is what I made from the contents of the cereal box—oat flakes—which I dipped into water and corn starch. My own Inca temple."

"Downright clever, Miss Multi-Tasker! Love you, girl!"

Nellie turned to Nan, and back to me, as if to say, why not love her, too? She stood there for a moment, and then retreated to her room.

"Oh, Jeff, I have to tell you about another phone call. Almost forgot. Kinda strange. Someone asking for you. He laughed—and then hung up. Weird, huh? Some kind of silly prank on you, maybe from one of your students?"

A pain in my stomach shot right through me. Mustache Man? But how could he get her number? No, it had to be someone else.

Hours ago I had thought of going over with Nan all the insurance policies we had . . . in case. But then I remembered something Charlie Parker once said about time—that time was on the wing. And even it those wings were broken, I had to take the time to find out. There wasn't a lot of time, to think about what I owed her.

It was time to fess up to Nan about my rendezvous with Mustache Man, that the cops would be with me, and he would be taken way, ending all our worries.

"Just make sure you stay here—until I call you, Nan. Lock the doors . . . keep the phone free for me to call you. Okay?"

"Jeff, do you have to do this?"

"Yes. It'll be okay. Time is with us. Just keep cool with Nel. Not a word. I'll be okay. Call you around seven. We kissed again, and I was out of there.

Chapter Thirty-One

5 p.m.

I stopped off at the Bleecker Street Tavern near Broadway to connect with Derek, according to plan. It was a place I often resorted to when I had to fortify my nerves, a step I sometimes took when I had problems with Nan, before I hooked up with Sasha.

Ellie Enright, the shapely *sympatico barista*, noticed I looked a little haggard. Trying to fortify myself, I ordered a short beer. Then I threw out a few bars of "Don't throw them looks at me—" fracturing a lyric from "People Will Say We're In Love," which I always sang with her when I was on the verge of going off the wagon. She'd been an aspiring musical comedy star twenty years ago—and was a serious listener now.

Then, an attempt at humor—"Ellie, what's the difference between the Middle Ages and now?"

"Beats the crap outta me," she said, wiping some beer glasses to a high sheen. "What, pray tell, Sir Jeffrey?"

"Nowadays, it's your vote that counts. In those days, it was the Count that votes."

"Not bad, Jeff. Now I got one for *your* middle ages."

"Let 'er rip!"

"What's five yer and five yer?"

"Yer what?"

"I'm asking you, Jeff."

"Beats the crap outta me."

"Tenure." Ha-ha! She followed this up with her tirade to get my ass in sling and go for it. So, I sat there alone with my mixed-up thoughts about my mortality.

None too soon, Derek popped in. We found a small table in a quiet corner.

He got right to the point. "Where we meetin' this mustachioed dude?"

"Down the block, at Kenny's Castaways, D."

"Hmm. Used to be a gay hangout in the 1800s, a den of iniquity called The Slide," he said with an elfish smile. "The cops tried to close it down, but too many city officials would've got their fingers burned . . . not to mention other parts of their anatomy."

"Well, Derek, guess what! The cops are gonna show up again— tonight! But, don't worry, time is on our side. We got 'em close on our tail, to move right in. You remember our old pals, Detectives Gerard and Jameson? They should be sitting in an unmarked car in front of Kenny's."

"Wait, how do y'know that dude will even show up, Jeff?"

"I told you, D. Yesterday, when I tangled with him in the park, he was miffed that I missed our first get-together. Yeah, I told you, he actually threatened me—and my family—if I didn't show up this time 'round."

"So, how do you know we can trust him now?" Derek gave his pocket a little pat. "I got my backup here, just in case—the penknife I used for carving my model Fulton boat, 'member?"

"Good!" But don't try to be a hero. That's why the cops are gonna be there."

Derek stifled a laugh. "What are they gonna do, move in on the kill? Hide behind the bar until you give them the signal to close in . . . ?"

"Well, hopefully not so melodramatic as all that. Let's just say that after our set-up talk, they'll be waiting at the door to haul in his ass when he splits."

"Gotta ask. How'd they know to be there at the right time?"

"Well, ol' pal, here's where you come in." I filled him in.

Derek was with that, up to a point. "Will they take him on the spot?"

"No, I don't think they have anything on him—yet. But they said they'd bring him back to the precinct for questioning."

"Great! That's a relief. Let's hope they find somethin' on him to keep him there for the long, long haul."

"Yeah, of course. Well, look, partner, it's 5:20. Time to hit the road. On the way, I gotta refill my prescription. Won't take a minute."

A half-way nod from him. He knew it was for my tranquilizers.

"And, get ready for this, D. I want to show you somethin' that's gonna knock your smelly socks off."

* * *

As we reached the drugstore on Bleecker Street, I asked Derek to wait outside for a couple of minutes while I picked up my prescription.

"Take a gander at these three Doric columns at the front of the drugstore. I'll give you a capsule history of this building when I return. I promise, it won't be boring."

By the time I returned, I had already popped in one of those cute little white pills. We stared at the building. "Focus on this for a second, D. This used to be the Bleecker Street Cinema, but you know what else? Stay with me on this—"

I put away the tranqs deep into my pocket and continued the story. "This same building used to be Mori's Restaurant, a very hip Italian eatery in the 1880s. Lots of celebs and theater folk hung out there to chit-chat and gossip."

"Mori's? Yeah, that name sounds a little familiar, Jeff. I think Tim includes that place on his Bleecker Street tour."

"Of course, it *should* sound familiar. Remember, when we were going through his binder at your place, we caught that word *Mor*— with an explanation point? We spotted it a couple of times."

"Sure. Yeah."

"Maybe that means there's something else important—really important—about Mori's. Can't figure it out . . . yet. When I went over Tim's notes about Mori's, I—"

"What's wrong, Jeff—?"

Suddenly, from the corner of my eye, there he was—Mustache Man—turning the corner on Thompson and Bleecker. Alone.

"We better vamoose over to Kenny's Castaways before he gets here!"

"Gotcha," I said, waving D forward.

Derek and I hustled in, heading for the seats that were in front of the bandstand. On the way in, we passed by the lavender electric sign that modestly proclaimed: "THROUGH THESE PORTALS PASS THE FAMOUS."

"How did they know about me?" Derek said deadpan, sticking out his chest in mock bravado.

Some locals and the usual mix of tourists were casually enjoying their drinks inside. Mustache Man followed us and sat down at our table, without saying a word. No one shook hands. But Derek tried to stare him down. I motioned for him to hit the bar for a round of beers.

"Who's this black guy?" MM asked. "I think I see him some place before. "You say we be alone."

"He's okay. My friend." I held off talking until Derek returned to the table with the beers. It was important he was with me on this all the way.

"Let's get this straight, right off the bat," I said. "My friend Tim described someone quite different from you. Tall, with a big scar on his face. It's obvious, you're not Antonio. Then where is he? And who the hell are you?"

This silent creepy presence next to me slowly rubbed his hands together, his sweaty palms emitting an acrid odor, like the malt I used to smell as a teenager working in a Milwaukee brewery. I couldn't stand it then either.

"Listen, we don't talk unless you tell us your name and explain yourself and your connection to—you know who I mean. Tell us *something* or we're outta here," I ventured, staring the man smack in the eye.

He uttered four words: *La Señora del Lago.*

Silence as we let that sink in.

Derek bent over to me, whispering into my ear, "That's Spanish for *Lady of the Lake*." I nodded, already figuring that out.

I motioned MM to talk, to say something, anything. Finally he let go, like water gushing from a broken pipe.

"Your friend, Tim, owed Antonio money for findin' him, how d'you say, the *old* book. Antonio, he go back to South America. promise I send him the money."

No trouble understanding him, even with his heavy Latino accent as he continued. "I find out 'bout Tim's death, so what to do? Not so hard to figure. Before, Tim tells Antonio he has a partner, see, in this deal, someone who works with him at, what is it called, Greene Cent name of your school, *sí?* I go to your school in SoHo, lookin' for you thinkin' you can help."

This guy reveled in his own cleverness, laughing as he continued his story. "I tell a guard at the school my cousin in Tim's class, he needs his grade, so I must talk to Tim's co-teacher. You. The guard he tells me your name—Jeff Gardner, right?—but says you not in yet I say to him I wait outside the school for you. What he look like, ask. Then he tell 'bout you. *Poco,* an' little heavy, N-Y-C T-shirt, Yankee cap, beard and mustache. You shave that off this morning, *sí?*"

I hated this guy, but that made me smile. My "uniform" look was my uniform, with or without the beard.

"So, I wait and wait for you, jus' outside the door, lookin' over ev'ryone who go in and out. *De pronto,* I see a cab comin' to the door. A man come out, lookin' drunk." He aimed his bottle of beer at me almost shoving it in my face.

"I look you over and think, could that be you? So, I wait a li'tle longer, 'til you leave the building, 'round four o'clock. Then I follow you *muy despacio* as you walk . . . slowly . . . to your building and come into the lobby."

"So why didn't you stop me?" I interrupted, trying to follow all this.

"I'm 'bout to. When I see you have visitor—you!" Now he was directing his remarks to Derek. "*You* was in the way. I say I want to speak to Mr. Jeff alone . . . in private."

Derek wasn't about to buy that. "You're a real hotshot, Detective Nancy Drew! How long you gonna go on with this bedtime story?"

"Jus' a minute. *Uno momento!*" MM took a deep breath. "I decide to come back next mornin', to give you, uh, a note for meetin' later, at a place we can go over things—alone!"

"You wait a minute, *uno momento!* This is too much! You did all that, even following me to the park the next morning?

"*Sí.* 'Portant to put it right in your hands!"

"Okay, now we know how you found Jeff," Derek cut in. "Sounds somewhat convincing. But I'm not so sure you're doin' this all for poor Antonio! Here's what I think is the *real* story. You smuggled him into this country for a couple thousand bucks, right? You fixed him up with a phony green card and fake name."

I could see where this was going, if D had it right.

"Antonio still owed you money for bringing him into the country. After Tim was murdered, he cut outta the country. So, *you, Señor* Mustache Man, are cashin' in where Antonio left off! Ain't that right? *Habla*—say somethin'!"

Enough petulant silence for Derek to go on. "There's a word for what you are—*coyote!* Slimy go-betweens who reap piles of money off cheap labor—"

MM was making me nervous, just sitting there like an Incredible Hulk, keeping mum. Where the hell were Jameson and Gerard? I reached into my pocket for my trusty pills.

Mustache Man's turn. "*Sí,* and their employers love it, love 'em, 'cause they add billions to the 'conomy—off workers' sweat. Peanuts for pay, no overtime, no holidays, no breaks—'cept all the accidents go down, no safeguards, nothin' 'cept hunger their families got to fight off. So t'keep 'em 'live, they work for nothin.' Nothin'! So when my friend finds somethin', somethin' 'portant like that book, well—"

Suddenly Derek jumped up. "Back up, *amigo!*"

MM shot up too, both very close to fists flying. I motioned them to sit down. They did. Derek returned to his own soapbox.

"How many illegals pour into the states a year? Twenty million? And then we spend billions for border security, stealin' resources from people who *really* need it! You're a damn, dumb drain on us, punk!"

"Whoa! Okay, okay, D, chill," I stepped in, gluing my eyes on the nineteenth-century ceramic floor, musing on why life couldn't be as neat as those little laid-out squares.

"No, Jeff! This slimy character has *mucho* balls rollin' in here askin' for money from us. Their kids come in here illegally, go to good schools—and then what—? A million of their high school kids *vamoose,* drop out ev'ry year! You sponges!"

"Sponges? I wipe you up with your lies!"

I didn't like those two guys going at each other, but, I admit, Derek had a point—complaining that so many "deadbeat" kids were doing that, while there was only a pittance for his Christopher Street homeless kids. Well, sure, I knew immigrant workers were exploited. And I just didn't see anything wrong with their kids getting a break . . . To calm things down, I ordered another round of beers for our table.

"Look, *amigo*, I do not come here to bull 'bout illegal aliens, as you call 'em. We are not aliens. We are human beings. My friend, Antonio, he work hard bulldozin' basement walls of that building. Hard, tough special work. *Sí*, he finds a treasure but he sell it to you for . . . peanuts. So I come to you t'get for him what *he* is owed—fifteen hundred dollars! So you pay me, and I send it to him, okay?"

"You mean, you came to get what you can steal!" Derek shouted.

"No, it's for his family, forced to live like a cellar rat here. That's why he go back to South America. Yes, life there's a struggle too, but least he be treated with *respeto*! So, you owe—"

"*Me,* pay? You gotta be kiddin'. Remember, it's Tim you should've dealt with—not me. In any case, Tim would've dealt with Antonio. Not you, whoever you are."

"But *you* and Tim—partners. Jus' as I am Antonio's partner. So now *you* are the man I deal with." MM pounded his fist on the table. "Pay up!"

"Well, I'm afraid you're outta luck, Mustache Man," I shot back, standing up. In the first place, I made no deal with *you.* Okay, out of respect to Tim's sense of fair play, and our partnership, yes, I would owe Antonio, but not you. No way! I don't even *know* you! I owe you nothing! My final word! *¡Finito!*"

He looked beaten. "If that is your choice—then, you gotta give back the book."

"Look you—surprise!—I don't even have the book! That simple! It was stolen! Right when Tim died! The deal is off! Do you understand now? *¿Sabe?*"

I must have spoken so loud that some customers at a nearby table started moving away. I sank back into my chair, suddenly struck by the absurdity of this whole thing.

His face turned pale. "I have to . . ." he said, pointing to his crotch. A little comic relief, I thought, but I was too wound up to laugh.

"Well, what?" Derek asked.

"I gotta go . . . you know." MM got up and vaulted over to the men's room.

"So rude. We didn't say he was excused," Derek, with more mock bravado.

"Is he really going to pee . . . or get a gun like Pacino did in *Godfather One*—or *Two*, I forget."

"Aw, c'mon, D, he's just peeing. 'Nature must obey necessity,' y'know, from *Julius*—"

"Yeah, I know. Well, Jeff, time for me play *my* part. We shouldn't have to wait 'til he gets too violent." Derek, right on, always hanging on the cusp of melodrama.

"Cut it out, D! Your imagination's working overtime," I smiled, feeling my confidence building, actually enjoying being the driller instead of the drilled. "Don't crap in your pants, my friend. I want to stick around to make sure this nightmare ends on a high note—for my family's sake. That's what *I* care about."

Derek sprang up. "Gotta see if the fuzz is still out there." He bolted for the door, slamming it as he ran out. Must've raised the eyebrows of some customers.

Just at that same time, MM swaggered back from the men's room and strode up to the bar, where he ordered a whisky. A quick shot seemed to bolster his feistiness. Seeing me alone, he spun fully around, shouting, "Last time I tell you! I want that money . . . or you know, you know, what's gonna happen—?" Looking like he was going to take on the whole crowd, he moved slow and easy back to our table. Almost daring anyone to take him on.

Some annoyed customers, sensing real trouble, paid their tab and left. Others moved back, waiting for the fun to begin. The bartender stared at me, extremely pissed, looking like he was going to throw *me* out. "Sorry," I called out to him, "just business. We're okay!"

Derek returned from outside, and plopped into the chair closest to this steaming has-been. A powerhouse now, he lifted his chin up to the hombre's face, as if to show off the tiny scar on his chin.

"Listen up, *Miss* Nancy Drew. You know, we *could* call the police. But, you wouldn't want 'em to kick *your* smelly behind outta the country, like they would've done to your friend?"

With a knowing wink, he turned to me and whispered, "They're right outside, waitin' for our signal to come in. Guess I'll havta stir things up."

Mute MM, run over by Derek's force, was peering up at the nineteenth-century Arabesque twirly ceiling designs above us, dancing in florescent light.

"Here's a very direct question for you," Derek said softly. "Did your friend, Antonio, the one who lived with the rats, did he kill my friend—my *lover*—Tim? Is that why he had to suddenly leave the country? Spill it!"

"I don' know what *you* talkin' 'bout."

"Like hell you don't!" D reached for MM's left thumb and squeezed it hard. "You're lying! You damn well know Tim was murdered!"

MM grabbed Derek by the collar and then let go. "Antonio has nothin' to do with it! *I* have nothin' to do with it! If you wanna know the truth, here it is. Antonio freaks out when he reads that Tim's killed. I tell you, he had to leave the country—fast—and that leaves me—his tight friend—to collect what's owed him."

Surprising myself, I swooped up a chair to prevent MM from killing Derek—and to throw in a little of my own payback for him stalking Nellie. But I was too late with too little—as MM tripped me, sending me to the floor, with the chair landing right on top of my chest before I had the sweet satisfaction of clobbering him.

About time! They ran in, the two cops, quickly pulling MM off Derek, pushing him up to a back staircase, where they swiftly handcuffed him. Yeah, a Bruce Willis movie, with *me* in the thick of it. And happening so quick—the few remaining customers scattering in all directions, glasses and bottles flying off the tables—reminding me one of the tiny windstorms I saw whirl around on a quiet street in my Wisconsin hometown—roaring in so fast and furious, then over in a couple of minutes.

We followed Gerard and Jameson out of the bar with their man, as they shoved him into an unmarked car, and sped off.

A Perfect Stranger

Chapter Thirty-Two

Wednesday, 8 p.m.

To get it over with, and to get on with my life, I cabbed down to Jameson and Girard's precinct station in the West Village to make some official statements about what went down at Kenny's Castaways. Then they dropped the double bombshell. First, the news about Mustache Man. The NCIC search picked up that MM—whose name (for at least the time being) was Carlos Hernandez—had a long string of prior convictions, and enough suspicious connections to drugs, mobs, and illegal entries to lock him up for years.

"That's only half," Gerard said, as I finished looking over the police blotter. An unidentified man was found floating in the East River the other day. We checked that out, too, all the way—it's your Antonio. Good, huh? "

Hearty handshakes from me. Nellie would be safe now.

"Look," Jameson added, still chewing gum, "you helped us nab this guy, Dr. Gardner, and we appreciate it. But, stop here. Please, no more Hardy Boy stuff for you or your partner Derek, about that book! It's too damn dangerous. Agreed?"

I nodded, shook their hands again, and took off for home. In the cab, I mulled over what they said. Yes, maybe I should stop playing detective—getting nowhere—with my list of suspects, the wall charts, and nosing around the tour. Everyone was on my back to stop—the cops, Nan, Sasha—maybe I should just do nothing, except pay attention to my tenure track, and to Nellie's safety, of course. I wanted to ease my mind for her graduation, and think about getting her a present, or maybe my usual sterling poem, ha.

"We're here, Mac," the young cabbie hollered through the pane. "Watch your step goin' out. I don't need no falls."

Heading for the elevator, I thought about the cabbie's warning. Again, the Law of Unintended Consequences. Simple things turn out just the opposite of what you expect. With both Antonio and MM out of the way, you'd think I could relax a little. No, with them out of the scene, I had to dig even further. Still a lot of questions, the biggest one now, how deep should I dig before falling in a hole myself?

Sasha practically jumped on me when I got back to my place and told her what happened at Kenny's Castaways and the police precinct. She immediately began checking out my head for bumps and bruises—and peeked at my healed toe. I won't deny I was in bliss with all this TLC. But my mind still weighed heavy on the book.

I went over the next day's tour itinerary, which reminded me to call my wife again.

"Nan, this is Jeff. You asked me to let you know about how I feel about Nellie going on tomorrow's tour. Well, here's my take on it—"

"I don't think—" Nan interrupted. "Not yet."

"Yes, I agree. This particular segment is a bit too adult for her. Better another time."

"Come over again, Jeff, soon . . . okay?"

Overhearing my conversation with Nan, Sasha ambled over with her sexy sway. "Listen, honey," she drawled, "how about *me* going on one of your tours? Doncha think *I'm* old enough? I got a personal day coming."

As she drew closer, how could I refuse? "Okay, Sash. You can come tomorrow. Meet the tour at about 11:30 in the a.m., at the Corner Cafe, if you want. But, listen, don't blame me if you don't get exactly what you expect." I planted a big wet kiss on her before she bounced back into the kitchen.

Seeing her flitting about in her tight white shorts and matching tennies, I was horny enough to give her my *full* attention, but just now I had other business to take care of, starting with returning phone calls from Rachel and my mother. I'd get back to Donny tomorrow.

Rachel wasn't in, so I left a message on her machine, inviting her to join the tour tomorrow. Why not? I thought. The more, the merrier. Besides, I recalled that she had something important to tell me. Probably about Donny's phantom committee to sponsor the book.

It took a little more gumption to call my parents in Florida, who too often had too little of anything positive to say about my life.

"How're ya doin', Mom?"

"I'm okay. But you, you dumb ox, I heard all about it. A couple days ago, Nan told me and your father that you're shlepping all around the Village looking for a . . . I don't know what. Are you *mishega*? Phi Beta Kappa, and you're so dumb? WHATEVER YOU ARE DOING, STOP!"

I told her I was good and not to worry. With Dad it was a whole different story. The first thing he wanted to know was why I didn't have a lawyer. Then he went into a tirade why I should've been one instead of a useless teacher. I admitted I made a mistake, by not getting a lawyer earlier. But now it didn't matter anyway, because the cops were no longer on my back.

"Of course they're off your back! You didn't do anything wrong, did ya, Jeff?"

"No," I said, but stopped there. It would take too long to go into all the business about Shady Lady and how it was related to Tim's death. Besides, it was really none of their business.

"Well, I'm relieved," Dad said. "How could *you* be involved in such funny business? You're not smart enough to be a crook."

"Thanks for the compliment, Dad."

"Listen, I know it's a long distance to New York. Sorry, I can't make the trip because of your mother's condition."

"Who said anything about coming to New York?"

"Well, if you're in trouble—"

"But, I told you, I'm not in trouble."

"Get a lawyer anyway, Jeffrey."

"Why? I'm not guilty of anything!"

"Don't shout at me! I'm not deaf—yet! Call Hiram, Jeffrey! He's expecting you to call."

I sighed to myself. It was too much. "Talk to you later, Dad. Kiss Mom for me."

Mom got on the phone again. "Kiss me yourself, you big dummy. I love you. You still goin' with that *shiksa*? Do you ever see Nan? At least *talk* to her? Hiram said you had to, once a week. Some kind of contract, right? Go back to her, and give us a new grandchild to come down here for me to play with. Kiss my sweet darling Nellie, too. Wait! What's this about her in a movie?"

"Huh?"

"Sex movie! Videos in her school!"

"No, way, Mom. Not Nellie!"

"Thank goodness. It had me worried terrible. You sure?"

"Yes. Wild rumor. Never could happen with Nel. Not her. Forget it."

"Good to the max! I'm sending her a big graduation present. I hope she likes the latest style in slacks. Stay well, all of you. Bye."

"Good luck on your tenure, Jeff! Don't forget to call Hi!" Dad bellowed.

Good luck on my tenure? He wished *me* that? The man who detested teachers, or was jealous of them because he had never gotten past third grade?

"Oh, by the way, Jeff," he said. "I'm takin' a Great Books class down here, with large print. Russian thinkers. I call 'em shtinkers. Still, I'm enjoying it."

"Wonderful, Dad!"

"Yeah, Jeff, gotta tell you. I'm on a committee—to choose the books we'll read. What d'ya think of that?"

I had my fill of committees at Greene Cent. Endless talking, no listening, and in the end, Max, though professing group cooperation, did what he wanted to anyway.

"Great Dad, let me know what books you choose—"

"I will . . ."

"Well, Dad, I'm glad you're keeping busy in your retirement."

"Trouble is, I never get a day off! But I tell you, Jeff, at least I don't have to take any crap from the beer bosses anymore. You were right on that score, them makin' a bundle, while we slaved away."

"Bosses can cause a lot of trouble."

"Yeah, I agree. Jeff, another thing. I had to wait 'til your mother went to the bathroom before I could say this. What's goin' on? Nan called just an hour ago, saying that you were in trouble. Someone menacing you?"

"Don't worry, Dad. It all worked out good."

"I'm flying up tomorrow—"

"No, I'm really fine. Really."

"I wonder. Bye for now, hear?!" Click.

I put the phone down slowly. Damn, they called Hiram. Then I got to thinking about Dad's committees—and Donny's phone call for me to join his new committee to vaunt the rare book—for his own sake. I was probably pissing him off, not getting back to him double time.

"They don't like me, do they?" Sasha complained, returning from the kitchen with a mug of coffee. "To them I'm no better than the Cuban maid that cleans their place every week. Well, screw it, I'm just a little Spanish illegal 'ho' to them, huh?"

Mentioning illegals, Sasha got me lost in thought about Mustache Man again. How we nabbed him. I still saw those chairs flying in mid-air. Not a pretty image.

"Where are you, Jeff? Stop thinkin' about yourself all the time. Come back to Earth . . . with me, now, if you catch my drift."

That seemed like a good idea. After all, I *had* broken the no-sex contract with Nan. Why not go all the way with Sasha, too? Indulge myself a little after a long barren stretch?

"You look kinda sexy with those shorts," I told her, giving her a little pat on her behind.

"Yeah, like maybe one of your students? I could pretend to be one of them now, if you'd like."

What fresh hell was this, some new-fangled arousal technique of hers? Picking up on my frown, she cooed, "Forget it. *Decansa!* I'm not gonna bite you. Least not yet."

She moved a teeny bit closer to me. I rubbed against those little white shorts, feeling her tush and squeezing it gently, while gazing down at her trendy Baby Phat sneakers. Yes, I was beginning to bulge, and she felt it rise.

"Hmm, good. That relaxing you?"

I pushed her away—gently.

"What's wrong? I thought you liked that kind of thing."

"I just don't want to go too far. Y'know about the contract I made with Nan."

Suddenly, she broke away, springing off the bed. "Nan. Nan. Nan. You're always yakking about Nan. And *him* too, that Derek!"

"What about Derek? Why are you bringin' *him* up?"

"Doncha remember? You text-messaged me from Christopher Street—two nights ago. You were talking with such, I don't know, *ardor*, about your new friend, Derek. And all the kids he's helpin' out. That he's such a *beautiful* person."

"Derek *is* beautiful. He's really helping those kids in need. *!Ay dios, mio!* you're so incredible! Nan mentioned the same thing about Derek! Both of you, so nasty about him!"

Sasha melted. "I'm sorry, honey. Listen, Jeff, I want to help. Maybe I can meet Derek on the tour tomorrow. How about a threesome?"

"Hey, ramp up the imagination! Why not make it a YouTube foursome? Nan too?" I kissed her cheek and got up.

"Jeff, sweets, how about a good back rub? Just like told times."

"A snap, Sash. Gotta look at my itinerary first. Twenty minutes, okay?"

Nodding her eager approval, Sasha started to meditate, as she gently squeezed her rubber stress-balls. I went into my bedroom and closed the door.

I thumbed through Tim's binder, tracking down any additional information I might use on the Walt Whitman leg of the tour coming up. Funny, pages 14-17 were missing. What's this all about? I went on, scrutinizing the pages with references to Whitman's "Children of Adam" segment. Some curious notes, scribbled in the margins—*Run-DMC*. A reference to a hip-hop group Tim liked a lot? I examined the marks closely again and thought about their significance.

Slow down! It might not be *run*! It could be any word, *sun, fun, shun*. Then I remembered yesterday catching another pair of initials in the binder, inside the margins of the segment dealing with Margaret Sanger. The initials *RJ*. At first I thought they referred to *Romeo and Juliet*. But checking now, I spotted the initials next to *RJ* were *DMC*, along with that word *run, gun,* or maybe *shun*—whatever. With exclamation points after *RJ*. And two words Tim had scrawled in between: *Ask Rachel!*

It suddenly dawned on me. *Reverend Johnson . . . Donny MacNeil . . . ask Rachel!* Well, okay, I would do just that—tomorrow. And, of course, now I had a better idea why Rachel needed to see me.

My cell went off, breaking my chain of thought.

"Dr. Gardner?"

"Oh, hi, Doree." What did she want at this hour?

"I hope this isn't a bad time to call you. I'm at the office working late, getting Dr. Raben's itinerary in order."

"What is it, Doree? Please get to the point."

"I found Mr. Hartknoll's notes for his class."

"Can't they wait 'til tomorrow?"

"Of course, Dr. Gardner, I just wanted to tell you I found 'em."

I mulled it over for a whole minute. God, did I almost overlook a chance to search for those missing pages from Tim's binder? "I'll hop over in twenty minutes, okay, Doree?"

Sasha stopped me at the door. "Where're you goin'? What about your back rub?"

"Have to wait, Sash. Something important came up at Greene Cent."

"Oh! One of your students—?" Umm, she was getting testy again, and I couldn't blame her.

"Nah. Keep your shorts on, Sasha . . . until I get back, for a nice back rub—even more." I threw her an air kiss. She gave me the finger, and I was out.

Chapter Thirty-Three

Fifteen minutes later

In the lobby of the school, security chief Jackson O'Rourke had a quip ready.

"Hey, Jeffie, m'boy, goat got your goatee?" Neat references to my current state of beardlessness. "Very punny," I said, tapping him lightly on the shoulder.

When I got to the fifth floor, sure enough, there was Doree, watering her beloved plants on the window sill. "You really have a green thumb," I said, admiring her geraniums.

"Hi, Professor Gardner," she replied, in that steady sugary voice of hers. "Well, they could use some more sunshine, but a douse of plant food now and then helps. I have those Shakespeare notes Mr. Hartknoll put together." She pointed to a stack of papers on her desk.

She glanced downward and slowly put some other papers in her desk top drawer. I noticed the heading on the first page, in large capital letters—PROF. RABEN'S UK ITINERARY.

"Couldn't help seeing that, Doree. Dr. Raben's trip plans in England? Lucky guy! Can I take a little peek?"

"I'm still working on it, sir, If you *don't* mind." She shut the drawer and locked it with a key she took out of her pocket.

I wondered about all the secrecy, but treated it lightly. Right you are, gov. I'm sure he'll share it with me later. Thanks, anyway, Doree."

"Anything else, sir?"

"Doree, two detectives wanted to know where I was Thursday morning, and I informed them I was with some students."

"That's right, sir, and that's what I told 'em when they asked me last Friday."

"Well, do you at least remember who I was with? I saw so many students about their term papers last week."

"I think I can, if I can look at your roster. I'll have to run it down."

"Thanks, Doree. But it can wait. By the way, is Mr. Hartknoll's cubicle still a crime scene?"

"Yes. You know, they took away his computer and some of the things that were in his office."

"I'm sure that the police are doin' a great job trying to track Tim's . . . you know."

"I suppose they are."

I knew how much Doree respected them, with her dad an officer and all. Once, during a department Christmas-Hanukkah party, she had shown me a photo of her sitting on his lap. She was holding onto a miniature star, smiling, evidently proud of the big man in blue. Although Doree rarely said a word about him, you could see that she idolized and sorely missed him.

"I'm sure your dad was a great officer, too." She nodded and smiled a bit as she jangled the keys in her pocket.

"Can I get into Tim's cubicle again? There's a special picture of him and me on the wall that I noticed the last time I was in his cube, and I'd like to have a copy of it."

"Yes, I suppose. But, remember, nothing can be moved or removed. Just make copies of whatever you need and put the originals back where they belong."

"I can do it myself, if you plan to leave soon."

"Well, I suppose I can open the door."

"I'd appreciate it. You're an angel, Doree."

I followed her to the adjuncts' office down the hall. On the way there, we passed a little alcove filled with glass-enclosed cabinets containing Max's personal memorabilia. He was a collector of Victorian antiques and turn-of-the-century fixtures, such as the old-fashioned water cooler and sink in the reception room. He even had one of the those ancient squawk boxes, allowing him to dictate messages on the spot to Doree from his office. But his great pride and joy—things of beauty forever—were his first-editions of Coleridge, Keats, and

Wordsworth, collected over the years, that now graced his office bookcases.

When he wasn't scowling at his staff about day-to-day pressing curriculum matters, Max Raben seemed to trust everyone. That was one of the reasons why he left his office door ajar when he was in there. He also wanted everyone to see the gleaming hardcover books that fairly leaped from his shelves. I wondered how many of them he had read from cover to cover, and which ones were first editions. The storage room off to the side, which he also always left open, spilled over with even more volumes.

Doree unlocked the office that housed Tim's cubicle. She said that if I just shut the door when I was through, it would automatically lock. Since I had to make copies, she'd leave the keycard right in the machine, located in the outer office.

"Oh," Doree added, "on your way out, just put all those Shakespearean papers in my bottom drawer when you've finished copying them."

* * *

Still on his wall was Rachel's drawing of Tim and me in Washington Square Park, playing Frisbee with Rachel and Nan. Tim had cracked some kind of joke about the Frisbee being a peaceful globe of adventure that we could squeeze in our hands. I carefully took the picture out of its frame to copy later.

My mission now was finding those missing Bleecker Blues binder pages. I looked in Tim's desk drawers. Nothing. Then I scoured through boxes in a closet. Nothing again. I rummaged through the papers that were left in the closet. Again, nothing. I looked over the empty bookshelves that had once been jam-packed with his books dealing with the period before the Civil War. Maybe now they were in some precinct storage room, waiting to be examined for clues. Who knew?

Thinking about these books reminded me of the talks Tim and I shared about the pre-Civil War era. He was always searching for new primary source material, and when that wasn't available, he'd subway up to the Schomberg Library in Harlem to hunt down sources. It was no surprise that both he and Raben essentially covered the same time period, but in different countries—and with different themes. Max wrote about overcoming suppression of freedom in nineteenth-century England, while Tim's focus was on overcoming oppression in nineteenth-century America. Both refused to get stuck in their particular periods, always relating their studies to today's shifting times and thoughts.

I made a copy of the picture and returned it to the wall, making sure everything was there just as I found. Then I shut the door tight, as Doree had instructed.

Just when I returned, she was locking up Raben's office.

"Don't forget those Shakespeare notes in my office. Remember to put the originals back into my desk drawer. I was going to type them up, but, well . . . it was hard to get back to it. I didn't even have a chance to look at them. Good luck, sir."

I waved to her in appreciation as she headed for the door.

"Just turn off the lights, Dr. Gardner. And shut the outer door." She left. Finally.

I consigned myself to a boring stretch of time copying the notes. But, as I was going through Tim's handwritten pages—hold it! I spotted something intriguing at the bottom of the pile—pages and pages of notes on the tour. Eureka!

I pulled those treasures into my sweaty-tinged hand . . . gently, gently.

A knock on the door. What now?! Doree back? Max? No, it was Jackson O'Rourke, making his dutiful rounds at the the close of day, sweetly whistling one of his favorite ditties, "I'll Take You Home Again, Kathleen," crooning like a pixyish leprechaun. "Anyone in there?" Was he checking things out—or checking *me* out?

I held my breath some more. Pause. Then Jackson's "Kathleen" whistling trailed off. Good! Gone! C'mon, I reminded myself, you asked for it, Gardner, playing private eye like this.

Wait a minute! What was I doing wrong? Why was I acting so guilty? As far as Doree knew, there were only notes on a Shakespeare course in her desk. She wouldn't have the foggiest clue that something else might be buried in them. I finished copying the class notes and returned the originals back to her desk drawer.

I stuffed all the papers under my shirt, below my belt, relieved that there was no bulge. I was safe for now, so get out, Jeff. Move your ass! I closed her drawer carefully, and bounced out of the office, like a kangeroo with a pouchful of happy offspring.

* * *

At a dingy diner on Sixth Avenue, I found an empty booth and spared no time going through my findings. There they were—pages 4-17 of Tim's personal binder! I took it all in, one glorious page after another.

Once finished, time to share all this with Derek, so I called him to join me. He showed up in ten minutes.

"Listen, D, this is hot! Remember earlier today, just before we headed for Kenny's Castaways, when we were at the drugstore, and I was telling you about Mori's—"

"Yeah, yeah . . ."

"Well, I just got a mother lode of Tim's papers from school, stuff bout Mori's and Douglass. Manna from heaven!"

"I'm in sync, Jeff. Keep talkin'. Go! go!"

"Okay. Here's what I found. Mori's, in the 1820s, was a semi-detached row-house. Dig this. Douglass may well have been hiding in the common basement as a runaway fugitive after first being sheltered in the David Ruggles home further downtown. With me so far?"

"Go!"

"Douglass wrote some heavy thoughts in his autobiography. Le
me see if I can find his quote. Just a second. Okay, here goes. T
quote: 'There I was in the midst of thousands, and yet a perfec
stranger.' "

"Man, that Douglass cat sure could wield a pen, Jeff!" he mar
veled, noisily sipping his iced latte.

"D, listen! After escaping to New York from Baltimore, he wen
on to New Bedford, Massachusetts, where an Underground Railroa
conductor helped him get his new last name—Douglass."

"So, his original name was diff'rent? Not Douglass? "

"Yes, he was born Bailey, Frederick Bailey. Douglass was a char
acter—a Scottish rebel—from a long poem, *Lady of the Lake,* by Si
Walter Scott. You still with me?" I gulped down my third cup of cof
fee. "Tim referred to his newly acquired edition of Scott's poem a
Shady Lady. Understand?"

"Yeah, but how does this book figure in the story of Mori's?"

"I'm coming to that! Later in his life, when he was in his sixtie:
Douglass—probably in the 1880s—returned to the building wher
he possibly hid as a fugitive. Only now it was a fashionable restau
rant—Mori's—which sometimes raised funds for serious causes lik
the ladies' millinery workers strike. And Tim thought Douglass ma
have donated his own signed copy of *Lady of the Lake* to raise mone
for them."

"Raise money? Yeah, I got it. But, Jeff, tell me, man, how did hi
book end up in Mori's basement?"

"Tim thought that for some reason, someone brought the signe
book down to the basement, where the kitchen was located."

Derek grinned. "Why there? Why not a Starbucks somewhere?"

"Shut up or I'll throw a chair at you! I don't know. Maybe a waite
grabbed it off a table and hid it in the basement for safe keeping
maybe behind some false wall or something. All we can conjecture i
that somehow the book, buried in a metal box, hunkered down i

Mori's basement kitchen. Layin' there through the years until Antonio uncovered it, while excavating for the new drugstore!"

"Strikes me as a solid theory, Jeff."

"Thanks. But, as you say, it's still just a theory, D. Anyway, I'll see you in the morning at CBGB's.

"You got it! And congrats again on your fab findings! 'Til later. Aba-daba-daba-aba!"

Chapter Thirty-Four

Thursday morning

At nine a.m., with the weather threatening, I met another group o
tourists in front of CBGB at the eastern end of Bleecker Street an
the Bowery. We convened in front of the famed punk rock nightclul
which, in fact, closed down for good, shutting its doors after a figh
with its landlord. The club owed a lot of back rent, impossible for
to raise the money to avoid eviction.

Hank Jankowitz exulted about CBGB and its influence on musi
and social mores for our times. Some of the tourists looked around
nostalgically no doubt recalling that this now-trendy neighborhoo
was once a complex mix of artists, bums, transvestites, derelicts—an
just plain humble, decent people like themselves.

Zip-zap, from around the corner materialized a Joey Ramon
wannabee, played by John, strumming his guitar. He was totally i
black—black hair, black sunglasses, and black motorcycle jacke
"Aba-daba-daba-aba—"

Muted laughter. He removed his sunglasses.

"Yeah, I know what you're thinking, Hank. 'That's not the Joe
Ramone *I* remember.' Well, you're right. See, it would be easy to sa
I was playing him, but there was only *one* Joey Ramone. So then ho
could I imitate him, then, if he was unique? I won't even try. Some o
you also might ask, 'Like, did it take courage to do all those origina
groundbreaking songs like the one I'm about to play?' "

Mindy handed Hank a cassette player and out blasted one of th
Ramones' classics, "Teenage Lobotomy." Shrill, loud, and de-lovely

The sound was clear, even if the words weren't, and the touris
ate it up.

"I'm sure this place has different memories for you," applican
Francesca coached the audience. "Yes—?" Mindy, Arthur, and I mixe

with the tourists, encouraging them to respond to the music, which they did, with glee galore.

"Horses, Patti Smith—just three chords—magic!"

"Gabba, Gabba, Gabba—Suicide band—pounding—"

" . . . Met my wife, Candace, at a concert right here—"

"God, on the bathroom wall, God—scribbled on the wall—*Dee Dee has the biggest prick*—"

It was then, in the midst of all this cacophony, that I noticed, rounding the corner—oh, my God—Nellie! Giggling!

"Nel, what the hell you doing here? Shouldn't you be in school?"

"Ah, come on, Dad, give me a break! The teachers have a planning-meeting today, so the kids are off."

"Wait a minute, Nell. You said yesterday it was only *half* a day. Anyway, I told your mother that this tour wasn't suitable for kids your age."

"Won't stay long, Dad. Just wanna see what it looks like."

"Whoa a minute! Does your mother know you're here?"

"Well . . . not really. But she knows I *wanted* to come."

"Well, she will now." I moved well away, hidden from Hank, as I made a quick call to Nan at her office.

"Okay, young lady, your mother will be right over! And she's really pissed off. You haven't heard the last of this. Just stay next to me and be quiet 'til she comes, alright?"

Nellie knew that I meant business, so she did what meanie-me told her—for the time being, that is.

Just the right moment, *she* popped out from around the corner—Derek—all dolled up as a hairy drag queen with a blowsy blond wig. She raised her eyebrows, fluttered her red polished nails and sashayed towards us. The glamor goddess wore oversized sequined eyelashes and a pointed studded bra. "I'm not Peroxide Blondie, but I am horny, honey!" The sound of a farty horn was emitted from Hilda's tape recorder, followed by a Sex Pistols' tune, accompanied by some bawdy high-stepping.

After a few more of Hank's nostalgic comments about Hilly Kristal, the owner who practically started the Punk Rock Movement, Hank called out, "Come on, everybody, we're movin' on. This is history!!"

As we started to move, scowling Nan pulled up in a cab and dashed to our daughter, grabbing on to her hand. Hilda aimed her beady eyes at me, no doubt wondering what *this* was all about. Hank, oblivious to this little side-drama, was far more interested in pushing the group on. I signalled Nan to cool down, not to make a scene with this domestic family spat in front of the tour group.

* * *

So, stowaways N and N quietly joined us as we hiked a block away to Margaret Sanger Square, on the corner of Bleecker and Mott, stopping in front of the massive red-brick Planned Parenthood building there. Okay, so far, so good. Rachel was waiting on the corner for us, as arranged, but I was sure as hell knocked out to see who came along with her for the ride—Stepdad Donny MacNeil, and also, sure enough, his eminence Reverend James Johnson. We had not been on the best of terms on Monday, when I had seen them last, but they seemed cool with me now—even if I hadn't returned any of their calls.

Hilda, noticing my added company to her tight number of tourists, took it all in stride, no doubt finding a golden opportunity to sell more tickets for the tour. At this point, Nan, to Nellie's delight, gave in—now both becoming an integral part of our ensemble.

Greeting me warmly, Rachel motioned me to the curb, away from the tourists, who were raptly attending to Hank setting the scene, 1920s New York. Donny and the reverend's eyes were on Rachel as she suddenly took a brown medium-sized envelope from her purse.

Her whisper felt strained. "Jeff, Donny and Reverend Johnson want to talk to you about the book. For you to go *in* on it with them. They'll explain."

"*With them?* What do you mean, Rachel, 'go in on it *with them?*' "

"They still think you have the book. That you're using your connections with the university to sell it, Jeff. But you can't do that without *our* permission."

"Who thought up that absurdity about my selling it to the university? Your two bleeping bodyguard buddies over there?"

"No!" She handed me the envelope. "My stepdad and Reverend Johnson just want to make sure this got to you, Jeff. There's a contract with Donny in there for you to look over. The book will have tremendous national interest. He needs to make sure you can help out." Donny and the reverend looked, to me, relieved that I had it, to do their dirty bidding, just as I suspected they were doing with Rachel.

"I'll see what I can do, Rachel. For you. And Tim."

"Thanks, Jeff. It means a lot to me." She signaled my consent to her two approving guardians, who were poised waiting at the edge of the crowd.

"Stick around, Rachel. I think Reverend Johnson will enjoy catching the skit we're doin' here."

"Sure, Jeff, but remember he and my stepdad want to talk to you later—about the contract—when you get a breather to look at it."

There was no time to check it out now, as Donny and Johnson strode toward me. Jankowitz was on his way too, to announce the next scene coming right up. When I put the envelope in my sling bag, Donny gave me a thumbs-up—which, thank you, I didn't feel like returning.

Jankowitz, chatting with Hilda, seemed to be okay with my family interlopers, who blended in easily with the tour group. He smiled warmly, as if saying, "Go for it, boy. Show 'em what you can do!"

He took a moment to tell me that he had some misgivings about how the scene was written. "I'm thinking of scrapping it. I had a nasty fight with Tim over it."

So that was what Derek had overheard Hank and Tim arguing about in the CWC, Ink office.

"Hey, let me know what you think of the scene—if it should stay or go," he said.

"Tim wanted to make a point through humor—biting humor," I said. "Just hang in, Hank, you'll see."

"But if it doesn't fly, out it goes, like a bad tooth, Jeff. Gung-ho, good luck."

As soon as Hank gave that sign, I jogged over to the other applicants, getting ready to lead the segment.

Hank turned to face his audience. "So, my friends, imagine you're back in New York of the 1920s—in this swarming, mixed immigrant neighborhood. Right here is one of the spots where Margaret Sanger addressed the immigrant ladies about birth control. Listen."

Francesca and Renee, adorned in colorful peasant dresses and shawls, stepped out of the Planned Parenthood building. Waspish-looking Mindy, playing the courageous Margaret, strolled out toting a packet of leaflets, eager to deposit them in the real mailbox on the corner. They greeted her with joy. Margaret smiled back.

"Hello, my friends, hello!"

Hilda handed Mindy a wooden box to stand on, as she eased into her role.

"Ladies, for centuries women have been the helpless victims of excessive childbearing—"

These words were not blatantly addressed to Reverend Johnson, but I could easily discern how they distressed him. Rachel, when she saw the reverend react so strongly to Sanger's words, bowed her head and inched away from him.

Mindy continued her Sanger role with glowing passion, " . . . a disease which brings poverty, unemployment, child labor, prostitution, war, and *undesired motherhood.*"

The last words evidently hit Rachel hard. She quickly backed away from the crowd. I walked over to her as she struggled to compose herself and asked what I could do. "Nothing," she said, fighting her tears.

"It's all over . . . I'll be okay. Just be careful what you do with what's in the envelope. Please."

Rachel returned back to Donny and the reverend. When I got back to the playing area, the man of soiled cloth continued glowering at me.

Nellie now, sitting on the ground smack in the front of the crowd, was clearly enjoying the proceedings, much to Nan's consternation.

Meanwhile, Jankowitz was casing out the whole thing, weighing the tourists' responses to the ongoing actions. They were quiet so far, evidently eager to follow the scene.

John, in vintage 1920's clothes, enters as Anthony Comstock, Director of the New York Society for the Suppression of Vice, accompanied by Derek, playing Elmer Plinkley—US Department of Justice. Arthur is a '20s New York police sergeant wearing a Bobby helmet. Oily Comstock instructs Plinkley to arrest Sanger if she goes through with mailing the birth control literature. Derek-Plinkley, in a squeaky high voice, croaks out, "Mrs. Sanger, I am here to advise you that this literature of yours is illegal and in direct violation of Federal Postal Code, Section 37 J."

Demure Francesca, playing a feisty Italian immigrant, Mrs. DeLucca, delights in hitting Plinkley over the head with an old-fashioned paisley umbrella. The crowd howls. Anthony Comstock pushes Plinkley away and strides up to Mrs. Sanger. "Madam, as you know, I have devoted my life to serving the Lord."

On this remark, Reverend Johnson lifts up his greasy head, all ears. John, as smug Comstock continues. "Why can't you see that those foul rubber objects you are surely recommending here are an affront to common decency? Allowing, even encouraging, these women to indulge and wallow in mere idle pleasure!?"

"Pleasure?" Mrs. Delucca, cries out. "You ever give birth? *Ascoltare*! My husban', he an *anarchiste*, he say 'government go away.' But what he give me, ahere in de belly—that's ahere to stay—!"

As she's saying this to Comstock, I noticed Reverend Johnson looking jittery again. Why? He motioned to Rachel to leave, but she holds firm.

The crowd reveled in the scene. Renee, playing Mrs. Torres, a young Latina immigrant, steps up. "Thass right. Eight months ago, well you know, my husban' quick, but I too slow. I try to stop, but he just go. I too tire and sleepy to say no. So, now we got nine, this one makes ten, or maybe twins. What happens then? Aw, too much kids, It never end, help me Margarita, *ju* my frien—!" Margaret, handing Mrs. Torres a condom, consolingly responds, "Of course. The *next* time."

My turn, shlepping in as the husband of a lady recruited earlier from the audience to play Jewish immigrant Sophie Feldstein. She's tugging me by my ear. I jerk back as she releases her hand, and then she picks on John, playing Comstock, and on Derek, playing Plinkley, who timidly squeaks, "Mrs. Sanger, it is now my duty to place you under arrest—"

The immigrant ladies, plus some of the tourists getting into this happening, block his way. Sophie orders me to step aside too and walks over to Plinkley.

"Let me tell you somethin', you *momzer*," Sophie barks. "Leave my Margaret alone, d'you hear? You see my husband here, Shmuel? Oy, Shmuel, such a stubborn mule for a husband I have got! A *keppel* on his head, *gurnisht* on the other spot—" Here she gestures vaguely to my crotch. Everyone got the hint, Reverend Johnson, not too thrilled.

Staunch Mrs. Sophie Feldstein continues (you'll forgive the expression), *hamming* it up: "He *shleps* me into bed, oy, he pounds me every night. I'll *plotz*, I'll call a cop, or else, watch out—I'll take a bite!"

Well, Donny MacNeil smiled a bit on that one, but Reverend Johnson seemed more annoyed than ever. Everyone else lapped it up, including my own two gals. Even Jankowitz turned on his moon-sized mile when he saw things were going so well. Sophie waited for the laughter to tamp down and then turned to me, letting me have it good, right In the *kishka*—guts:

"So Shmuel, do for me a favor, please, just put away that tool. Give me a vacation. Go and spend a week in shul. Want to make me happy? Hold it two weeks, 'til it's safe. Then, amen, it will at last feel kosher, not *traif!*"

Applause broke out like an unplugged dam. The tourist who had just portrayed Sophie took a show-stopping bow.

Comstock has no choice but to arrest Margaret when she dumps the letters in the mailbox, causing all the immigrant ladies to protest nightily. They try to block Comstock and Plinkley as they lead Margaret away to jail. Renee, Francesca, and the woman recruited from the audience bombard Comstock and Plinkley—they're going to "prevent" their friend Margarita from being hauled away.

Smiling, Margaret informs them, "Don't worry, my friends, I'll be back. And for now, you know what you must do." She waves to them as she's carted off, then suddenly stops. Facing the ladies again, she sings out with bold conviction: "Prevent, prevent, that's our intent. You can, my friends, of course. Protect your worth and plan each birth. The future will be yours!"

The tough trio of immigrant ladies run after her and smack kisses aplenty on Margaret's blushing cheek.

Applause in the background pleasantly jarred my thoughts back to the present. Jankowitz generously acknowledged the actors. He, Hilda, and the applicants passed out a sheet about Sanger with her picture and her quote: "Stone walls do not a prison make, nor iron bars a cage."

Hank shook his head.

"Anything wrong, Hank?"

"Yeah, me."

"Sorry."

"That Sanger scene sure was some sweet number—and I had the balls to tell Tim it was too corny. How stupid could I be, arguing with him?"

"I don't know, Hank. But no time to fret about it now."

"You're right, Jeff. Let's go—onward!"

I remembered Derek letting me know about the quarrel between Tim and Hank, but the word that stuck with me now was "sweet." Something was tickling my brain about it . . . something . . . sweet.

Chapter Thirty-Five

A couple minutes later

Hank proudly announced the tour's next stop: Walt Whitman, a few blocks down on Bleecker and Broadway.

It was real high to see Nan on the bright side, and of course Nellie was beside herself with glee. But there was also the ominous silence of Rachel and Donny, and the "righteous" anger of Reverend Johnson, calling what he had just witnessed "blasphemous, the whole scene, stupidly one-sided!"

He pulled me over to the curb. When we were well away from the others, he asked, "Why are you doing this? Why are you making Rachel cry? I was appalled by that scene! Don't you see how upsetting it was to her?" Glancing over to Rachel for a second, he added, "Maybe we should just forget the whole deal about the book!"

Donny MacNeil motioned his friend to cool down. Coming up to me, he said, evenly enough, "You really upset Reverend Johnson with that last scene. But don't let that interfere with our contract. This national treasure is too important to lose over a silly argument like this. I'll talk to him."

I hastily excused myself, not wanting any more interference with the tour, and signaled Nan, mingling with the group, to come over to the side of the curb.

"What was that all about?" she asked.

I pulled the brown envelope out of my sling bag and handed it to her. "It's about this. Here, hold on to it," I told her. "Give it to your brother Hiram. Now, get back to Nellie. And both of you—go home!"

"Okay, Jeff, but I—"

"I'll explain later, Nan. Keep your cellphone open." I hugged her.

Stuffing the envelope into her purse, Nan cried out, "Come on! Are you gonna tell me what this is all about? You're getting crazy again."

I wanted to, but no time now. Sasha, coming down the street from the other side, evidently saw Nan cozying up to me, and didn't look too happy about it.

Nan grabbed Nellie's hand, pulling her in the other direction. "C'mon, Mom, I wanna see more of the tour, Mom! Can I please? Hey, learning can be fun!" She wasn't going to take no for an answer, refusing to budge.

"Get over here, Schlepp!" Jankowitz yelled at me from across the street. Derek, with him, waved me to join the group right away.

"Next stop, the Corner Cafe at the corner of Broadway and—where else—Bleecker Street. Join us there," I called out to the rest of the group.

The Fab Four—Mindy, Arthur, Fran, and John—were waiting for me to catch up with them.

Sasha, sprinting at a fair clip, pulling up to us, cried out, "Sorry, I'm late." She avoided looking directly at Nan, while Nellie gave her the once-over.

"Too much to tell you now, Sash." I pointed to the cafe. "See you in there. I got you a reserved seat. Enjoy." Sasha, peering warily at Nan and Nellie, stepped into the cafe.

"Looks like you got your whole *posse* here tonight," Nan said. She pronounced it like a woman's private part. Nellie's face turned red.

"I told you to go home, Nan! What are you doing!?"

"I'm gonna see what you're up to—"

"No! I told you. Go home!"

"No way! I *told* you I was gonna check this tour out."

"Well, then, at least give me that envelope back."

She did. "What's so damn special 'bout it anyway, Jeff?"

Silence. I stuck the envelope back into my sling bag.

"Not going to tell me? Something to do with Tim?"

"Well, with a book—"

"Book? What book? Something *you're* writing? For your tenure?"

"I'll tell you later. Everything. I promise. Go home now, you two. Go!"

"No."

She stepped defiantly into the cafe with Nellie, who clapped her hands joyfully. Vain me knew the real reason Nan refused to leave. Seeing me so cuddly with Sasha was maybe too much for her.

I spotted MacNeil and Johnson heading our way, with Rachel pulling along behind them. What's this? More unfinished business?

Hank was at my side. "With your toe all healed, I guess now I'm catchin' up with *you*. Top job so far, gang," he said to all of us affectionately. "You know, it's going to be murder picking one of you to replace Tim for the job. You're all doin' so fine. You four Americans are not so idle. Ouch!"

Deftly maneuvering his wheelchair, Jankowitz easily mixed with the tourists inside the Corner Cafe.

When I looked at Rachel, flanked now by her two virtual prison guards, she seemed like a million miles away in her own world. What I suspected now made sense from the way Johnson stuck his claws all over her—the letters *RJ,* in Tim's binder—Reverend Johnson—next to the words, *Ask Rachel.*

The reverend's eyes were on her like a searchlight. Did she really think he wanted to see the book exhibited as a national treasure, or was he just out to score a windfall for himself? Then it hit me. The Law of Suspicion confirmed. When it hits you, you go for it. What I suspected just made sense from the way he was looking at her and the way he was talking about her.

I didn't have to ask her now. It all fit. Tim had paid for his sister's abortion, leaving him stone broke. That's why he needed me to help pay for Shady Lady! Obviously the reverend didn't want to leave any trace he was involved with Rachel's child. The slimy bottom line— did that mean he was compelled to rid himself of Tim?

Chapter Thirty-Six

11:30 a.m.

It was no surprise to see Max Raben and Doree perched at a common table in the back of the cafe. For a possible grade change, Max had promised Renee to check out her contributions to the tour, specifically the Shakespeare segment that she designed.

A few more bubbly tourists poured in and took their seats. They were treated to some little pizzas and a fantastic penne salad with ricotta and peas.

In a corner, near the entrance, Nan and Nellie sat at a table that faced Sasha, who was sitting alone. They did not acknowledge each other. Rachel, Donny, and the reverend were in the back, on the other side of the cafe, squeezed in between the tourists' tables. *Full house,* except no sign yet of Lazon, whom Derek had invited.

A very unassuming young man in slacks and polo shirt, one of the managers of the Corner Cafe, greeted them, before turning things over to Hank. Stroking his white beard as his own little signal for everyone to stop chatting, Hank wheeled himself over to a spot where he could be seen and heard clearly by everyone. "Now you're in for a surprise," Jankowitz crowed, addressing the tourists. They quieted down, and he began his spiel: "Folks, in the late 1850s the basement downstairs housed the famous Pfaff's Underground Beer Cellar, a bohemian gathering place for vagabonds, poets, and, ah, tourists like you. And, like you, they gawked and gossiped about the famous and infamous assembled. Do you know who its greatest literary star was?"

"You, Hank?" a mischievous tourist yelled, accompanied by a ripple of laughter.

"No, not quite," Jankowitz teased. "Pfaff's literary star was Walt Whitman, who often carried a large green book, in which he wrote many of his *Leaves of Grass* poems."

Hank softly stroked his beard, and then, with great theatrical flourish, donned a greyish vest. I pretty much guessed who'd play Walt this afternoon.

As the tourists enjoyed their sparse, but creatively-concocted meal, Derek joined some of the regular waiters, who were wearing butcher-type aprons and elastic garter bands around their rolled-up white shirts. Renee Alvarez, doubling as one of the waitresses, looked pert in the same long skirt she had worn as Mrs. Torres during the Sanger segment. Her paisley, brocaded apron was a sure crowd-pleaser. Derek's new paste-on handlebar shadow mustache was pretty prominent—if it didn't fall off. He sang out brightly, along with the real cafe waiters—and, sorry to say, not always on key:

The vault at Pfaff's where the drinkers and laughers / Meet to eat and drink and carouse / While on the walk immediately overhead / Pass the myriad feet of Broadway . . .

Expecting to see Lazon enter, Derek's eyes were on the door while he sang along, strumming his guitar. And sure enough Lazon did, breathing heavily and apologizing profusely to him. Pleased to see Lazon sit next to Nellie, Derek quickened his song, the waiters repeating the verses several times, huffing to keep up with him.

While they dined and exchanged banter, Jankowitz explained that after the main repast, everyone would see and hear a dance set to a poem Whitman penned right here. He mentioned it was a homoerotic poem, that Whitman was gay and actually wrote the poem about *men* in love—but would be danced today by a man and woman.

The tourists took in the background information as easily as they had absorbed the penna in their salads. In a raised cranky voice, a tourist asked, "You mean Walt was *queer?*" His wife hushed him. Hank, amid some friendly laughter, said he thought he had made that clear.

"Good. So am I," the questioner admitted. *"Drinkers and laughers . . . laughers and drinkers,"* he sang out, from Whitman's poem. More good-natured response. Nan and Nellie were lapping it all up. Imagine!

Raben and Doree, Rachel and the reverend, Nellie and Lazon, Nan and Sasha. God, I thought, the irony—*all of 'em together* in one unseemly place, a restaurant on Bleecker Street. Yes, my very own social network, all bunched up together! But unlike birds and ants and other species, designed to work together, the only purpose I could detect here was for the assembled to make me nervous. How would I manage to maneuver this, all these paired opposites sitting in the same space, yet separated in so many different ways, like little detached islands in the same choppy sea? The ol' Law of Coincidence again, I guessed. Some pundit said there was always room for coincidence. I guess this was the room. Sasha looked so lonely at her table that I stopped off to say hello, and then did a quick hop and skip over to Raben and Doree. "Where's the bathroom?" Raben asked. Not waiting for an answer, he excused himself, looking like he was going to explode any minute.

"What brings you guys here?" I asked Doree matter-of-factly.

"To see you act." Turning to me, she said, "I think what you're doing here is awesome, sir."

We chatted a bit until Raben returned, noticeably relieved, a beer in hand. He came off like a smug cock of the walk as he settled down.

"And you, Max? What's up with you?" Meaning, like why was he sitting so snugly in that chair looking like Nero, ready to throw out a thumb or two at my performance?

"Oh, I'm with her," he chortled. They seemed to be really enjoying each other's company.

I gently shook Max's hand on the way to Nan's table again. Nellie was busy explaining—actually pantomiming—her oatmeal box project to Lazon, who seemed to take it all in, as if breathing in the incense pervading the air. I know no one had planned for them to be such instant friends. Still I thought she just might be the magic engine propelling him to return to school.

Hank informed the crowd that a dessert would be coming, some kind of apple turnover they might've enjoyed at Charlie Pfaff's German/French style restaurant back in the 1850s.

In a small tidy room off to one side, I glimpsed Derek and Renee preparing for their performance. He was wriggling into his costume, a colored T-shirt, matching shorts, and a flowing blue sheer scarf wrapped around his neck. They joked about the "naughty nature" of the poem they were about to dance.

"Love that scarf, Derek. I'll whoop your booty with it," Renee teased.

"Yeah, but take it easy," he said, blushing a bit. "Hey, there's already plenty of that sexy stuff in his poem. Walt's liberal friends, like Ralph Waldo Emerson, begged him to ditch the erotic poetry in his *Leaves* collection—but he wouldn't listen."

"Yeah, Whitman wouldn't take any *guff* from the establishment," Renee rejoined.

Hank, as Whitman, made that point clear now to the audience, as he addressed Arnold, playing the eminent author Emerson. "Ralph, I'm tellin' you and your other buddies from up Boston way that if you cut out the sex, you cut the book off from its root."

Sasha lit up at that remark. Her preoccupation with matters sexual, already evident, was working overtime.

Hank resumed in his own voice. "You know, folks, Whitman is venerated today as one of America's grandest and most innovative poets. Well, I think the philosopher Arthur Schopenhauer was right on the money when he observed that every original idea is at first ridiculed, then vigorously attacked, and finally taken for granted—years and years later." A sly nod from Max.

Instantly becoming Whitman again, Hank got into a little tiff with Arnold/Emerson over the title of one of his poems: "To A Common Prostitute."

"It's a fine title, Ralph," Whitman, said, "and it properly fits the poem. I thought you'd agree with me on that." Emerson tittered.

Applause. If Hank had called on me, an Emerson ally, I would've challenged Waltmore. Well, we had to move on.

We applicants and the actors waited eagerly for Hank's signal for the dance to start between Derek and Renee. We were glad everything was going well so far. Then, out of the blue, Renee clutched her stomach and started gurgling, retching hard. I think the sight of Raben sitting in the audience must have given her the willies. After all, Max was the one who had okayed the F she got in Tim's class.

"I'm gonna heave," she gasped, rubbing her stomach.

"I'll get you to the bathroom!" Derek offered.

"No, you gotta go on, Derek. Now!" she moaned.

"Alone? How *can* I?" he replied.

"You gotta, Derek. Go on. Do it solo. Go—!" Renee kept repeating, as she headed for the bathroom.

Derek spun around to Francesca and Mindy and asked if one of them could fill in for Renee now. When they declined, he turned to John.

"You do the dance with me, John. Didn't you hear Hank? How he said Whitman wrote the poem for two men anyway?"

"No way, man!" John said. "Are you off your effing rocker?"

I felt it coming, but I was not quick enough to escape Derek's riveting eyes.

"Then you, Jeff, be my dance partner! Tim would've liked it."

I shook my head, convinced Nan would not be greatly impressed if I did that.

I checked on Renee in the bathroom and heard her retching again behind the locked door.

Derek just stood there like a lamppost, wondering, I guess, if he'd have to go solo—if I didn't help. Hank promptly called us out to the side room when the tourists got antsy for the show to begin. Derek rattled off to Hank his idea—that I'd be filling in for Renee.

"Huh?" Hank responded. "The *two* of you do the dance? Interesting."

"Yeah, Hank! C'mon, our tour's about what really happened in history and—"

"But," Hank cut in, "that was then—"

"Well, don't let history get stuck in the past!" I said.

Hank slowly raised his thumb up. "Go for it then, Jeff. But hurry, hop on stage!"

I was set. Except for one minor detail—I didn't know any of the steps.

Chapter Thirty-Seven

A few minutes later

Hank, still as Whitman, commenced writing in his oversized green book, then paused, waiting for us to come out to perform. Off to my right, I noticed Derek had moved to a corner. Springing up and weaving in between the tables like a butterfly looking to alight, he settled right in front of me and touched my hands gently. I had nowhere to go except forward with him, trusting that he would guide me through.

The lights faded and came up again, the throbbing music starting slowly.

Hank said the words on beat and with surprising feeling as Derek and I began the sensuous *pas de deux.* Surprising myself, I was an easy enough follower.

Hank matched his—Whitman's—words to our heated, languorous movement. At first, just a trickle of laughter from the tourists. Then as the music—and words—settled in, so did the audience: *Hair, bosom, hips, and bend of legs . . .*

Derek wound up the dance smack in the direction of Rachel's table, ending right in front of the reverend. Sensing what Derek was doing, she seemed embarrassed and wary. Reverend Johnson lowered his head, but Donny MacNeil burned his eyes into both Derek and me, as the sultry dance stepped up.

Love-flesh swelling and deliciously aching / Limitless limpid jets of love, hot and enormous, quivering jelly and love, white-blown and delirious juice / Bridegroom night of love making surely and softly into the prostrate dawn / Undulating into the willing and yielding day . . .

It was over. Derek nudged me to bow to the applause. Sure, the appreciative tourists clapped like mad. Yeah, for them it was a ball, but hell, what a mess for me. My toe was okay though. Nan sat stone-faced at the table on the other side, her arms folded angrily across her waist. During our dance, I had spotted Nellie with her head down on the table, sneaking a peek now and then. Now Nan pulled her up from her seat, and, in a flash, without a word to me, they were on their way out of the cafe. Did I see Nellie give me a thumbs up as she exited? Yes! She *liked* it! I was wowed—it looked like *she* herself was ready to dance with Lazon right there.

As my two gals started for the door, the reverend and Donny Mac-Neil rose abruptly out of their seats. Rachel started to get up too, but Johnson must've said something that made her, robot-like, sit down. The two men darted out the door with me close behind, to ward off any trouble for Nan. On my way out, Raben tried to stop me.

"No, I gotta go, Max! Be right back!"

"Hold on, Jeff. I got to tell you something. I liked it. Really! Make sure you include this tour stuff in your tenure defense. Could be solid gold for a grant later. Really fine."

Whoa there! Was he serious or just putting me on? Max was being either too good to me or was a very good liar.

I nodded and ran out. Down the block, I spotted Nellie hanging on to Nan, with the two ghouls closely in pursuit.

"Back off! Leave her alone!" I shouted, approaching them like a drunken Vandal.

"No need to be alarmed, Mrs. Gardner. Just hand me the envelope," the reverend said, as he approached Nan. We saw your husband give it to you. Now we would like it back. That's all we want. It's ours."

I stepped in between my family and the two pests. "She doesn't have it, " I said, pulling the envelope from my sling bag, waving it in front them like a juicy bone to a ravenous dog.

"I do have it, and it stays with me! So keep away from my wife and daughter!" I motioned to Nan and Nellie to head home, but they just ran across the street, turning back to look at me. Nan got busy on her cellphone.

"Don't worry," Donny said. "We were not gonna touch 'em. All we want is the envelope back, if you please." He reached for it in my hands, but I pulled it away.

Lunging for it again, he cried, "Stop foolin' around, Gardner! Just hand the it over—and we'll call it quits!"

"Sure, you want me outta the picture. Just like I want both of you out. Well, here, Major Donny, take the damn thing." Laughing, I tossed the envelope into the air. "You're welcome to it. Take it with you to hell! Double time!"

"*Thank you,*" the reverend said, scooping up the envelope from the pavement.

"Now, go 'head, get outta here. You go to hell, too, Reverend. 'cause, I know the truth, what you did to Rachel! Not a nice thing, you bastard!"

"No, you don't understand. Don't be so quick to judge!" Johnson said, creeping close to me.

"Oh, I understand perfectly."

"No," he hissed. "The devil tempted us, but the Lord set us right again, and when I get the book, everyone will see I stand for righteousness." He ended so softly I could barely hear him, as close as he was to my face.

"You stand for nothing! They'll see what you did to her! Stay away from her!" I spit out, making sure Donny, a few feet away, heard me. I started across the street.

"Wait a minute," he said, catching up. "You're saying Reverend Johnson did something to my daughter? Is that what I think you mean?"

"Yes."

Donny turned back to the reverend, whose silence was answer enough. But he looked anxious to leave. Donny turned to me again. "You better be right 'bout your accusations—"

"About your friend, this pious, so gentle reverend, *with* your daughter?" I answered, staring straight at him. Donny replied by smashing his fist into my stomach. Twice. I doubled up and fell on the sidewalk, as they made their getaway.

* * *

I looked up to see peering down at me Nan, Nellie—and Rachel too, who had probably wandered out of the cafe to check up on her father and Johnson. Some pedestrians started to gather, but I managed to fend off most of them off as my anxious angels helped me back on my feet.

The reverend and Donny were half way to the end of the block, on Broadway, when they turned around and observed the little crowd forming around us. From a distance, Johnson signaled Rachel to join him. Right now.

"I'm not your pet dog to summon!" she shouted. "Not anymore!"

As I saw the two snakes crawl away, I yelled at 'em with all I had left in me, "Cowards! Shameless cowards!" They just kept on walking away.

Whether they heard her or not, Rachel's message was clear. Visibly shaken, she turned to me. She wore no smile of victory as I took her hand. Nan jumped in and offered her a place to stay for the night.

The two women and Nel started home, linking their arms together. They all looked back a couple of times as I made my way to the cafe door and watched them disappear around the corner. In a matter of minutes. Poof. Gone.

A cop emerged from an approaching squad car and inquired, "Is there anything wrong, sir? We got a call about some trouble."

I stared blankly at him, muttering, "No problem, officer. Just a little altercation. It's been resolved."

"Are you sure?" he said, looking at me like I was one of those inebriated Bridge and Tunnel jocks from New Jersey.

"Yes," I nodded, clutching my groin.

"Okay, then. You better get movin'. All of you. Clear the sidewalk, please," he said to the dispersing crowd. "Now I can get some breakfast." Looking back a couple times, he headed to Wendy's, across the street.

Holding my stomach with one hand and my other palming my groin, I caught my reflection in the cafe window and took a minute, before entering, to compose myself. On my way in, I made out Max holding up a piece of his breadstick in a salute, totally unaware of the drama that had just transpired outdoors. He probably thought I was on break or rehearsing outside for the next scene.

Sasha was pissed. "Where'd you go? To be with *her*, I bet! To comfort her, poor thing. She couldn't let Nellie see that lively dance—full of life, so she left. And you *had* to run after 'em. To be with *them*. Of course."

"Well, Sash, I was a little preoccupied . . ."

"Where were you, Jeff? I was lookin' for you! Hey, why you holding your stomach? Come on, Jeff. Talk to me!"

"It's okay. It's just the lousy food. I'll tell you later. Everything's cool, Sasha. The tour's about to continue. And I have to go." I was in no mood for another sidewalk confrontation.

Derek and Lazon were hanging out downstairs with some of the friendlier tourists who were eager to see what would be next on this crazy tour.

"Renee okay?" I asked, covering up my own pain.

"Yeah," Derek said, "we'd been goin' over our lines for the Shakespeare segment comin' up—her big date with the Bard! See you outside in a few."

I went upstairs with Lazon. He flicked his hand on my shoulder. Firmly. Confidently, it seemed. "You got a mad neat daughter, Dr. Gardner. She asked me what I wanted to be when I, like, grow up. You know what I said?"

"What?" I breathed in deep, feeling again the sharp pain in my groin again.

"Maybe an awesome teacher . . . like you."

After Lazon said that, I glanced over at Raben, who was still chatting away with Doree. I wondered if he had heard the boy's remark—if he was thinking the same thing. It would've been nice.

My cellphone went off. Eyes-in-back of his head, Hank saw me open it, so I had to make it fast.

"Popster, we just got home. We're worried sick about you, me and Mom. Are you okay? It's all my fault, that I sneaked away—"

"No, no, sweetheart. You have nothing to do with this, nothing at all. I'll explain everything later."

Nan was on the line now. "You gotta get yourself to St. Vincent's in a cab! You could have injuries. Hurry!"

"I'm fine. Don't worry. I'm back in the cafe again, getting ready to move on. Gotta get on with my job. I love you."

A pause.

"Why are you doing this, Jeff? We want you to come home."

"I made a promise I'd do the whole tour."

"But why? It's too risky—insane! First, the man who threatened Nellie, and then, that other man who hit you! Come home, now!"

"Ah, Nan, the tour's almost over. It's even good for my teaching and—"

"Teaching?! Get a grip! This is no learning curve, no way. Jeff, where are you going? I'm coming—"

"No! That's it. Stay with Nellie. Oh, Nan, we have our group counseling scheduled for Saturday. Think we can cancel?"

"I don't know . . . maybe. Take care of yourself. I'm worried sick about you."

Hank's eyes were on me. I shut off the cell. At least they were home. I wished I was with them. But I had some business to finish.

Chapter Thirty-Eight

1 p.m.

When the tour resumed at the corner of Bleecker and Mercer, a light rain was already beginning to send Renee up the wall with frustration and panic. Some of the tourists were dreading the possibility of a really heavy downpour. Hank gathered the group around a street sign and riffed a bit about Brigadier General Hugh Mercer, a Revolutionary War general, who had been killed in 1777 at the Battle of Trenton. "Forget the rain," Hank kibitzed. "At least we are all alive and will soon experience another lively, unforgettable performance—courtesy, thank you, of CWC, Ink."

Renee was depending more than ever on her Shakespeare "Rapsody" to cancel the failing grade Tim had given her for plagiarizing her term paper. In addition to her acting stint, of course, she figured Raben would appreciate her research, writing, and comprehensive analysis regarding community street theatre and home-grown culture,

"Tomorrow's the last day for grade changes. Shoot, I can't afford to be rained out now!" she lamented. "Dr. Gardner, I think I'm gonna throw up again, 'cause I don't know if I'm up to doin' this."

"Look, Renee you can't get behind the beat. Sometimes you have to latch on to these second chances and run with 'em. It's sort of like a second serve in tennis."

"Uh, second serves are usually weaker—"

"So forget tennis, Renee. You're playing a different game here. Here's an idea, okay? With all these street objects in your skit—you're helping people look at things in a different way, expand themselves and their imaginations. That's good, darn good."

"I never thought of it quite that way."

"See how your thought waves are already changing into good vibes . . ."

"You really think I can—?"

"Yes, you can make a new start. Go for it. Put your heart into it."

"Thank you, Dr. Gardner."

"Aw, come on already. Call me Jeff."

Raben, standing a few feet from me, was giving us a quick look-over, wondering, no doubt, what I would do with her in her scene. Doree was still close by his side. Sasha gabbed with John, the young actor, while Lazon seemed to be all alone in his own world. Good mentor Derek gave him an occasional nod of encouragement for staying with the tour.

I joined Jankowitz huddling with the tourists. Referring to the tidy, two-story red-brick apartment building in front of us, he asked them if they had ever heard of Henry Miller. One tourist got the name mixed up with the playwright Arthur Miller, who had recently passed away. But the rest of us knew Henry Miller for his books that got banned in the 1960s. And, in fact, there was a history-making obscenity case that decided it was perfectly okay for people to read so-called smutty books, such as his *Tropic of Cancer,* that had literary value. And this apartment building here was once the home of Grove Press, renamed Evergreen Press in the 1970s, that published a number of Henry's so-called prurient books, as well as such authors as Edward Albee and Alex Haley.

Janice, a feisty middle-aged black woman, who worked across the street at the cleaners that Sasha used, suddenly appeared on the scene, garbed in a long black shawl and a glam red rose on her all-white flowing Victorian-styled night gown.

"Hi, Janice," Sasha called out, waving energetically to her. An aspiring actress, Janice looked forward to shining in this next act, as small as her part was.

In a deep resonant and commanding voice, Renee explained to the assembled what we were about to experience dramatically.

"Now this building has a deeper history, y'know," Renee declaimed. "In the 1820s and '30s, it was the home of the famed African

Grove Theatre. And the publishing company once had their office on Grove Street. That's why, in the 1960s, the publishing company named their company Grove Press. What a great coincidence! The African Grove Theatre, an all-black company of super-talented thespians, enacted a wide-ranging repertory of comedies, musicals, and a heck of a lotta Shakespearean plays, which included *The Tempest* and *Hamlet*. As a tribute to this famed playhouse, what we're about to see are the beginning and end of the *Scottish* play."

Searching for a sign of Raben's approval, she looked over to where he was standing, diligently writing notes on his clipboard.

Janice joined Mindy and Francesca, both in all-white garb, to instantly become the Three Weird Sisters, dancing around the trash basket-cauldron, which had sat on the corner, innocently unnoticed until now. After circling slowly around the cauldron three times, the women intoned in one loud, creepy voice, " 'Fair is foul, and foul is fair!' "

Renee let out an eerie shriek. " 'A drum, a drum!' " as John tapped out an African rhythm on a big drum to the cadence of the ladies' gravelly sounding, " 'Hover through the fog and filthy air.' "

Then Janice and Mindy cried out in a witchy-synched voice: " 'When shall we meet again—In thunder—' "

On that last word, Derek, accompanied by John's dissonant drumbeat, strummed a lightning-sound riff on his guitar that chilled to the bone.

The ladies continued their ominous chanting, waving their brightly-colored scarves in a smartly unified rhythm and tempo. With my tambourines picking up the beat, I joined the others in the dizzying cadence that heightened the intensity of the words.

Hovering around the cauldron-trash can, as the tourists assembled around them, they threw scary objects mentioned in the play into the can, but with equivalents like candy corn for teeth of wolves and large Afro-combs substituting for scales of adragon. " 'Witches' mummy, maw and guff.' " Through it all, they chanted those time-honored words, " 'Double, double, toil and trouble; Fire burn and cauldron bubble/ Cool it with baboon's blood,/Then the charm is firm and good.' "

On the last line, Renee and the rest of us gathered the spectators into a tight circle. Max had squeezed himself next to Doree. I was beginning to realize that maybe something was going on between them, maybe like a father-daughter thing. I knew how deeply she missed her own father. So, it made me feel good that she was close to Raben in that way—if it was only that way.

I smiled too early. Bang, the clouds suddenly darkened with a humongous clap of thunder. Hank motioned for the tourists to make a beeline dash to the little park across the street, while he remained with us. Max and Doree, bless 'em, also stayed. The ladies three continued chanting in the rain, and Derek, John, Lazon, and I hung in right with them as they shimmied around the self-styled cauldron, singing, " 'The weird sisters, hand in hand/posters of the sea.' " Renee lost no time cajoling the tourists who had remained through the downpour to chant with her in unison, " 'So foul and fair a day I have not seen!'" Around the fourth or fifth time of repeating it, the rain suddenly stopped and the sun peeked out of a chilly gray cloud.

I had to give it to her. Tim had mentioned that Renee was a real go-getter, who he predicted would be a dynamo upstart in the corporate world some day. I felt she deserved a half-way break on redemption road. So far, Max seemed to be enjoying her efforts. A hopeful sign for her—and for me, too, her *ad hoc* mentor.

About half of the tourists who had fled to the little playground across the street returned. Those of us who decided to chance it in the rain were thoroughly drenched, with Hank looking especially miserable trapped in his wheelchair. Ballsy Renee, of course, continued on, in spite of this sorry wet spectacle.

With ceremonial flair, Janice wrapped her wet shawl around her shoulders to instantly transform into Lady Macbeth. The emerging sun cooperated, too. For how long was anybody's guess, even for the all-knowing witches.

" 'Yet there's a spot,' " Janice, as Lady Macbeth, cried out, gingerly rubbing her hands together. Now, lifting her head and stretching out her hands, she continued:

" 'Out damned spot! Out, I say! One: Two: Why then 'tis time to do't. Hell is murky . . . ! Yet who would have thought the old man to have had so much blood in him? . . . Here's the smell of the blood still: All the perfumes of Arabia will not sweeten this little hand. Oh! Oh!' "

Janice still hadn't caught most people's attention because of the annoying showers, but the tourists who had stuck around loved her tacky bit of theatrics, and I did too. She took a little bow and exclaimed, "Thank God for the African Grove Theatre!"

Applause rang out as it might have at the Globe Theatre. Well, maybe not quite. Janice graciously acknowledged the loyalty of the audience, to whom she modestly said, "I got to get back to the cleaners and take care of some more spots." Some laughter and more applause. She was a hit, a palpable hit. Renee kissed her on the cheek.

Renee strode over to me and also gave me a light kiss. "Thanks for believing in me, Jeff. Like Lady Macbeth, I've been, uh, going through some depression and insomnia lately."

"It's okay, Renee. I know about that, first hand. But you'll do great on your next act too," I said, hugging her.

Janice was starting to cross the street when Derek called her over to join us.

"Janice, I was wondering if you could stick around for another half-hour."

"Another thirty minutes?" she asked looking warily at her watch. "I dunno . . . Amet, our manager, needs me at the store. I can check."

"It'll be another chance to act. Trust me," Derek said.

"Where? Here?"

"Right around here, where it might have happened."

"What? What happened?"

"Come right back, I'll fill you in. It's about our man Frederick Douglass."

Chapter Thirty-Nine

:15 p.m.

Douglass?! Are you kidding, D?" I whispered to him, pulling him ide. "No scenes about Douglass now!"

"Why not?"

"If the creep who stole the books sees a scene like that, he'll know e're after him. It'll blow our cover!"

"No, I think my idea will work, man!"

"Forget it! No way!"

I took another step toward him. "Whoa—I'm serious!"

"You whoa—! Just listen!" He took a step toward me.

Hank, sensing tension between Derek and me, stepped between s. "Cool down, guys! Let it go. You're still onstage. You know, spectors are always watchin'. Act professional!"

"Okay, Hank, okay," Derek said. He was still glaring at me when Iank left.

"Derek, I just don't think we should call attention to the book by oin' a scene about Douglass."

"Cool, down, Jeff. Listen to my idea at least. Remember the Iousetrap scene in *Hamlet*? Where that shrewd dude tries to catch 1e conscience—of that king? Well, dig it. I just saw him. Donny IacNeil. Look over there. He's back, standin' near the curb. See im?"

Surveying the scene, I nodded. "Sure enough, D. Returning to 1e scene of the crime . . . Oh, so calm and decent now."

But wait 'til he sees this next scene, Jeff. Man, even the rain won't ash away his ass-face guilty puss."

"Really? Well, we'll have to see—"

"I figure we can stick something in our new Mousetrap scene showing he killed Tim—with poison!" Oh, this man was really o fire! I had to cool him down.

"But we don't know that for sure, D—!"

"That's why we gotta do the scene—to find out! Any ideas?"

It was worth a try, but I still wasn't sure. Sleuth. Actor. Now playwright. I had to think fast. But I had to put any new scenari on hold, now that Renee was beginning her act. I wanted to b close to her in case she needed me. Spotting me approach her, sh began on a high note. "Gather around, wham! Poetry's about t slam!" she called out, motioning for the tourists to come closer an enjoy the fun.

Lazon volunteered to be first and rapped a poem that everyon seemed to like, a nice tribute to Shakespeare. Applause for the youn bard, as Renee turned to me and repeated the kid's last words, "Wit a mad-good leader like you, I will love Shakespeare anew!"

"That works! Thanks, Lazon," Renee enthused. "You're a buc ding poet and, like, you sure did show it! No argument—better tha 50 Cent!"

About five or six volunteers spun out their poems on the spo Renee offered some closing remarks about the eternal spirit of cr ativity, good vibes for peace and love—because, in the words of th Bard, "the charms are wound" again. She looked so relieved whe Raben gave her a hearty thumbs up.

Calming down a bit, I decided to cool it about the Mousetrap. just couldn't think of anything good enough at the spur of the mo ment. So, I ventured to take the bull by the horns, and check o Donny, standing all alone, by the curb. What did he want? Why ha he come back—and alone this time?

He held his hand out to me. "Sorry, Dr. Gardner. I guess you wer right on about Reverend Johnson. Trust me, I'm going to take care c him, and see that he gets his." Donny seemed contrite, claiming tha he knew nothing about the reverend's scummy behavior.

I nodded okay because I believed him. But I still felt concern 'bout Rachel. What was the Major going to do to make *amends* to 'er? She was the real victim here.

"Oh, and another thing, Doctor. About the contract. It'll have to 'e rewritten now that circumstances have changed, you know, with he reverend out of the picture. Teaming up, we'll make the best use 'ut of the book. Win-win!" He looked nervous when he said it, covring his mug with a plastic smile.

Okay, my turn to play with him. "Major, I really don't know what ou're talkin' about."

"The contract, the contract," he repeated, his voice getting louder nd faster. "For you to come in with me. Just you and me." He was weating hard.

"So what about the new committee you're forming?" I asked.

"Uh, we'll be in charge of that together. No problem there."

"I don't *think* so," I said. "Tim made a deal with me, and I mean o stand by it. Why don't you go back home to your reverend and, he both of you, get down on your scabby knees and pray? And ask or Rachel's forgiveness, while you're at it. You're gonna need it!" Donny slunk away as I bounced back to join the group.

Derek stepped up, with Janice, back now, and Renee at his side.

"Forget it, D," I whispered. "Donny split. No need now. Go back o plan A."

"That's okay," he said, disappointed. "But somehow I think Donny's connected to Tim's death—so we gotta get to the bottom of hat."

"We will, we will," I said, pleased to find that he was still so gung-o. "But now you gotta go on with the scene you planned."

"You don't mind us doin' Douglass?"

"Go right ahead. I'm with you. Just don't give the barn away about s chasing after the book. Got it?" He nodded.

"Hey, folks," Derek cried out, as the tour group regrouped around im, "if I could have your attention. Please."

Everyone was eager to give it to him. Jankowitz too.

"You know what our man, the Big Bard, said, 'Life is but a walkin shadow.' So, I ask you, my friends, isn't this what we've been doing a the time, making these shadows on Bleecker Street come alive? In realit and imagination? For example," Derek continued, "it is conceivable— we don't know for sure, but maybe, just maybe, one of the Africa Grove actors helped Frederick Douglass, back in the day when he wa a young man named Frederick Bailey, escape to freedom 'round her Yes, could've been right here, right where we're standing, in actual fact.

"For real?" one of the wide-eyed tourists asked.

"Maybe. Because some of those actors in the African Grove The atre were secretly Underground Railroad conductors in disguise. Nov let's try something cool. John and Jeff, here, will play slave catcher on the prowl, tryin' to find the slave Frederick Bailey, soon to becom the free man Douglass. Renee and Janice, there will be stuff for yo to do. Arnold, Mindy, Fran—hang in there—you'll rock on Freedor Road too!"

What the hell, he was taking over! Even Hank was impressed Well, why not? I was game to play along. Umm, me, play a slav catcher? Something new, alright. Gotta put it on my old acting ré sumé. Derek handed us a couple of long sticks to be our rifles. Janic draped the black shawl from the Lady Macbeth scene over her heac while Renee wrapped a large sheet around her waist to serve as a skir

"Ready, you slave catchers?" Derek asked, facing the tourist grou head on. "Oh, before we begin, there's a little song I'd like to teac y'all. You can clap along to it, too, if you feel the spirit, rock it out! He sang out with a spirit that still amazed me!

Oh, Canaan, sweet Canaan . . . I thought I heard 'em say there were lior in the way . . . and I don't expect to stay much longer here!

God, the words Tim and I had sung during our last class at Green Cent! I wondered how *he'd* feel seeing all this, with me a proud par of it.

Derek didn't have to ask everyone to join in the song again. They were eager to go with it, sweet and pure. Settling down, I gave it all I had.

But as our luck would have it, just as the scene started, a tremendous crack of lighting and the heaviest rain I had seen in years unleashed itself from the heavens above, the darkness descending like a thick wool blanket over our eyes.

"Shit, there goes my grade down the fucking drain," Renee moaned.

"Everyone, get to the shelter across the street. Move!" Hank commanded, directing the scene like a cool Cecil B. DeMille knock-off.

Folks from all directions barreled over to the park restroom area across the street that contained a small canopied breezeway between the two public lavatories.

"Derek! Jeff! Help me with this!" Renee yelled, unwrapping the large sheet from around her waist. Good—this time she was making sure Hank got over to shelter.

"Cover Hank. Don't let him get drenched!" I shouted.

It was clear he was moving too slowly, as Hilda struggled to make headway, pushing, pushing the wheelchair hard through the driving rain.

"Hilda, let me take over," I cried out, thrusting her to the side. "You—Derek, John, Mindy—hold the sheet steady over Hank, while Fran and I push. Let's go! Go!"

"Can I help?" Sasha asked, running over to my side.

"Yes! Thanks, Sash. All of you. Stay close. I'll need you to help boost him over the curb." It was a crazy, curious sight—Max, Doree, Lazon, Derek, Janice, Sasha, and God knows who else—all clumped together around the crawling wheelchair as we slogged along to our destination.

At the curb, I yelled to anyone who could hear that we needed to work together now. "Come on, guys, when I give the word, gently lift the wheelchair off the curb and set it down on the street—carefully. Steady now . . . steady . . ."

On my signal, anxious hands lifted the wheelchair a good six inches off the ground. Good—but that kicked up another problem. The chair wobbled at a crazy tilt—back and forth, back and forth.

"Ah, ah—!" poor Hank cried out from under the sheet, freaking out he might be dropped.

"Don't worry, Hank. We'll set you right. Steady, steady. . . ." I tried to assure him, as we finally managed to set the wheelchair upright on the pavement. But why was Hank still whimpering?

Then I noticed it—a trail of blood from an ugly gash on his side was pouring onto the street, mixing with the incessant, uncaring rain.

Chapter Forty

2:30 p.m.

Everyone scattered like squealing mice after the ambulance had raced Hank to the hospital. Feeling way down, I returned home and got into some dry clothes, then called Derek. He wasn't home, so I left him a message. Next, I tried Sasha, who was. I had to unload myself.

"Poor Hank. I feel terrible about what happened to him. It's my fault really."

"No, Jeff, it isn't. You're not to blame."

"Yes, I am. And you know, I've had it. I'm through with all this. I mean it."

"Well, good, honey, I'm glad to hear that."

"Yeah, but now I've got to get to the hospital to check on Hank."

"Hope he's alright. Give him my best."

"Of course, Sasha. Call you later."

"Take care, Jeff . . . I love you."

When I arrived at St. Vincent's Hospital an hour later, I was relieved to find out that Hank's injuries were not life-threatening. Still, the day's events shook me up bad. I wasn't surprised to find Gerard and Jameson in the waiting room. They reported Hank was doing okay enough to answer their questions, and they'd be visiting him soon.

I gave them my take on what went on in the park. Trying to keep what was left of my composure, I reached into my pocket for a pill, but remembered I left my bottle at home—a soggy crutch. Then I sprang the question at the top of my mind. "Did you find the weapon?"

Gerard said that they'd it found it on the street, a small kitchen knife, but the fingerprints were washed away by the rain.

"That knife was intended for me—you know that?" I exploded. "Not for the old spunky guy down the hall! Kind sirs, people have been creating havoc to get a hold of that book—and there's still no trace of it. Tim was killed for it. Whoever did the knifing is connected to Tim's death. God, isn't it crystal clear to you that someone wants *me* out of the way, that I'm the biggest obstacle to whoever stole the book?"

His response was plain and simple. "We know, Dr. Gardner, we know. But don't you remember our phone conversation yesterday? Advising you strongly against playing detective, that getting more involved in the open like you do could put you in danger? You made yourself a magnet, and now look what happened. Surprised?"

No, I wasn't. Strangely, I now felt oddly intoxicated by it all, even with me as the target. Maybe it *was* worthwhile to take these risks. Those mavericks taking chances on Bleecker Street weren't the only ones to do so. Besides, I had a growing hunch that we were getting closer to wrapping it all up.

So I told them I wasn't going to quit. I know, I know, moments before I was already to hang it up—now I had to keep going. Was I crazy? Up and down crazy, all the way.

So I dove right into it. "Any suspects?"

"You mean for the knifing? "

"For *anything*!" Raising my voice in a hospital was not a good idea.

"We're still tracking it down, getting closer," Jameson went on. "We've been keeping tabs on various people for a long time. 'Specially you."

"You were?!" I asked, amazed. "How so?"

"Your wife's been calling us a lot." Gerard said. "Like that cop who checked on you in front of the Corner Cafe."

"Nan called him?"

"Yup." Hmm. Looked like Jameson was easing up. Wow, Nan! She made the right call there back on the street.

Hilda, coming out of Hank's room, gave me a look registering no great love—a fact that was not lost on the cops. Was she blaming me for what happened to Hank?

"Why don't you go in first?" Gerard suggested. "We need some alone time with Mr. Jankowitz."

"Thanks, officers. I won't be long."

A huge bandage covered Hank's entire right thigh. Otherwise, he seemed in surprisingly good shape from the tumbling—and knifing—he'd just gone through.

"Hi, Shlepp," he said, not especially cheerful. "Good to see you again."

"How you feeling, Hank? You don't look bad at all for all the Olympic-size somersaults you took."

"A cut better than this morning, Jeff." He started to laugh, but stopped abruptly. "Listen, I better not crack up over my own jokes. Makes me jiggle my insides like jello."

"You're quite a cut-up, Hank."

"Well, Jeff, whoever did this to me sure has a funny sense of humor."

"Yeah, boss. Hey, you can joke about it with the cops waiting to see you. They want to make you 'Star of the Week.' "

"Okay, Jeff, very funny! Now I gotta get serious. I won't be able to get back to the old fort for a couple of days, or maybe weeks. Who knows when? I was gonna ask you—"

He paused, searching for the right words. "You know, Jeff, that you're doin' a great job with the tours. The people eat it up big time. So I won't beat around the bush. We'd like you to join us at CWC, Ink."

I smiled at Hank, but didn't know how to answer him.

"I was gonna ask you anyway, Jeff—to take over the Bleecker Blues Line 'til I'm ready to return. I know you're ready for it."

"Hank, I—"

"Your style, Jeff, I like it. You're good with people . . . and you sure know your history. What d'ya say?"

"I dunno, Hank. Gotta check my teaching schedule. I plan to cover Tim's summer Shakespeare course at Greene Cent."

"Sure, Jeff. Anything." His pouting lips showed his obvious disappointment. "Oh, I know you're all hooked up with that college that Tim was involved with. He only worked part-time for me. But still, can't you take my offer? At least for the summer? A challenge! Work up some new ideas for the tour, like Tim was doin'?"

Hank smiled warmly. He wouldn't let it go. "I'd ask my family, Jeff, but who's to ask? They're gone, all scattered." I promised him I'd go to Greene Cent and look at the schedule, then give him a call.

An orderly came in to take the food order for tomorrow's breakfast. Hank made some snappy checks on the menu and whisked her out.

"The crap they serve is a poor excuse for chow. Just oatmeal. Not even a hard bagel with a little butter. Shit. I still got my teeth, for goodness sakes!" A hearty laugh from the old guy with the shining bald head. I laughed easy with him.

"Yeah, and you know what?!"

"What?"

"They won't let me have any sugar on the pissy oatmeal. Nuts to that!"

It looked like he might start cracking up. Silence.

"So?" Hank looked hard at me, with his patented broad smile.

"So, I'll let you, know, Boss."

"At least, can you fill in on the tour for tomorrow?"

I nodded. "Sure. No problem, if I can fit it in," at the same time occurring to me that I had my little tenure meeting the next day to bone up for.

"Well, Hank, I gotta be goin'. Don't forget these two friends of ours, Gerard and Jameson, are waiting to see you. So I'll just tip-toe outta here and leave you in their capable hands. Take care of yourself,

Hank Jankowitz—the Maven of CWC, Ink!" I gently grasped his big hands. "I'll let you know my schedule."

I knew that the cops would get nowhere quick with Hank as a witness. He was just the accidental victim of circumstances here.

On the way out, I asked Gerard if I could stop by the precinct later to discuss an important matter.

"Oh, is it about Donny MacNeil, the guy who knocked you around? Nan told us—"

"No, not him."

"Then who—or what?"

I told them who I believe killed Tim—and who tried to kill me.

One word did it for me. Oatmeal. And that gave me an idea on how to trap the killer.

Chapter Forty-One

4:00 p.m.

First thing I did, after getting home, was call Nan and Nellie to put their—and my own—minds at ease. Big mistake! Nellie's nonstop crying made it hard for me to get a word in edgewise to her mother. And Nan kept insisting that I drop by—like *now*. Later, I assured her, later. I called Sasha to hang on for a couple hours and I'd meet her at my place. There were things we needed to go over. Finally, I tried to reach Derek, leaving him a message to call me asap.

After a hop-to lunch of whatever leftovers I could dig up in my fridge, I called the police precinct, letting G & J know I was on my way.

Fifteen minutes later, we were all settled in Jameson's cramped office, where I unleashed my idea in full.

"I don't know, Jeff," Jameson cautioned. "That will involve an awful lot of risk on your part. Of course, we'll be right with you, next to you almost, but still—"

"I'm okay with that," recalling our great teamwork snaring Mustache Man.

After a few minutes they came back with another cop and proceeded to wire me up. Took all of a minute.

"Gotta ask you again, Jeff. You in? Think carefully. We do want you to help us wrap it up, but remember, it's very risky."

"Yeah," I said, picking my words carefully. "Well, I'm doin' it for Tim. I can't let him down. I got into this from the moment I agreed to go in with him with the book, and—"

"Don't, Jeff, it wasn't your fault."

"But, I—"

"But nothing," Gerald interrupted. "We're not priests or shrinks Jeff. If you want one of those other guys we could arrange it. That's easy. This will be harder, but no doubt, more effective. To finally wrap it up with you as a part of the team in a big way. Your choice . . . . Well, you in or out?"

I nodded in silence, taking it all in. "You're right. I'm not finished until his killer is nailed." I was shaking.

My cell. Okay, I told myself, calm down. Nellie again. Not giving up. Talk to your daughter. She loves you. Be a *mensch*. Jameson gave me a thumbs up to take my time.

"You okay, Popster? Mom and I can't stop worrying." She was crying.

I held my breath all the way to ten. Sasha would be proud of that. "Yes, I am, dear. I'll be fine. See you this evening. I love you . . . your mom, too."

I looked up at Gerard, who gave me another thumbs up and big smile.

When the cops started wiring me, I literally felt it, that what I was going to do was for real. The patch on the wire squeezed my chest, pushing me on to something I had to go through with . . . if we could pull it off. I'd know soon.

"Let's go over the plan, Jeff," Gerard said, " 'specially the security guard's role. Got to make sure both window and door stay unlocked."

"O'Rourke will come through," I assured them.

"Do we pick up the print on the way over?" Stupid question. When else could we pick it up?

They nodded confidently, then excused themselves for a minute.

The plan was smart enough—when push came to shove. I hoped I'd be strong enough to carry out my part of it.

When Jameson and Gerard returned, it was weird to see them decked out in outfits that looked like window washer uniforms. But the guns inside their pockets had nothing to do with cleaning. Except for finally cleaning up this whole wretched case.

We headed out.

Chapter Forty-Two

5:30 p.m.

The rain had stopped and the sun was out again. I squeezed into a corner of the unmarked car and we were off. For a few minutes, the quiet excursion uptown afforded a little time for reflection.

This morning, when Hank complimented Tim's Sanger scene as "some sweet number," something buzzing in my head bothered me about him saying that, but I couldn't make any sense of it.

But then in the hospital, it suddenly came clear to me, when Hank said he hated his morning oatmeal without sugar. So, it boiled down to *oatmeal*, the key that began to spring the case wide open.

I recalled Nellie's loving obsession with her school project—two different results developing from the same oatmeal box—a peep-hole camera from the box itself and an Inca temple made from the box's oats mixed with glue and paint. That got me thinking about the way two different sides of a personality can converge, for good or evil. That sealed it right then for me.

Now, almost in pitch silence, we drove to the Ronin Gallery, midtown, where I picked up a framed print of the great Kiyochika of the Meiji era. The young sales clerk who wrapped it was pleased by the suddenness of her sale. Jameson paid for it out of the city coffers, a cheap price for the trap it was going to set. We drove downtown.

As we got close to Greene Cent, we spotted Joe Chiang, the intern from the Daily News, outside the building, still hunting for any kind of hot leads. He looked beat, exhausted. But here he was coming toward me, full court press. "Dr. Gardner, Dr. Gardner—if you have a minute, please. My newspaper got a call this morning from the Frederick Douglass Museum in Maryland about a book that a Donovan MacNeil and you are pursuing, to be donated to that museum. Care to comment?"

"Ah, not now, I—"

Gerard whisked him out of the way as we entered the building. Joe didn't know it, but the scoop of his young reporting life was waiting for him—if he'd only just stick around for the next hour.

I nodded my usual hello to Jackson O'Rourke, by now my certified accomplice.

"Working late, Jeffie? Getting squared away for your tenure meeting tomorrow?" His wink acknowledged he was a proud member of our improvised "assault" team, ready to go. "Or are we meeting up today?" he murmured.

"The boss still here, Jackson?" I asked innocently enough, masking the mixed emotions pulling me apart. Raben had always been good to me. Yet, what he did to Tim, so horribly inexcusable.

Nodding to Jameson and Gerard, like an old pal, Jackson assured us that Max was upstairs.

"Everything 10-4, top to bottom?" Gerard asked. "The inside window and door both unlocked?"

Jackson gave the detectives a stealthy thumbs up. "Yes, thanks to our efficient cleanin' lady! Everything's under tight control, sir." Jackson saluted briskly.

The detectives headed for the service elevator to ascend to the floor directly above Max's office. I kept my cellphone on, poised at speed dial. They needed about five minutes to secure their positions.

On the way up on the regular elevator, I thought about what Joe had just mentioned, that maybe Donovan—Donny—was on the up and up after all. That he wanted to put the book to use for the public good.

In the reception room I said hello to Doree, a bit surprised to see her. She looked so bedraggled. After the first rainstorm debacle this morning, I thought she vowed to make an appointment this afternoon to get her hair done, Well, apparently she didn't, or couldn't yet. A problem, how to get her the hell out of here without forcing it.

"What've you got there, sir?" Doree asked, spotting my large package.

"Going-away present for Professor Raben," I explained. "A surprise. Mind if I put it there?" I asked, pointing to a tight space behind her desk.

"Not at all," she said, carefully taking the print from me and placing it where I had suggested.

"Careful, is *trés* expensive." We shared a little laugh.

"Hey, Doree, you still goin' to that fab hairdresser in the East Village that Sasha suggested?" Careful, Jeff, don't overplay this. "I mean, not that you need it—"

"Yes, I have to leave now—that hairdresser likes us to be prompt. Just finishing up some work. Never ends."

There they were again—those "top secret" papers—"Professor Raben's UK Agenda," sitting here on her desk, dying for my inspection. "Can I take a peek? Hope you don't mind." Picking up some loose pages from her desk, I started to scan them.

"No, sir, please don't. I'm not, uh, finished yet." She fairly tore the pages from my hands and threw the entire report into her desk drawer. "Sorry!" She didn't look a bit sorry for her hasty grab. No matter. I had seen enough on the first page to confirm my suspicion: *Day #1, presentation of special "North Star" discovery.* Right. "North Star" had to be Raben's code for Frederick Douglass, who had founded that abolitionist newspaper in New England.

She turned on the old-fashioned squawk box on her desk to let the old man know I was here, and she was off to her appointment.

Then to me: "I'll be leaving now. Have a good evening!"

She headed for the door and was gone. I sighed a huge one as I locked the outer door. Plan A was back on track.

When I entered Max's office, he was, as usual, at his desk, skimming through some notes.

On his desk there were piles of books, and, of course, his favorite chess box, the one he claimed his Oxford professor Isaiah Berlin had given him completing his Ph.D. dissertation long ago in England.

"About time you got here, but I know you were, uh, *preoccupied.* We really need to go over your tenure talking points for tomorrow."

He cleared the papers from his desk and, folding his hands, looked at me, grim as a trapped gopher in its own hole.

"That was something today, Jeff. Everything started so fine. We were all having so much fun. Then, the rain, and that ghastly sheet under which we were supposed to take cover—and, of course, that gruesome stabbing. Who could have thought . . . ? Sorry, I just couldn't get mixed up in it. Not in my DNA. Had to leave. You understand, of course. Anyway, glad *you're* fine."

I nodded amen to that. But, you bastard, why don't you ask about Hank too?

"There's a lot of work I have to do before I depart for the UK. That's why I got out of there in such a hurry, like a jackrabbit. Didn't want to get involved in a lot of questioning and things!"

Yes, I remembered him, hobbling away with his cane, his diligent Doris at his side. A sight that could've split my gut, if Hank's bloody body hadn't taken all my attention.

"Packing for tomorrow's trip, Max?" I asked, glancing casually at some of the books he was going to take along.

"Yes, I leave right after your tenure planning-meeting tomorrow. I know it's going to work out fine for you, Jeff. I'm on your side all the way. "

"Classy chess set," I said, admiring again its ornate casing. "Professor Isaiah Berlin gave it to you, right?"

Max moved it away gently. "Yes, when I beat him at his own endgame."

"Must've been somethin'. A rarity."

"Yup. I was such a young *pisher*, so full of myself. You know what he did after I won? He just presented me with this chess set, pure and simple. Yes, somethin', huh? I guess he liked me. Like I like you, Jeff."

"Ditto from me, Max. In fact, I have a little something for you. You could say it's a going-away present. Just a sec, I'll get it."

Max loved the print. I mentioned that a smart woman helped me pick it out.

"Fine woman, Jeff. You know, you and Nan should get back together. Most assuredly."

He unwrapped the package and looked lovingly at the mysterious Zen mountain landscape. He said, "Thank you. It's beautiful. Really spellbinding. Fine!"

I smiled at that. "Where do you want to hang it, Max?"

"Here, in my office, of course."

"Great idea! But speaking of taste, Max, how 'bout a little toast to your trip?"

"Sure, I'll drink to that," he said. "I'll whip up two milkshakes—*sans* sugar, of course."

No sugar, of course. But something else. Deadly.

"Two of my sensational non-fat shakes comin' right up, Jeff!"

Max got to jabbering about Nan, how great she was, going on and on to praise his own wife, who, despite her chronic sickness, was willing to make the trip to England. He seemed to be in such an up mood as he examined the print more closely.

"Jeff, you know what one Japanese painter long ago asked? Or maybe he was Chinese. I can't recall. 'Is the painting in the hills or are the hills in the painting?' Nice observation, right?" That was Max. Gloating on the details when convenient for him.

"Honestly, a little of both, I imagine, Max." As we gathered around the print, he handed me my drink and thoughtfully a napkin, too.

"A toast," Max said, "to the beauty in the hills, or is it the hills in the beauty?" Again, he was amused by his own witticism. Hilarious.

Without indulging, I put my drink down.

I placed the print on his desk, next to his chess box, and stared at it, then shifted my attention to the box, and finally to him. As I started to open the box, he nimbly flicked my hand away.

"How did you know?" he asked quietly.

"Law of Opposites, Max. Hiding something so rare in something so familiar."

"No, this chess box is not so common, Jeff. But I see your point, the least inspected, the most unexpected . . ."

I reached for the lid, but Max did not stop me this time. There, the holy grail I had been chasing the whole week, Shady Lady in all her rare glory! I picked it up, gliding my hand down its speckled grainy cover. Douglass's signature was so clear, the familiar bold likeness of the master writer himself. And the inscription! Seeing it there, I heaved a strong sigh, the *real* thing at last! Like a lighthouse beam, my eyes fixed on those incandescent words: *With this book I have a new name and hope for everlasting freedom. Frederick Douglass.*

Carefully thumbing through the book—delicately, oh so delicately, all there—in good condition, no, top-grade condition, not a smudge on it, wholly, completely intact. I breathed deeply. The plan was still on course. I looked up and waited a second.

Chapter Forty-Three

Max leaned over. "Tim said it was okay for me to have the book. To take it along to London. He wished me well with it. He did, Jeff. We made a deal."

"Come on, Max. That's not my understanding. Give it to me straight."

He started to finger the chess box, like it was a new-born baby.

"Jeff, hear me out," he said, lowering his voice. "You know, back in the Middle Ages, European kings took to this immortal game of chess as sultans and emirs had done centuries before them. Did you know that? In Normandy, the French king, Louis the Sixth, I think, in the midst of battle was suddenly seized by an enemy knight. 'The king is taken!' he shouted. You know what the king replied?"

"Got me, Max . . ." How long did I have to wait before this man broke down and said what the wire on me needed to hear? Yes, that he was guilty of theft—and murder?

"What, Max?"

" 'Ignorant and insolent knight!' " the king replied. " 'Not even in chess can a king be technically taken!' "

I paused for a second. "It's time, Max. Checkmate!"

"What do you want from me now? Get to the point!"

"It all added up. *You* told me, Max. When I was here on Monday, you didn't want to hear anything I said about the book Tim had found, remember? In fact, you refused to even listen, forcing me to change the subject. Your silence about the book spoke volumes. You know, yourself, it's *not* what's reported in history that's always the most important, but it may be just the opposite—what's left out. All you really seemed to be interested in, then, was your chess board. You said you really played some fine moves. And all this time I was reading your face tryin' to figure you out. You were really seeing all the great moves alright, not with chess, no, but with the book. Well, weren't you?"

"No, no, you're mistaken. I really cared about Tim. If you think I'd ever harm him, way off. Just the opposite. Remember, I got him a promotion here. *Full-time.*"

Suddenly Raben made a feeble, pathetic attempt to wrest the book out of my hands, but I was never going to let him have it again.

"Jeff, did you know this? Listen," he said, "at our celebration for his promotion, Tim plucked this glorious book from his briefcase, and showed it to me. A few days before, he had mentioned that he'd recently acquired a rare book—something I'd definitely be interested in. And he was right. I couldn't believe my eyes when I finally saw it. I told him if I could somehow have it, it would be the crowning height of my lifetime, giving me new hope to carry on with my work."

"Well, did he make some kind of deal with you?"

"Yes. We shook hands on it. Like gentlemen. Gentlemen-scholars. Doris prepared two of my low-carb shakes to clinch the deal. I told Tim I would take the book to England, and we would share the credit. I told him I didn't want any money for the discovery, which was his."

"Just the greedy *fame*? That right, Max?"

"It was a fair deal, Jeff. Tim was bright,and also a bit ambitious. I would help him make all the right connections, you see, with the advancement of unique scholarship . . . great grant possibilities— super fine opportunities!"

"Why couldn't Tim get that honor all for himself?!"

"Well, maybe he would've, Jeff, had he—"

"You're lyin', Max! Tim didn't give you the book to take to London. He showed it to *me* right after he left your office. In fact, he took it back home with him . . . and then it was stolen. Which brings us back to my main point, Max. Something went wrong, didn't it? Horribly wrong. For some reason, Tim withdrew from your deal and that's why he took the book back. This must've made you go crazy. Crazy enough to kill him!"

"How dare you! Okay, goddamn it, I did borrow the book, but I did *not* kill that young man!"

"You had to, to get the book. Admit it. You poisoned him some-how, with your non-fat fucking shake!"

I wanted him to say it. Say it, Max, say it!

He got up slowly and stared out the window. maybe conjuring those Parliament buildings again . . . or Westminister Abby? Or Dou-glass himself wandering through the cobbled streets of London, back in history, so long ago?

Did he hear one word of what I said? No, he just droned on. "The people abroad, in England, all those inestimable top-notch scholars. When they see me hold this up, my discovery, they'll be so quiet, Jeff. You'll hear sighs in the audience . . . you'll be there, too, won't you? And then there'll be applause throughout the whole cavernous room. 'Max Raben's done it again,' they'll be whispering to each other. 'Max's done it.' "

"Max, you're chasing rainbows."

Silence in the room. No whispering. No applause.

In any case, the London trip was just a dead dream now. Not only was he canceling his annual Dickens lecture, but his life as he had known it. He was going to jail.

Say the words—that you killed Tim—and bring this ordeal to an end! Say 'em, Max!

"Keep the book, Jeff, and good luck with it. Now, if you'll excuse me, sir, I must finish my packing. And thanks for the print. Thank you so much." Planting his cane securely on the floor, he got up, cir-cled around the desk, and started for the storage room.

I couldn't very well let him go there, so I pulled up a chair, fast. "Sit down, Max. It's all over!"

"Didn't you hear me? Keep the book, Jeff. You deserve it. But think again about the deal I made with Tim. It would be the same with you as I offered him—tenured full professorship, on your terms. And a chance to run our unique new youth outreach program. Tim would want you to accept that."

Max picked up his drink and waited for me to join him. "What's the matter, Jeff? No toast after all that I offered you?"

Another pause as he saw I wasn't buying. He swallowed the rest of his drink as mine went untouched.

"For goodness sake, Jeff, think of your family. Your little girl. Give her a break. Money can buy good opportunities for positive growth. You can help people with money."

"Max—"

"Well, what do you think? Will you go for it?" he asked, his eyes fixed squarely on the book.

I remembered Tim telling me to "*almost* touch it," that is to be careful handling the rare book when he had first showed it to me last week. In the most gentle way, I picked it up lovingly, and then placed it back on the desk.

"Tolstoy had it right, Jeff, you know."

"Tolstoy?! How the hell did *he* get into the act?"

"Because he said, 'Everyone thinks of changing the world, but no one thinks of changing himself.' "

"Max, all I need for you to do now is tell the truth."

"The truth? How dare you presume to be my moral conscience when you're guilty of the same thing? *You* stole this book from those immigrants and now blame me for doing the same, you heads-in-the-cloud hypocrite! I'll tell that to the committee tomorrow, that you're a vindictive low-down thief, and you'll never get another teaching job anywhere!"

He kept looking at the book, wanting to take it back, like he had won his point. I blocked his hand. There was a brief tussle of our hands, like a little dance of folding paper dolls, but even more pathetic when he uttered a faint "You selfish fool, you could've had it all, like the deal I made with Tim."

He started out of the office door, with me right behind him. The door opened before he even reached it. Doree. Wearing a raincoat, the same one she wore when she pushed me into a car. Her words, full of stark hatred, were directed to Max. "*Deal* you made with Tim? Bullshit!" Flexing her gun, she came at me like a whirlwind.

Chapter Forty-Four

Immediately after

Gerard and Jameson, their automatics in hand, burst out of the storage closet. Doree, too fast for them, shot Gerard, who fell to the floor, stuck her gun against my head, and hollered to Jameson. "Drop it, or he'll get it worse than your partner! Drop it and kick it over here!"

She pressed the gun harder on my skull. Jameson held onto her gun, but amazingly Doree knocked it out of her hand. I took a hard, deep breath.

"Now, kick your gun over here! No tricks!"

Jameson did.

"Stop! That's far enough. Now, move back. Go!" Doree kicked Jameson's gun into the other corner. She moved her gun slowly back and forth between Jameson and me, as we stepped back. Max lowered his head down on his desk.

"Put away your gun, Doree," I said calmly. "This can all be settled peacefully. First, we have to take care of that man on the floor."

"My dad's gun," she boasted. "Yeah, my dad taught me how to use it—"

"We got to help him," I pleaded, pointing to the blood on Gerard's vest.

"Shuttup! I wouldn't mind doing it again. I've been waiting a long time for this, Dr. Gardner! Too bad I missed you with my little knife in the rain, but I got this!" She brandished her handgun in the air like she was in a film noir. Sickening.

"You heard me. Bullshit, Dr. Raben. You lied! Mr. Hartknoll did *not* give you that book. I *stole* it for you. And you said you would take care of me if I did. You'd take me to England with you and your old lady—for me to nurse her—dole out her heart medicine and clean her drecky bedpans. But *you* weren't planning to take me to Merry

England with you, were you? You didn't even buy me a plane ticket. Did you forget about that? You're not very good on keeping promises, are you, sir?!?"

Pure venom glazing over the last word.

"She's crazy, Jeff," Max whispered to me.

"Crazy, am I? Mr. Hartknoll—Tim, as you call him—didn't want to give you the book, and he didn't want your "deal" for promotion either. You're the insane one, Dr. Raben! I heard it *all* from the squawk box on my desk. *Everything* you were talkin' about! You asked him for the book—and you'd see to it that he got a promotion to full-time status. Well, he turned you down, flatter than your wife's tit. You toasted him and wished him success anyway and said you'd sponsor him for a full-time position, even though he was to keep the book."

"That's *not* the way it happened, Doris!" Raben shouted. "Not at all!"

"It's *exactly* the way it happened, you old fart, and you know it! When Timmy—as I will now call him—left this office, you begged me to find the book in his apartment and bring it back to you here. 'No, problem,' I assured you. I told you I would do it. And I kept *my* part of your greedy deal!"

A pause. Raben didn't deny it, just shook his head back and forth.

Jameson held up her arms and made a move toward Doree.

"Stop," she screamed, "or these two are dead ducks!"

Jameson stopped and said it softly, "Come on, Doree. Look, I'm unarmed. We'll do everything you say, but give me the gun before—"

"Before what?" she asked and spun around toward Jameson. Gerard was bleeding badly.

"Why, Doree, why? You seemed like such a *nice* person . . ." I was groping for the right words to say, but when I heard myself say that word, I almost threw up.

"Why did I kill Tim—or why am I going to kill you?! 'Cause I hate you! Both of you! Tim killed my dad. This was the raincoat my father wore on patrol duty in the subway. When your palsy-walsy

Timmy and his teenage hoodlum friends in Brooklyn jumped the turnstyle, my dad chased 'em, and he fell from the platform. Your great buddy could've saved him, could've pulled my dad back from the rail. But that chicken-hearted little shit ran off like the miserable coward he was, leaving Dad totally helpless before the oncoming train."

I remembered Rachel telling me all that at Tim's funeral, but I never connected that the transportation cop was Doree's father. Now it made sense—her cradling her father's picture in her office. Tim's last words came back to me, at the mailroom. Then I thought they were *tour is*. No. *Doris,* he was telling me then. *Doris* . . .

"But, It didn't end there, on the tracks. The grief of living with that through the years killed my mother, too. Your friend Timmy broke her heart!" she cried out.

I took another step toward her. It didn't make sense. "Your mother? I just talked with her the other day! Does she know that you're doing this, Doree?" I asked in the most non-threatening voice I had. "Think of her, Doree, how she feels about you."

"Not true! Didn't you know, Jeff? Her mother died ten years ago," Max said. "You can't believe one thing this vapid, vicious girl says."

"Shut up, old man! I am not a girl! I am a woman! I am a woman seeking justice!"

God, she's a total schizo. Faking her mother's voice the other day fooled me completely. Careful. I decided to tamp it down, say nothing. She could actually pull that trigger without any warning, as she'd done on Gerard.

"Doree, what Tim did—or did not do—back then was not pre-meditated—"

"Premeditated, premedicated, what the fuck's the difference! NOTHING was what he did. NOTHING to save my dad!! But what I did was certainly premeditated. Yeah! Following Tim's tracks those many years, even entrenchin' myself in his stupid life in this dump, waiting . . . waiting for the right time—"

"Doris," Jameson jumped in, "I'm talking to you like a woman. Woman to woman. There's a man there who needs our help—"

"Yeah, like my dad needed help . . . and didn't get!"

"Then think of your mother, she wouldn't want you to—"

"I know how Mommy feels about this, Jameson. She'll be dancing in heaven—finally, at long last, getting her total justice. Not only Timmy getting his due reward—but you, too, Dr. Gardner. Doin' all those things with him, teaching those dumb-ass classes together. Real hot shit, weren't you together? Real stars! More bullshit! Well, I'll give your friend Timmy this—he just made me think about it more, transcribing his Shakespeare notes last summer, all about Hamlet avenging the death of his father. That was good enough for me!"

I couldn't let that one pass by. "Okay, Doree, let's say you're right. About Tim and your dad. But listen, In *Hamlet*, a lot of people die at the end who are not to blame for what Claudius did. So why are you picking on us, Doree? We're not to blame for what happened to your dad. We're not!"

"Can we cut all this crap about *Hamlet*?" Raben said, lifting up his head from his desk. "It isn't the time! Do you understand, Doris? This man is bleeding! I'm pleading with you to get a hold of off yourself, and I beg you to—"

"Just one thing more, Dr. Asswipe! Once you realized that Timmy was hesitating about handing you the book, who did you turn to? Me! The one you always turn to when you want a favor. The one everyone turns to! You know, I did you a favor by putting Tim out of the way so fast—so I could bring back the book to you, yeah, like in *Hamlet* again—'The moment is all!' Right?"

She turned away from Max, back to me. "You were Timmy's friend, weren't you?! You worked together."

"Sure, Doree, I was. But—"

"But nothin'! You are nothing. Nothing! So you can cut the *crap!*"

She turned to Gerard, who was trying to sit up. "Stop his bleeding!" I yelled. "Use the silk scroll on the wall!"

"All right, don't move. I'll do it!" She reached for one of Raben's Japanese silk scrolls hanging behind his desk, ripped it off the wall and tossed it to Gerard. "Here, make yourself a tourniquet. And don't ever say I am not compassionate."

Gerard managed to stanch his bleeding, but not his seething anger. "You . . . you won't get away with this!" he whispered, finishing his tourniquet, the scroll now drenched in blood.

Jameson made a slight move toward Doree, who waved her off with the gun.

"I told you. Don't try anything, hear? Remember, detective, you didn't do a finger-liftin' fucking thing to get justice for my dad!"

The arrows of revenge that fly in the dark and strike the innocent; Francis Bacon said it and Doree was living it. What could I do to get her to change the arrow's direction away from us? I was desperate for anything that might work, even Sasha's calming-down techniques— anything to buy some time for Jameson to take action.

I looked over to Jameson, waiting for some of kind of signal to move. She motioned for me to hold off.

"Doree," I said, "look, this is going to sound funny, but I want you to take a couple of deep breaths now and—'"

"Shut up! Shut the fuck up, you loser! You don't even have a job here. And you're not gonna get tenure tomorrow, doc. I heard fatso over here talkin' to the big cheeses upstairs. They're gonna dump your ass straight down the toilet! But before that I'm gonna—" She cocked her gun like an old pro. How many times had she seen her dad do it? She could tell I was about to pee in my pants, which would have brought another big smile to her miserable face.

"Shut up, all of you! I'm not done!" she shouted at Jameson. Then she turned to Raben, waiting.

"Doris, I appeal to you one more time. Please—!" Raben whimpered.

"No, I told you, you're not off the hook, fatty-pie, with all this wise-ass bullshit I've had to take the last five years. I only stayed on the job once I found out Tim came on the staff—to be real close to him—"

"I had nothing to do with his murder! Nothing!" Raben shouted to the heavens.

"Oh, no? Let's bring it home to last Thursday morning," she said, an ugly leer on her face. "Tomorrow will be one week to the day. I saw you, Max, making nice with Timmy."

She said his name in a little baby voice, dripping with sarcasm.

"Your door was open as usual, and I saw you so cuddly-wuddly together. Aww—I heard you, fatty-pie, say it—that Timmy could hold onto the book and he'd still be promoted at Greene Street Cent. When you sent for me, I saw you shaking his hand. Shakin' hands with that lousy killer?!"

"Yes," Raben said, tears welling up in his eyes. "I shook his hand. Yes! Tim was a good man. I respected his decision, his integrity, his refusal to be bought off."

"Max, you're not denying that you tried to make the deal, are you now? Are you?" she asked in that nauseating sing-song pitch.

"I had *nothing* to do with you *killing* that young man. That is the truth!" Max cried out. He was sobbing uncontrollably.

"Oh, poor Dr. Raben. But *you* told me, Maxie, to prepare two glasses of your favorite non-carb shake to celebrate Tim's new promotion to full-time. I went back to my desk and made the shakes, and I saw you and Tim laughin' it up and having such a good, swell time, and then I looked down at the photo of my dad on the desk, and *he* wasn't having such a good time, was he?

"So I took out my little bottle of sleepin' pills—that would finally give me a night of rest, once a good number of them were inside Timmy's stomach. Facing my dad's picture, I slipped those crushed buggers into his milk shake, then added some delicious fruit to the mixture—so no one would know, right? No one would know," she repeated, in a whisper. "Not even you dumb cops," she said, pointing to Jameson and Gerard. "My dad would've made mincemeat of you!"

Raben shook his head in disgust.

"Don't look so pissed, Max. You're the guy who wanted me to find the priceless book, you greasy, greedy pig! 'Integrity?' That's not a fucking word in your hyped-up vocabulary! Even though you told Tim to keep the book, the fact is, *you* wanted it. In the worst way! I don't know how I ever put up with you when you started playin' me with all that bullshit flattery of yours. 'Oh, Doris, I will show you the world, your eyes will open to the wondrous glories of the past and future!' Oh, yeah, I did all your bidding. I did everything, including hiding Timmy's personal papers for you and— "

"Not that way! You're crazy! I'd never have wanted you to kill TIm! How could I?" Raben's wail pierced the room.

She turned to me. Good! I was close to Max's desk. If I could throw something at her to distract her—maybe Max's fancy chess case—I could get that gun.

"You might want to know Dr. Gardner, how I got that book. A piece of cake. I had Tim's key, yeah, *his* key. He trusted me with it, when I did his work in his apartment. It was just a question of finding the right time. *You* gave me that, Jeffrey-boy. Thank you! Last Thursday morning, after you taught that class with him, Tim called his parents to celebrate the news of his promotion. Oh, so fine, right, Maxy! The students were clapping so much for you and that scummy friend of yours. Why, beats me. Then you, Max, invited him up to his office for the celebration, and that was when I gave him what he deserved . . . a real treat!

"Oh, and to top it all, Tim went back to his cubicle, and you had quite a scene. I heard it all on the intercom. You thought he was drunk from all that party wine. You went nutso with your own jealousy of Timmy and got into an argument. Yeah, hurt your toe. Oh, I was so eager to help you, remember? So I came a-runnin'."

I glanced over to Jameson, her eyes signaling, not yet, wait . . . wait . . . This nut had us covered. But for how long? How long could I take Doree, going on and on?

"When Timmy and you headed for the infirmary, I took a cab back to our building and sneaked in when the doorman wasn't looking. Then I put on my neato disguise, my father's old raincoat, and retrieved the key to Tim's apartment. As I waited for him, I 'tore up the place,' as you say, to make it look like a real robbery and continued to wait for him. When I heard him turning the key in the lock and enter the dark apartment, I stood still, ready to pounce on him. He was too out of it to stop me pulling his briefcase from his hand. Grabbing it—a snap!—I knocked him to the floor and breezed off to my apartment, stashing my raincoat and his briefcase . . . a few minutes go by and I hear the siren—all clear to make my grand appearance in the lobby, right, Jeffo?"

She laughed with a little bow of her head. "The rest, as *you* say, Max, is history."

Jameson remained cool, her face frozen in anticipation for the break she was looking for. What else could I do except ask—when?

Max nodded. "But I had nothing to do with killing him. *You* did that, you miserable nut!"

Raben was making me nauseous, too, with his self-serving blather grinding on and on. He moved closer to Doree, but I restrained him. Jameson also made a move, an ever so slight one, which Doree caught, waving her back. She was helpless as long as Doree had us covered. But for how long?

Doree turned to Gerard, now on the floor. "Pretty neat, huh? My dad would've been so proud of me getting away with it. Yes, very neat!"

"Neat enough to fry you," Jameson said. "Back-up is on the way. Don't do anything more or—"

"Or what—what *you* gonna do? You should be ashamed of yourself. Both of you, helping guys like this. You call yourselves cops?! Betraying my dad like that! *He* was a *real* cop! You're nothin' but worthless patsies, sticking up for these two college creeps."

I inched my way over to Max's desk, trying to find an object, anything, to throw at her. "Why me, Doree? I never harmed you."

Doree saw me staring at the book next to Max's chess set.

"You? Here's what I think of you! Look!"

Quickly she grabbed the milk shake, opened the book, and splattered the drink all over the title page. It soaked in, in a split second—the priceless words of Douglass were now a blurry soggy clump, rendering the book worthless.

"No!" I cried out. I was paralyzed to move, to think, to do anything. I moved to get the book, to wipe off the dripping liquid, to save its soul, to save mine. She pushed me back, holding her gun steady.

"Good! That was *his* book and you were *his* buddy, Dr. Gardner! *Always together*. And you knew I had it in for him, didn't you? After the funeral—on the train, remember? You told me you knew what Timmy had done when he was a teenager, leaving my father like that, alone on the subway train tracks. So when you started lookin' for his killer, I knew I had to get rid of you too, like pretending to get stuff for my mother, sharing a cab up to that CWC inky bullshit company, and pushing you into that moving car. Yeah, it was me alright. I just didn't push you hard enough." She laughed again, harder, and held onto the gun even more tightly.

I wasn't listening to anything she was babbling about. My heart was with the damaged book, a dream obliterated, destroyed forever. "You fucking bitch, you just destroyed history! You destroyed a people's pride, you—!"

Doree stepped up to me and pushed the gun into the side of my head. "Get away from the desk. I see what you're tryin' to do, sneaky one!"

"And the speeding car on Hudson Street that almost mowed Derek and me over?" I asked slowly, "How did you pull that off?" I was stalling, trying to think of a way get to the book, to save something of it.

"What car? I don't know anything about no damn speeding car on Hudson Street. But the knife in the park . . . sorry I messed up and got the old guy. And as far as your new pal Derek—I'll get him too!

"Doree!" I screamed as loud as I could, pointing behind her, "Your mother—"

"What?" she yelled, just like they do in the movies when that old trick is pulled. She bought it, turning around, yeah, but only for a second.

This time she pushed the gun even harder into my head. Yes, I was a goner for sure, my last thoughts about Nellie diving into the lake at summer camp. I was looking down at her from heaven, if I made it there.

"Got you!" she screamed back at me. "Makin' fun of my mom, like that! What you *all* did to her! Got you!" Just as Doree took aim, Jameson moved toward her as she pressed herself on my body, ready to pull the trigger. I pushed her away, but not hard enough. "Got you, got you, got you!!" she screamed as Derek burst into the room and dove headlong on top of her.

"You got nothin'!" he shouted.

With her head squashed against the floor, Doree was not in a position to say or do anything.

"How's that for an entance?" Derek said, holding her down. Her gun was on the floor. Doree made a move toward it, but Jameson stomped hard on her foot. Still, Doree managed to get the gun in her other hand and point it at me. Then she turned it around and stuck it at her own head. "Happy Birthday, Dad! See you in heaven."

The gunshot filled the room.

Chapter Forty-Five

Right after

Three squad cars and an ambulance arrived quickly after the shooting. Gerard protested he wanted to go back with Jameson, not in the ambulance with Doree's body.

"You motherfucker!" Jameson yelled, as they wheeled the body out to the ambulance. Exhausted, or not, she tended to her partner with full energy.

I tried to piece it together. There it was, plain as day now, the "Law of Inner Thoughts" Isaiah Berlin had referred to—the crucial ones in history, the inner events, the most real ones, are the most painful, but seldom revealed by the ones most hurt. Doree had lived all those years with her dad's cruel, unfair death ravaging her mind and soul. And her mother's crazy crackup resulted from that event, leading to Doree's twisted search for justice.

Derek naturally tried to turn the solemn mood around. "Jeff, that entrance I made—just in the nick of time, huh?" "Yes, one of the greatest theatrical entrances in human history. Holy Houdini, how'd you do it, anyway, Derek?"

"When I visited Hank in the hospital, he mentioned that you were goin' to Greene Cent—"

"Yeah, but I didn't tell Hank *when* exactly."

"No, but I decided to head you off at the pass anyway, pardner.'

"Law of Unlikely Coincidences rearing its head again." We laughed together.

The cops shared my well-earned sigh of relief that the worst was over. Max, however, stood mute.

"Got to take you in, old man," Jameson said, cuffing him.

After flicking the sweat off my face, I hugged Derek. Hard. For maybe a minute. That's a long time compared to almost losing your life in a second.

"Hey, buddy, how 'bout a drink—on me!" Derek offered, a bit too cheerfully.

"As long as it's not a carb shake!"

Jackson O'Rourke emerged from the door, his face showing a mixture of satisfaction and regret, seeing Max being led away.

"Good job, Jackson," Max sneered. "I heard you opened my storage closet window for those snoops. Thanks loads, Brutus!"

"All part of my job, sir," Jackson smiled slightly.

Motioning to me and Derek, Jameson said, "We'll need some statements. You two have to come down with us. And, we have to unhook you, Jeff."

"A snap," Derek laughed.

She turned to him. "Thanks, both of you. My partner thanks you, too—" She was back to chewing her gum. Great.

"One minute," I said. I went to Max's desk and picked up the chess box. "You might need this."

Jameson put the remains of the decimated book into a plastic bag. "Yeah, we'll take this too. Sorry, Doctor, this happened."

I took one last look at the soggy mess. Our glorious Shady Lady was gone, and I saluted her with a tearing heart that had witnessed and withered from two deaths in one week.

Stiff-lipped, attentive Jackson O'Rourke, cautious to the hilt, flashlight in hand, led the three of us out of Max's office.

Chapter Forty-Six

Saturday, A week later

Next stop, the drugstore on the corner of Bleecker and LaGuardia Place. The tourists, in light summer garb, gathered around us.

"This used to be Mori's, a very popular Italian restaurant in the 1880s, where the Brad Pitts and Meryl Streeps of the day hung out," Derek called out, with confidence enough to match the sun's brightening rays.

"But even before that, in the early 1820s, it was a connected pair of two modest row-houses. Just maybe, it might've been here where the great abolitionist Frederick Douglass was hiding after escaping to New York from Baltimore," he continued. I winced when he said that. It wasn't historically accurate. No one really knew, even back then, where Douglass hid in New York. Or where there may be other autographed copies of his book—hidden away somewhere.

What was really important for the tour group to know about Douglass was his life story—the pains he endured as a slave, his longings to be free, and his accomplishments as a free man, all of which Derek conveyed with gusto to the assembled.

"I'll play him later," Derek said, glancing over to me for approval "when we show you how, uh, he might've escaped from Maryland—to find his way here. The exact escape routes were kept secret," he clarified. "Well, in any case, I think you'll dig the performance a lot."

Same old Derek, never one for false modesty, even if he didn't need to boast now. After all, he was now the man in charge of leading the Bleecker Blues tour. I helped him out on weekends.

"And I'll show you how Caroline Ruggles, a leading actress of the African Grove Theatre—and related to David Ruggles, a conductor on the Underground Railroad—might've saved young Douglass from the clutch of slave catchers," Renee said. She was also working as part-timer on the tour. "It's pretty certain, mind you. But no one knows what *really* happened." I was glad she added that.

I didn't like the tour playing around with history. One of the reasons I decided to consult on this tour and work weekends was to keep things as close as possible to historical veracity. At least pretty much to the mark, of course, with the usual dramatic license taken. To fill in the blanks, I was working on finding some other verifiable slant on the African Grove Theatre for Renee to act out. History was not only about the people who made it, but about the people who reported and wrote it. For the so-called victors, usually.

"And speaking of Douglass," looking over to Derek, "that wasn't always his name, you know. When he ran away from Baltimore to New York at the age of twenty, his slave name was Bailey, Frederick Bailey. His risks were many, matched by many rewards."

I went on to elaborate how Douglass got his new name from the name of a character in a book called *The Lady of the Lake*, a long narrative poem by Sir Walter Scott. Pausing for a second, I added, "Well, when Douglass returned to New York City when he was sixty or so, there's a *possibility* he may have spoken in this very building at a benefit, to raise money for a ladies garment workers strike."

I remembered Tim was in the process of bringing to light the shadows of history that still lingered here on Bleecker Street. The new tour groups had to know this.

My cellphone rang. Would Jankowitz have had a fit if he knew I was using it while leading one of his tours?

I did, a couple of times, to catch up with Jameson and Gerald. They let me know that they were finishing gathering evidence for Max's trial coming up next month.

"Who's that? Nellie?" Derek asked. "That was some graduation she had yesterday! It was somethin', seeing your dad there, and you guys huggin'."

"No. It was Rachel. She's runnin' a little late, be here any minute."

Tormented by two men who should have been her champions— her father and her minister—Rachel was still coming to painful terms with both of them and trying to move on. She was planning to live in Manhattan and clerk in a law firm and also hoped to take summer art courses at New York University. To keep Tim's generous spirit alive, she was looking forward to working later with me and Derek as a counselor for homeless kids. As for the reverend, his church bid him an unfond farewell. Period.

"Jeff, you're workin', so chill with me," Derek said. "When you gonna come on board full time as a full-time tour guide?"

"Hold on, D. The tenure planning committee at Greene Cent has been postponed a couple of weeks. I'll let you know then."

And, in her own intense health-kick way, Sasha watched my back too. I felt bad about our splitting up, especially since she was my godsend last week. She took it surprisingly well, even offering to remain good friends. I'd look forward to that.

Some people, we all know, never get the help that Douglass and others on this street got. Doree was one. There was no one around to help her when things went badly for her family. Thinking about the false front she carried all those years jarred my mind. If she had only reached out . . . reached out for someone to help ease her tortured mind.

So what about Nellie and me? And Nan—if she wanted me back? It took a week of running back and forth, up and down this street to show me how much I needed her and lover her.

Nellie bought me a big green moleskin notebook, the same color as Whitman's. She suggested I should write down this story, all that had happened in these "awesome" past few days. Or maybe I should just do some research on Douglass. Raben once maintained I might write something for tenure about Douglass's early adventures in New York. That would take *mucho* investigation, a recounting of all the secret help he got. Yeah. I might call it "Shadows on Bleecker Street."

Hey, here she was coming now, to see me in action, my facial hair all grown back, my toe and head, up to par. A couple days ago, we had celebrated my Big 4-0, combined with her graduation party.

"Hi, Popster!" Nellie, called out in delight, as she approached us, leading her cute little schnauzer that I promised her for graduation.

"I'm gonna play Margaret Sanger when I go to camp tomorrow . . . for the talent show at the end of summer!"

"Oh, no, you're not!" We hugged. "This is my daughter, everybody—and her little pal Snoozy!" I beamed.

She was onto something that I shared with pride, and had drawn my strength from. How much I was indebted to all those brave iconoclasts, those spirits of Bleecker Street, on my tours—Lenny Bruce, Charlie Parker, Thomas Paine, Walt Whitman, and of course Margaret Sanger—all who had risked their lives for their freedom of expression.

Rachel, carrying her sketch pad, joined the tourist group, waiting, like everyone else for the scene to start. I handed her a book with a photo of Mori's as it looked maybe a hundred years ago. She looked forward to sketching it later.

"There's a lot to see and I got to finish my packing for camp, Dad! C'mon! On with the tour!"

I waved to the tourists, and for Derek, and Rachel to come closer.

We were ready to do the scene about Douglass escaping into the building in front of us. If that, indeed, was the building. Could've been. And could've been where Douglass came back to fifty years later when it was Mori's restaurant. But did he have the book with him that gave him his new name? Well, that remained to be settled.

Then I joined Derek and Renee in the song that Douglass might have sung as a young man on the go for freedom. The one I had sung with Tim, another spirit of Bleecker Street, not so long ago. And I hoped he was hearing us good now.

Oh Canaan, sweet Canaan . . . I thought I heard 'em say . . . there were lions in the way . . . and I don't expect to stay much longer here!

We all moved on.

THE END

Authors' Note

We hope you enjoyed reading *Shadows on Bleecker Street.* The more we learned while researching and writing it, the more we appreciated the cultural icons whom we integrated into both Jeff's street and inner journey. Mavericks like Douglass, Whitman, and Sanger not only were the forerunners of social justice in their times, but they also have left their activist and artistic imprints on many generations that followed. It makes us wonder where such leaders are today and who they will be in the future, not only in our country, but world-wide. So from the Greenwich Village in our story to the ever-expanding global village, we hope our novel has given you fresh opportunity to think about how such icons interact with issues that are vital in people's daily lives. Please let us know what you think of the book and send any questions you may have to further enrich our mutual journeys. You can email us through the Puck Press website.

Thank you.

Milton Polsky and Warren Wyss
www.shakespeareinc.com

About the Authors

Milton Polsky is a prize-winning playwright and author of over twenty books. He has taught writing and theatre at New York University and City University of New York. His latest book is *A Shakespeare Trilogy*, published by Puck Press. He lives on—where else?—Bleecker Street. **Warren Wyss**, a contributing author to *From Silk to Oil*, and a literary editor, has taught writing, literature, and film and theater studies at a number of institutions in New York City. He has worked in the tour business for over twenty years. Milt and Warren serve as co-chairs of the UFT Players, where they have had a number of their plays produced, including *What the Dickens!*, published by Players Press.

Frederick Douglass